Praise

"*What Start Bad a Mornin'* is a breathtaking novel. Amaya Lin, loving mother, wife and caretaker of many, has built a life that is on the verge of collapse when a hidden past sweeps in. I was riveted by the revelations that followed, stunned by the conclusion. Carol Mitchell is a writer of immense talent and this is a stellar debut."

— Cleyvis Natera, author of *Neruda on the Park*

"With *What Start Bad a Mornin'*, Carol Mitchell casts light on immigration's most unsettling predicament: the tension between the life you leave and the one you create. In vibrant prose, she demonstrates how an unacknowledged past will never die, as well as the power—and cost—that comes in surviving it."

— Courtney Angela Brkic, author and memoirist

"With luminous prose, Carol Mitchell tells the story of every Caribbean immigrant, indeed any immigrant, who has had to remake a life they have known in their homeland for the uncertainties in the US where race is often the determinant for success. *What Start Bad a Mornin'* leaves the reader with empathy for the passions that drive the ambitions of the vividly-drawn characters, and, at the same time, it is a cautionary tale about the consequences of repressing childhood trauma. A compelling debut novel."

— Elizabeth Nunez, author of *Prospero's Daughter* and *Now Lila Knows*

"*What Start Bad A Mornin'* is a tense, gripping tale of a woman's unwilling spiral into her own locked past. As her protective layers of amnesia are inexorably stripped away, the pillars of her life tilt, crack, and crumble, forcing her to question everything she believes about herself as she scavenges for the truth: What is real? What is mirage? Amaya's journey of self-discovery takes her thousands of miles, real and newly recollected, from her ordered existence in Virginia, USA, to the Caribbean island of Trinidad where she lived as a student and met the man who would become her husband, and finally to Jamaica, her birthplace, where the threads of a turbulent political and personal history intersect and converge in a tapestry as violent as it is revelatory."

— Charmaine Rousseau, author

"One sentence spoken by a stranger becomes the thread that unlocks decades-old memories for Amaya, who has been living as if her past never existed. Carol Mitchell's debut adult novel is brilliant storytelling that deftly weaves a tale of cross-cultural Caribbean life, trauma, and survival. I couldn't put it down."

— Nerissa Golden, *Ordained for This* and *In Plain Sight*

"In carefully measured spoons, Carol reveals the details of Amaya's life, keeping our interest piqued, holding our attention until the very surprising ending. Richly characterized, mystery and intrigue, buried memories and glaring revelations, this story of family, displacement, loss, and immigration keeps you eager to get to the next page."

— Opal Palmer Adisa, *The Storyteller's Return*

"*What Start Bad a Mornin'* grapples with themes ranging from quiet domestic desperation to the perils of the immigrant experience, from latent racism to the literal violence of politics. The character dynamics are complex and interesting; the entanglements sometimes heartbreaking, sometimes heartwarming, sometimes frustrating, sometimes cosy, all the beats of genuine human interaction. A compelling, meditative, and well-paced journey."

— Joanne C. Hillhouse, writer

"Carol Mitchell's novel, *What Start Bad a Mornin'*, is sublime and intensely compassionate. This debut is uncompromisingly Caribbean; yet, it sings of the America into whose arms immigrants collapse with the intention of rising above the selves they once were. Mitchell's complex characters are enmeshed in an intricate web of classism, racism, colorism, and nationalism— sometimes under the same roof. The intangible and unnamable elements of one's abandoned home follow these hopeful immigrants wherever the future finds them. This is a story of grief as characters sow seeds and must forsake the harvest. This is also a story of triumph. Each sentence is carefully crafted, polished, and captivating. *What Start Bad a Mornin'* is glorious and downright unforgettable. Mitchell's craftsmanship is astounding. This is a book you'll want to read more than once."

— Katia D. Ulysse, author of *Mouths Don't Speak*

WHAT START BAD A MORNIN'

A NOVEL

CAROL MITCHELL

2023

Published by Central Avenue Publishing, an imprint of Central Avenue Marketing Ltd.
www.centralavenuepublishing.com

Published in Canada
Printed in United States of America

1. FICTION/African American & Black/Women
2. FICTION/World Literature/Caribbean & West Indies

WHAT START BAD A MORNIN'

Cloth: 978-1-77168-354-8
Ebook: 978-1-77168-355-5

1 3 5 7 9 10 8 6 4 2

Keep up with Central Avenue

what start bad a mornin'

*When the caterpillar completes its cocoon, it dissolves into a
soupy mess and emerges a new creation,
memories of its past existence a faint imprint on its DNA.*

CHAPTER ONE

Five minutes past five; I was going to be late. Only fifteen minutes left to pick up Aunt Marjorie before she had a meltdown. Having finally extricated myself from my last meeting, I waved goodbye to Taylor as I rushed past the main reception desk. She was on the phone, but she smiled and mouthed, "Bye, Mrs. Lin."

I hurried down the hallway to the elevators and entered the first one to open. It was empty. *Thank you, Jesus*, I breathed. I pressed the Lobby button once, then pulsed on it three or four more times, even though I knew my impatience would not make the doors close any faster. Finally, they slid together, and the embossed gold sign reading "Gil, Lin and Associates, Attorneys at Law" was replaced by my reflection in the metallic surface of the doors.

My appearance surprised me. I resembled someone in control of their day. My eyes were steady and I looked respectable in what my husband, Brian, called my uniform—a striped, long-sleeved button-down silk shirt (pink and gray that day) tucked into black work trousers. Observing my calm exterior did nothing to dampen the churning in my brain. I ran my hand over my short 'fro then dropped it just as quickly when I saw the mess I was making of my hair. I could almost hear the seconds ticking away before the box lurched and began its ten-floor descent.

Don't stop, don't stop, don't stop, I chanted in my head, tapping my foot to the rhythm of my thoughts as if doing so would speed up the elevator or prevent it from stopping on any other floors. It was not an unreasonable request, even at five p.m. This building was occupied primarily by law firms, banks, and investment firms, all businesses where leaving work before nightfall was unthinkable, unless you were the boss. Or the boss's wife.

When the elevator shuddered to a stop and the doors opened on the main floor, I pulled my briefcase firmly onto my shoulder and glanced at my watch.

Eight minutes past five.

As long as traffic was no heavier than usual, I should be able to make up the five minutes I had lost, and arrive on time to pick up Aunt Marjorie. Even when she was having a good day, she barely tolerated the Ramus House. The staff told me she watched the clock like a child counting the minutes to recess. At five-twenty, she would be sitting near the checkout desk, straight-backed, gripping her handbag in her lap and radiating impatience in such powerful waves that even the staff, trained to manage the many manifestations of dementia, kept their distance.

Sunlight forced me to close my eyes as I stepped outside. After eight straight hours indoors, it was easy to forget that daylight persisted. No matter how many fluorescent fixtures I had installed in my windowless office, there never seemed to be enough light for me.

I inhaled deeply, like a newly released prisoner sampling her freedom, but the breath was dissatisfying. As was typical of a Virginia summer, the combination of heat and humidity thickened the air into a soup-like consistency that barely filled my lungs. People always assumed that because I grew up in the Caribbean the heat would not impact me, but without the cooling sea breeze, the heat here was oppressive, and even after more than twenty years, I had not got used to the Virginia heat.

Nine minutes past five.

I headed to the car, my thoughts vacillating between the meeting I had abandoned mid-discussion and my tardiness. Some days it was hard not to resent having to drop everything, every day, and turn my attention over to Aunt Marjorie's needs. The clip of my heels on the pavement drummed a soft beat of accompaniment to my thoughts.

As I passed Brian's car in his reserved spot just outside of the building that housed our offices, I regretted parking in the overflow lot. An article in one of the women's magazines we kept in the office recommended parking far away from one's destination as a way of incorporating exercise into one's routine. My doctor had put the fear of God into me at my physical last month. I was not overweight, she had said, but I needed to exercise.

"You can't avoid everything that might be coming to you as you age," she had said, "but with regular exercise and good eating habits, you can help your body weather the aging process better."

I wanted to take the advice seriously. Caring for Aunt Marjorie had given me some insight into the way I did not want to age. I did not want to be so completely dependent on anyone, ever. But I had not been able to find time for exercise. Something always tugged at my time: work; managing the household; caring for Aunt Marjorie; advocating for my son, Taiwo; tending the garden . . . each a heavy stone in a sack I carried around with me perpetually. Whenever I considered putting the burden down, guilt would overcome me. Who would put the effort into caring for everyone like I did?

I strode past the footprint of our office building, then past two other buildings that occupied the same compound. The overflow lot was deserted, quiet except for the occasional chirp of an unseen bird in the surrounding trees. As I walked past a large golden raintree, a breeze shivered through its leaves, releasing a blanket of yellow flowers. I stopped, paralyzed by a memory that flowed into my brain in shadows, watercolors, and whispers.

The large poui tree that had belonged to Aunt Marjorie's neighbor in Black River, Jamaica, had frequently shed its flowers onto her yard. I recalled rolling in the leaves as a girl, covering myself in the delicate flowers, feeling their velvety softness against my skin. I heard Aunt Marjorie complain: about my soiled school uniform, about my lack of decorum, about the audacity of the neighbor's trees in encroaching on her garden. But her voice held no conviction, her scoldings halfhearted as if her only real annoyance was with herself, for not joining me. I relished the imagining for a moment, lingering in my carefree joy, turning the memory around in my mind as if it were a precious jewel, each petal a gem with which I could purchase a segment of my almost-forgotten past. *Would these flowers have a similar effect on Aunt Marjorie?* I wondered. The sight might trigger memories that would transport her disintegrating mind to a place where she felt secure, if only for a few minutes.

Aunt Marjorie. "Crap," I swore under my breath. I looked at my watch. Eleven minutes past five.

I picked up my pace again. My footfall was quieter now, dampened by the fruit, the flowers, the leaves that littered the ground, and my guilt about being late, which pounded in my head in a familiar rhythm.

I spotted my black sedan covered with a dusting of pollen, which effectively nullified the cleaning Taiwo had given it on the weekend. I fished my keys out of my briefcase. Brian had drilled a safety routine into my head when we bought our first car. Initially, I dismissed his earnestness as paranoia born of growing up with his mother in a relatively remote area in Trinidad, but over time his lessons sank in and became part of my normal. "Always have your keys ready, the key pointing outwards in case you have to use it as a weapon. Check your surroundings before you open the door. If you see someone suspicious, don't get in the car. Keep walking."

And so, just before I arrived at the car, I turned.

A woman stood behind me. She was about two car lengths away. Her head was down, and the sun glinted off of the plastic shine of her black handbag as she fumbled in it as if looking for keys—which was odd because my car was the only vehicle in this section of the lot.

There was momentum in her stance; her body tilted forward a few degrees as if she had been moving and had only stopped when I turned. I looked at her a little more closely. Her sweater was baggy, its neck misshapen as if accustomed to sitting on a larger body, and her tight black pants ended just a

4

little too high above her ankles. *Like she's expecting a flood*, I thought.

A vague sense of discomfort fluttered in my stomach but I dismissed it. *She can't be planning to mug me. Who would wear a bright orange sweater in August to mug someone? Plus, I can definitely take her.* Although the woman was taller and larger-bodied than I was, there was a softness about her that suggested she was not here for a fight. She raised her head, and our eyes made four. She regarded me with a clear, steady gaze. I searched her face, trying to figure out what she could possibly want from me. She was young, with full cheeks that filled out her oval-shaped face, and skin as smooth and unblemished as the shells of the brown eggs I sought out at the grocery. Her hair, braided in a style a few weeks past fresh, was pulled back and would have made her face look bare were it not for the large gold hoop earrings hanging from each ear. My left hand reached up to touch the small gold hoops I had worn for longer than I could remember. I knew those earrings. They were the earrings Caribbean grandmothers passed down to the granddaughters on whom they could pour the love and indulgence they had not dared show to their daughters.

The young woman opened her mouth as if she was going to speak, then closed it. Her bottom lip curved up and her lips settled into a pursed shape that transformed her face from stranger to familiar as if a switch had been flipped.

The desire to flee rose from deep in my belly and pushed against me like lava trapped inside a mountainous dome. I unlocked the car, opened the door, and entered in one fluid movement, locking the door once I was inside. Securely in my car, I looked at her again through the pollen-dusted window. I was sure I had never seen her before, but my heart pounded in my chest, the sound drumming in my ears as fear filled my body. She approached the car. She formed her mouth into a word: "Stop" or maybe "Please."

I did not want to hear her voice. Every ounce of my being rebelled against allowing her any closer, yet I lowered the window just enough for breath and sound to pass through.

"I have no cash," I said.

"Me name Angela. I'm your sister," she replied.

Her words did not impact me in that moment. It was her accent—smooth, rich, and thickly Jamaican like a buttered slice of hard dough bread—that clumped in my throat and threw me spinning backwards into my seat.

A wave of black rose in my line of sight.

A wave of black that cleared only to reveal a memory of Brian and me standing in shoulder-to-shoulder silence on the Pitch Lake in Trinidad, watching the silver shininess of a twenty-five-cent coin sink into the asphalt until it disappeared into a wave of black.

A wave of black that left my head too heavy to remain upright. And so, like the coin, I succumbed, leaning back onto the headrest and closing my eyes.

"BUT THIS LITTLE piggy had none . . ."

The voice was female, lilting, playful, pregnant with laughter. I was tiny, lying along the length of an arm, my head in a palm, my body along a forearm, and my legs dangling on either side of an elbow. The sun scattered in blinding streaks between the leaves of a tree—a mango tree, the scent of the ripening fruit sweet, almost overpowering. I struggled to stay in the moment, to stay in the baby's head, because I was in there, but I was also everywhere, looking down on myself through the woman's eyes, looking down from a larger vantage point, aware of everything at once: the trees, the clouds, the sun. But in the baby's space I felt security, warmth, and love, definitely love. I looked up towards the woman's voice, her face shrouded in the shadows, a dark blot in the midst of the sun and the trees. One by one, my toes were being tugged, and now it was my smallest toe's turn.

"But this little piggy . . ."

The voice paused again.

"This little piggy . . ."

Another pause. I held my baby body taut. Anticipation bubbled inside me like soda in a shaken bottle pushing against the cap.

I had done this before.

"This little piggy went weeeeeeeee all the way home."

With the last phrase, a hand descended on my tummy and tickled me. I shrieked with delight. The woman laughed, throwing her head back. I strained to see her features, to know this person. Light touched her face, revealing first her forehead, then her eyes. Tears ran from her eyes to her cheeks. I did not notice when the tears turned into bright-red rivulets flowing down her face, until her laughter convolved into an ear-shattering scream.

CHAPTER TWO

I opened my eyes then closed them against the light, a wave of nausea rising briefly in my stomach before subsiding. I opened my eyes again, slowly this time, focusing on my hands: pale palms upturned on my lap as if in supplication. My head ached and my heart raced in response to the macabre vision. *It was just a ridiculous dream,* I told myself, even as the sense of déjà vu lingered. When my eyes adjusted to the light, I raised them to look out of the window. Angela was no longer there. I blinked, then looked left and right, scanning the parking lot for a sign of her retreating figure, a flash of orange and black to prove she had been real. Stillness was all I encountered. Even the trees, whose branches had swayed just moments before, manipulated by the breeze, were motionless.

Where could she have gone? I was sure I had only closed my eyes for a few seconds, but when I looked at the dashboard clock, it read five-sixteen. Three minutes had passed since I got into the car. *Crap.*

What the hell just happened? I raised my hand to rub an itch on my right cheek and it came away wet. I touched the left side of my face. Tears, one from each eye, ran a sticky trail down each of my cheeks. I looked at my fingers, half expecting them to be dyed red, but the liquid on my cheeks was transparent. Why was I responding to this woman this way? Passing out? Tears? I had never lost consciousness before, not that I remembered.

Maybe I was dehydrated, I thought. I had not had time for anything but work since a quick bite at lunch. And since Aunt Marjorie had come to stay with us, exhaustion had become more a physical trait, like a droopy eyelid, than a temporary state of being. But to faint? Three minutes lost just like that because a strange woman with a Jamaican accent claimed she was my sister.

Sister. I released a long steups, then I laughed. I had not steupsed in such a long time; the motion was therapeutic, and the sucking sound cleared my thinking. I had no sister. I had grown up as Aunt Marjorie's lone ward. She had taken me in after my parents died when our house was destroyed by fire. A childless widow, Aunt Marjorie had raised me with all the love she had been able to deliver. That was all I knew. No one talked about the tragedy, and I had been too young to recall it. That woman, Angela, had to be at least fifteen years my junior. She could not be my sister.

My phone buzzed; the Ramus House showed on the caller ID. I took a deep breath and started the car.

Bob Marley's voice poured out from the speakers. His *Kaya* CD had been on repeat in the car for at least two weeks. His music soothed Aunt Marjorie and somehow always seemed to have the salve for whatever bothered me as well. That afternoon, the Universe chose the song "Running Away."

True, so true, I thought in response to Bob's insistence that I could not avoid the realities of my own life. My thoughts drifted back to the strange woman. She might have been an employee walking from a nearby bus stop or a vagrant looking for someone to fleece for money. It was more likely the latter. Her ill-fitting clothes suggested poverty. When we first moved to the US, we had lived in Washington, D.C., cramped into Brian's uncle's home, and one of the things that endeared me to Virginia was that here, I could escape the poverty that littered the streets of Washington. The destitution visible in D.C., concentrated as it was in the bodies of people who looked like me, was discouraging. It challenged the vision of the American prosperity we had migrated to find. We had sacrificed so much to get to the US and faced so many disappointments on arrival that I could not stomach the daily reminders that we might fail.

But over the last ten years or so, I had seen hallmarks of human struggle seep out into the streets of Northern Virginia as well, primarily in the form of begging at busy intersections. The reality that panhandling was no longer uncommon in our area did not, however, explain why someone would be trying to solicit money from passersby in an isolated parking lot. And the nearest bus stop would have dropped the young woman on the opposite side of the compound. And then there was the fact that she was definitely Jamaican. What were the odds of that in this neighborhood?

I inhaled deeply and focused on the highway ahead. I became aware of my body, bent forward as if my leaning could make the car move more quickly. I forced my shoulders to relax and sat back against the seat. I had less than ten minutes to pull myself together and be ready to deal with Aunt Marjorie. I needed to be in control when I arrived.

IT WAS FIVE-THIRTY when I pulled into the Ramus House's parking lot. There was an empty spot next to the reserved spaces, so I was parked and inside the building in a matter of a minute.

I flashed my driver's license at the exhausted-looking woman at the main desk and signed Aunt Marjorie out.

"She's all yours, Mrs. Lin," the receptionist said.

I looked past her down the white corridor to a row of chairs along a wall. Beyond the chairs was an open hall where I could see a scattering of tables with people seated around them. The sounds of talking, moving chairs, and shuffling feet floated towards me but seemed to fall into a hollow as they reached the spot where Aunt Marjorie sat alone.

"Auntie," I said. I smiled, hoping my expression was more cheerful than I felt.

Aunt Marjorie stood. She held her handbag in both hands in front of her chest and looked me up and down. Only her eyes moved. That single glance transported me to my childhood and I saw myself standing hand in hand with her, my head just reaching the top of her waist as it did in the only photograph I have with her, the only photograph I have from my childhood.

"I was just about to catch bus," she said, then pursed her lips. "I don't have no change." She gestured forward with the handbag. "But I know sey Mr. Gregory woulda trus me a ride to Black River."

I ignored Aunt Marjorie's glare and enveloped her in a hug. "I'm sorry I'm late. Please forgive me, Auntie. I'll take you home," I whispered, my mouth directly against her ear. Her vanilla-scented lotion filled my nostrils and infused my cells with a sense of home.

At first her body remained as stiff as the metal support of her handbag, which poked into my breast. A moment passed and I had just about resigned myself to the idea that this was going to be one of our more difficult evenings, when her shoulders dropped and the tension drained out of her body like water rushing down a drain after a clog was removed. She released one hand from her handbag and folded her arms around me.

"What I go do with you, eh child?" she said.

I closed my eyes, breathed in her scent again, and allowed myself to relax into the embrace. I pretended that I was once more the one who was being comforted and cared for.

LATER, AFTER I had settled Aunt Marjorie in front of the television to watch her soap operas, I went out into the backyard. I walked down the middle path of the fifteen-foot square garden plot that sat between the main house and our tiny guest studio. I lowered myself to the ground in the very center. I folded my legs one under the other, clasped my hands under my chin, and closed my eyes. Up until that point, I had suppressed the image of the woman in the parking lot, but now she reemerged, her face simultaneously foreign and familiar. It was not that she looked like anyone I knew, but seeing her expression felt like getting on a train heading for home. But home was not a place, not Jamaica or Trinidad or Virginia. If I knew what home was at all, it was Aunt Marjorie, Brian, and Taiwo, no one else, no sisters, no one. I shook my head, hoping the motion would clear the muddle swirling in my brain.

I let her claim echo in my mind just one more time. *Sister?* A ball of saliva filled my mouth and I forced myself to swallow. What kind of sister would desert me when I might have been passed out or dead from shock? Maybe she had been scared? *Why was I rationalizing the actions of a clearly deranged woman?*

I opened my eyes and surveyed the garden around me. The orderliness usually gave me comfort, helped me to center. I had pruned my rosebushes so they grew long, bare stems topped by tight balls of leaves from which they flowered profusely. Each plant enjoyed exactly the space and sunlight quotient it needed to thrive. The beds on the right caught the morning sun and featured a wide variety of herbs—anise, bay leaf, chamomile, cilantro, dill, and more—arranged in alphabetical order except for the companion plants. I had dredged up the lessons Aunt Marjorie taught me when I was a teenager about growing unblemished plants without pesticides, and placed chives and basil where they could provide pest protection to the others.

Each time I relocated: Jamaica to Trinidad; Trinidad to Brian's uncle in Washington, D.C.; D.C. to our first then second then third home in Virginia, I started my garden anew, but this one had somehow known it was the most permanent, and it showed in the way the plants obeyed my instructions. Even the sunflowers stood ramrod tall, sentries daring any trespasser to enter, and the creeping herbs: mint, oregano, and thyme, grew within the confines of the rows in which they were planted as if they understood that in this garden, unbridled expression was not valued.

A shadow drifted overhead and I looked up at the dwarf palmetto palms, their fronds swaying. They were both my greatest success and my greatest failure. In each of my previous gardens I had experimented with a palm tree, and in each I had failed. I desperately wanted to recreate the illusion of freedom I had once felt while sitting under a palm tree in my backyard, the fronds filtering light and air into the precise quantities that fit my physical and mental needs, but each winter the palms had succumbed to the cold. Then I discovered the palmettos. These were now thirteen years old and stretched past my five-six frame to an impressive six feet, tall enough to shield the garden from the outside world and to make me believe in a sense of permanence, believe that I might never have to abandon another garden. Somehow, however, as I placed them in the ground, I must have transferred my anxiety that they would not survive, because they were the only plants in the space that defied my strict control, reaching thin branches towards the sky and beyond the garden wall as if trying to escape.

I breathed deeply, allowing myself to drift along with the palm branches. I had never before been at a point where I envisaged my life in one year's time as clearly as I could anticipate tomorrow. Life looked less like the slow-moving hurricane it had been for most of my forty-one years and more like a pleasant stream doggedly carving out a deep, predictable path. And then came that woman. Asphyxiation was the closest description I could dredge up for how one glance from that stranger had felt like a hand reaching through my brain and down into my heart, searching for something I could not give, reaching, squeezing, until I felt as if I could not breathe.

Earlier, as I prepared dinner, as I tended to Aunt Marjorie, as I greeted Taiwo when he arrived home from work, my intentions had been focused on the point at which I would escape to the garden. I had seen myself opening the gate, entering, breathing in. I expected that being in the garden would cleanse the memory of what had happened that afternoon or give me clarity, understanding even, but I was there and none of these things was happening. What I felt instead was an intense anxiety about the encounter and the way it seemed to hint at a past I could not identify. I inhaled sharply, stemming the memory of the woman. As I exhaled, I wondered if the entire incident was an aberration, a ripple that would fade into a distant speck, or if it signaled a major change in the direction of my life.

I stood, massaging my knees, which had grown stiff from being forced into a prolonged fold. After a gentle flex of my back, I picked up the spade, strode into the bed of herbs, and began to dig.

I started with the thyme.

CHAPTER THREE

The garage door rumbled as it rolled open, announcing Brian's arrival. I glanced at the kitchen clock. Eight-thirty, exactly as he had promised when he called. Aunt Marjorie was sleeping, Taiwo had retired to his room, and the house had only just settled into a quiet that demanded nothing from me.

Standing at the kitchen sink, I breathed in deeply then out slowly, savoring the last few minutes of solitude. Brian would not enter the kitchen through the garage door but would instead go outside and walk counterclockwise around the property before entering the house through the front door. When I moved in with him into his mother's house in Trinidad, he had related how his father used to walk the perimeter of their home every night, checking for snakes that might have threaded themselves through the diamond-wire fence. As soon as his mother had agreed, around age five, Brian had joined his father on the nightly sentinel, and when his father had died seven years after that, Brian had continued the patrol alone. It was such a part of his daily routine that he had patrolled the property line of each home we rented in our early days in Virginia and continued when we acquired a house and garden of our own.

His attachment to family and routine had always been comforting. Brian surrounded himself with photos going back four generations, the oldest one a fading black-and-white photo of a tall, middle-aged man of Chinese descent wearing a suit, flanked by his wife and three children. The photo array was one of the first things Brian put in place whenever we moved from one home to another, carefully wrapping—when we left one place—then unwrapping each framed image himself and placing it on the living room center table.

Through those photos, Taiwo knew his paternal grandparents even though he never met his grandfather, and his grandmother, Mrs. Lin, had died when he was six. He seemed to feel something akin to affection for them, the tension that had existed between him and his grandmother when she was alive erased by images of her smiling at him from the frames.

All I could offer from my side of the family was an aging aunt with few memories of her own. It was Brian who insisted that the one photo I had of my extended family, the one of Aunt Marjorie and me, accompany us with every move. Some days I wondered why Aunt Marjorie—in fact, no one in the small town of Black River in Jamaica, where I had grown up—ever thought to fill me in about my parents. The truth was that they might have told me, and I might have lost those memories like so many others. I recalled with clarity every moment of my life as Brian's wife and Taiwo's mother, but as I moved along the path from Jamaica to Trinidad to the United States, my memories of Jamaica fell away like a bridge crumbling behind me. The absence of photos was partially to blame for the missing pieces in my life. Without that photo of Aunt Marjorie and me, I might not recall anything of my childhood at all.

I did not spend much time dwelling on my past. Brian's mother, on the other hand, had been very concerned about my lack of a history she could use to determine my worth. This came to a head one morning, twenty years ago, when we were still in Trinidad.

Maracas, Trinidad - February 1983

I had moved into their house three weeks before, homeless, unemployed, and pregnant with Taiwo. I was still struggling to settle in and that morning I had opened my eyes, disoriented, exhausted, wondering what had awoken me, and soon realized it was the gnawing of my stomach—empty. *Which is best for the baby, rest or food?* I wondered. Food, I decided, and forced myself to my feet. I made my way towards the kitchen.

I descended three steps into the sunken living room, which lay between the bedroom and the kitchen. The pointed leaves of the two large potted palms that flanked the steps scraped against my arms. The living room sat in the center of the house, encircled by the dining room, kitchen, and bedrooms, and so the sunlight that surrounded the house struggled with limited success to infiltrate this space. Instead, it was lit day and night with artificial lighting that cast pasty gray shadows over the heavy antique furniture and the photos, many old and fading black-and-white, that covered every flat surface. Whenever I entered this room, I tried to imagine myself nursing a child on one of the Queen Anne armchairs. The idea filled me with despair.

How will I raise another being when I don't have a real grasp on who I am?

I was at the bottom of the steps when I noticed someone else was in the room. Mrs. Lin was still at home. If I had known that, I would have remained in bed until she left. She had accepted my presence in her house with a graciousness that barely veiled her displeasure. Her slights were so subtle I could not complain about any specific act, but her animosity was clear. On the day we met, she ran her eyes over my body, pausing on my burgeoning belly before returning to my face. She pursed her thin lips as if she had been contemplating a smile but changed her mind midway. She sighed, her nearly flat chest rising high then falling as she expelled the breath with considerable effort. I had shivered, feeling as if a trail of red ants had walked over me, never biting but leaving an imprint of tiny feet, a persistent threat against my skin. After that, I had avoided her as much as was polite, but more than once, I overheard her complaining to Brian about my laziness in stage whispers obviously meant to reach my ears.

That morning, her face was heavily made up and she was dressed for work in the skirted version of a gray business suit, but from the way she lounged on the living room loveseat, her stockinged legs up on a deep-maroon velvet cushion and crossed at the ankles, it was clear she was in no hurry to leave. I had entered the room in barefooted silence. She had not heard me, and I was about to retrace my steps when her words stopped me.

"Yeah, dat's what she said. No family."

She was speaking on the telephone. Curiosity glued my feet to the ground.

"How I supposed to know why she don't have no family? She just show up from Jamaica and sink her hooks into my Brian." She listened once more. "Of course, I warned him . . . but anyway, I have to put up with her now. She carrying my grandson."

She must have sensed my presence. She looked up and our eyes met. Her chest rose in an intake of breath then stilled. She knew I had heard her words. She exhaled.

She swung her feet off the couch, sat up, and spoke into the phone.

"Listen girl, I got to go to work even though I really not in the mood today."

She placed the phone on the cradle.

"Good morning, Amaya," she said.

"Good morning, Mrs. Lin."

Mrs. Lin rose from the couch and walked over to where I stood. I became uncomfortably aware of my disheveled appearance. I was still in my night-clothes—a short, light-blue, sleeveless cotton nightgown—and my afro was a mess of unruly curls. For a moment I saw myself in her eyes. I had been brought to her homeless and almost four months pregnant, as unappetizing as a sumptuous dinner laid out on a toilet seat. I was, from our first meeting, a problem to be solved.

I held my head high, considering what I could say to redeem myself in her eyes. We were the same height, so she met my gaze head on. She stopped close enough that I smelled the musky scent of her perfume. A wave of nausea and exhaustion pushed at me, and I had to will myself to stand still and maintain eye contact. A lock of hair strayed near Mrs. Lin's right cheek like a dark shadow on a pale background. She tucked it behind her ear.

"I hope you know you hit the jackpot, marrying Brian," she said. The flat tone of her voice belied the venom of her words, as did the cool expression with which she regarded me.

I remained motionless against Mrs. Lin's onslaught.

She sighed then continued, her voice low in volume and in pitch. "You know, in 1806, my great-great-great . . ." She stopped to count on her fingers, revealing short, carefully manicured nails. "Great-grandfather came to this country on the *Fortitude*. They were pioneers in a way, came before the indentured laborers. My great-great . . . my ancestor was from Canton. Most of the others who came with him chose to return to China when they realize the conditions under which they would have to live here, but my ancestor and his wife chose to stay. Maybe Port-of-Spain reminded them of home along the Pearl River. I don't know. I never been to China. Maybe they love the idea of starting over in a new place. Maybe they eat some cascadura. You know what they say: if you eat it, you have to die here." Her lips curled into a half smile, but her eyes remained cold.

"Our line almost die out. My great-great-great-great-grandfather's children all died without marrying, except for the youngest, who was able to find a suitable match once indentured laborers started coming from China in the 1850s."

I tried not to react but my eyes widened slightly. I understood that by "suitable match," Mrs. Lin meant Chinese. Every statement she made emphasized the counterpoint of my reality. I was not Chinese. I had no idea who my great-great-great-great-grandfather was, where he came from, or anything about my ancestral line. When Mrs. Lin's ancestors arrived in Trinidad, my ancestors were enslaved, unable to *choose* to return home because the conditions in the Caribbean did not meet their expectations. The collective memories of my people were eroded by the trauma they endured. Perhaps that explained my ability to forget the history of my own life in Jamaica. I wondered what this would mean for the child growing in my womb. Would he care about his ancestry on either side? A slow ache rose in my back as if a fist were tightening around my spinal cord. I considered walking out of the room rather than standing there to suffer the indignities of Mrs. Lin's suggestion. While I weighed the likely repercussions of such an action, she continued.

"May I be completely honest?"

I waited a beat then nodded, although the question was clearly rhetorical.

"I was the first in my family to marry someone who wasn't fully Chinese. My parents accepted Eugene. His father was Black but he was hardly around, and Eugene's mother had raised him and his brother in the Chinese tradition. Eugene knew how to come knocking, how to court me." Her gaze drifted upwards as if she were watching a movie in which she starred as a younger version of herself. Her mouth curved towards a smile, and a youthful softness relaxed on her face just for a moment before her expression hardened again. She refocused on me.

"I anticipated Brian would marry a Black woman. All of we living here together in Trinidad. Black, Indian, Chinese. None of us truly belong. And there are so few of us Chinese here now. We have to be Trinidadian first and Chinese second. But you . . ." She leaned in closer. "You not even a Trini." Mrs. Lin released another labored sigh.

"I wanted to get that out in the open, so you know how I feel about this . . . this situation. You're bearing my grandchild and marrying my son, and even though it happened in the wrong order, I'll accept you. I hope I'm not making a mistake. And . . ." She paused and bit her lip, the first real hesitancy she had shown since she began speaking. "The baby better look a lot like my side of the family."

Tears welled in my eyes, and my right hand tingled with the urge to slap her pale, smug face and actualize the sting those words had left in my mind. Mrs. Lin stood before me, her head slightly tilted and her lips pursed, her expression taunting as if to say, "What are you going to do about it?"

I evaluated my situation once more. Brian loved me, but I had seen evidence of the power his mother exerted over him with a lead so gentle he seemed unaware he was being controlled. Would he choose me if it came down to it? I was not sure, and I could not risk a major disruption before we were legally bound. *Three weeks until the wedding,* I told myself as I turned and fled the living room. I stumbled on the steps and reached out to steady myself, grabbing a handful of palm leaves in the process. I thrust the plant away and heard a thud as it hit the floor. I envisioned the pot broken, the soil flowing deep, dark reddish-brown onto the cream carpet, but I did not pause to right it.

Safe in my bedroom, I thought about my hunger, my stress, the pain in my back, the stumble, and prayed that the baby was okay. I curled up on the beige sheets as tightly into a fetal position as my belly would allow and imagined myself stranded on a seashore, water rushing towards my feet as tears and unsated hunger pains wracked my body.

CHAPTER FOUR

Fairfax, Virginia - August 2003

The ocean sounds in my daydream receded, only to be replaced by the splashing of falling water. The faucet was on, near its fullest pressure, and the sink was filled with suds, covering my arms from my forearms to my clasped hands. I lifted one hand and turned the water off just as Brian passed by the kitchen window, a silhouette in the summer twilight. The click of his key in the lock was followed by the sound of his feet stamping off dirt on the mat. I sucked in my stomach and squared my shoulders, prepared to present a defense for what I had done to the garden. I would never admit that I did not understand my actions myself.

Should I tell him about the woman in the parking lot? The intensity of the incident was already beginning to dull. I was no longer sure of the woman's features or even if I had heard her right when she called me "sister." Had I really blacked out for three minutes or just misread the time? Brian would stir things up again, ask questions I could not answer. He would speculate about why I had such a visceral response to a stranger, present theories for why the woman might have seemed familiar. He would nag at the coincidence that the woman was from Jamaica and insist that she wanted something from us. And if I told him that she had claimed to be my sister, the doggedness that made him a good lawyer would rise to the fore. Irritation stirred in my stomach at the thought of his interference. *Why mention it at all?*

Brian stopped in the kitchen doorway. I did not turn around, but I could feel his eyes focused on my back.

"Night, Maya." He paused. "You trying something new in the backyard?"

I turned. His slight six-foot frame only half filled the doorway as he stood with one hand rested on the doorjamb, the other loosening his tie—another nightly ritual, this one meant to convert him from boss into husband and father. The transformation had been necessary when Taiwo was young and every one of our spare moments was filled with worries about his development. In those days, we ended up talking and thinking about work, regardless of how he was dressed.

I nodded slowly, solemnly.

His lips were half-raised as if he was undecided about whether to approach the matter of the garden with humor or concern. He must have noticed my somber mood because apart from a slight elevation of his eyebrows, he said nothing more about the mounds of dirt and discarded plants at the back of the house. He crossed to where I stood and kissed me on the forehead—ritual three—before washing his hands and sitting at the kitchen table to eat the dinner I had laid out for him. I joined him, clasping my hands in front of me to keep them still.

"How was your day?" I asked.

There was a pause as he chewed and swallowed the mouthful of rice and peas he had put in his mouth just as I asked the question.

"Good," he replied. "Fruitful." He paused, a forkful of chicken halfway between his plate and his mouth. "The team finally finished the summaries for the Framtiden deal, and they haven't found any issues. You know I don't believe anything really done until the ink dry on all the signatures, but this? This looking real good."

I had been in the meeting when the senior associate updated Brian. The Framtiden deal was the kind of opportunity that did not happen often for a barely medium-sized Black-owned firm like Gil, Lin and Associates. We would be representing the interests of a successful Swedish technology firm as they made their entry into the United States market, and the billable hours we had expensed so far had generated more income in three months than any single deal of the firm's twenty-year history. Brian's partner, Geoffrey, had hit it off with one of their top executives on a flight from LA to D.C. and since then, almost everyone in the Corporate division had been involved in making sure we got the contract. Geoffrey repeatedly assured Brian that Framtiden was fully committed to using our firm, but Brian personally scoured every detail of the deal, balking at the possibility of even the slightest error. The serendipitous way in which the opportunity had come to us made him feel that we could lose it just as easily.

"How the rest of the meeting went?" I asked. Perhaps it was a reflection of my unsettled frame of mind, but I was unable to resist reminding him that I was in the conference room when the associates gave their report. His slight was unintentional, but not unusual. I was the firm's administrator, officially managing the business side of the law practice for ten years and unofficially for much longer. But without a complete college education in an environment where the number and caliber of the letters after your name directly impacted your billable rate, I was still just the managing partner's wife, and sometimes even Brian seemed to regard me as a secondary member of the team.

"Good," Brian repeated. He rocked back in the chair just slightly, his hands behind his head. His plate was empty now, his knife and fork in the six-thirty position. He sighed, and his eyes closed for a moment longer than a blink. "Dinner was delicious. Thank you." He sighed again, and this time it seemed like he was exhaling a heavy weight from his soul. "Daven brought up your idea to include shares as additional payment in the agreement with Framtiden. Josh and Martin disagreed. They really got into it."

I bit my lip on the inside and my tongue swelled towards the salty taste of blood. I had suggested that we tie the firm's compensation from the deal to the Swedish firm's success at a meeting last week, but I had had to leave for my daily trek to pick up Aunt Marjorie before I could make my case. Framtiden had a long and steady track record in Europe. They wanted to position their sensor products in the American market, and I had a hunch that the market for their products would explode. Owning shares could mean a steady stream of wealth for the firm, which we could leverage to smooth out the peaks and valleys we sometimes experienced between large contracts. Even though we had been in business for twenty years, as one of the few Black-owned law firms in the country, we continued to hustle for new clients. Requesting an ownership stake seemed an obvious way to structure the deal, but the suggestion had been ignored, at least until Daven, a second-year associate, picked up the cause.

I looked past Brian and into the darkness that had settled outside the kitchen window. I remembered my feeling in the garden, the premonition that my life was headed for a disruption. Maybe this was it. A good change . . . a major coup for Gil, Lin and Associates.

I swallowed hard. "It's a good idea. What you fraid of?" I said.

Brian sighed and ran his hand through his hair. "I don't want to seem . . . I don't want the firm to look like we're opportunists, trying to chook out they eye. This is the biggest deal Gil and Lin has seen in twenty years. I don't want to lose it because we're greedy. All they want is a law firm to guide them through the process of entering the US market."

"But they need more. And they should work with a firm that will be an ongoing partner, not just set them up and walk away. They have to get through a set a red tape with taxes, product liability, contracts, hiring, patents, immigration. We can do all that in-house. You and Geoffrey built that."

"We sure did," Brian said with a wry smile. They were in the process of refocusing the areas of practice on business law and divesting the firm of the criminal and litigation departments.

"We should be invested in their nonlegal success as well," I continued. "It's done all the time with start-ups—stock in lieu of payment. Framtiden is a start-up in the US. I know you can make them see that."

"You self know what we up against, Maya. We are the one percent and not in a good way."

"They aren't American."

"They still see color."

"Yeah, but Framtiden don't have the baggage Americans have when it come to working with a Black-owned firm. We can't operate from a position of fear forever."

"This is such a huge deal. It can break us . . ."

"Or make us," I interjected.

"True. But with the cultural differences, the language barriers, I feel like I'm back at UWI answering questions on a final exam I ain't study for. One misstep could sink us."

"Or make us," I repeated. "You are ready, Brian. We are ready for this." I moved to stand behind his chair and rubbed his shoulders. Leaning forward, I placed my chin on the top of his head. He had aged well, kept himself in shape, his stomach trim from regular cycling. The only signs of his forty-five years were the circles of tiredness around his eyes and the slight thinning on the top of his head where I rested my chin. As I disturbed the strands of hair, the scent of his shampoo drifted up to my nostrils. "We are going to do this," I said softly. The image of a video conference floated into my consciousness, the serious expressions on the faces of the men around the table in Sweden grainy, but I could sense that they had confidence in Brian.

The silence in the kitchen was charged with our collective thoughts. I knew I had not assuaged his doubts. While Brian was confident in his abilities as a lawyer, he would not trust any external validation that did not come in the form of a legally binding agreement. His disillusionment with our place in the United States had begun before we left Trinidad.

Washington, D.C. - August 1983

When he learned that Brian's mother had won the Diversity Visa Lottery, Uncle Joe, Brian's father's brother, had painted a picture of the US economy decorated with enthusiastic stories of the recovery from recession and all of the people he knew who had got hired "just like that," the snap of his fingers echoing loudly over the phone. Then we discovered, in the months between his graduation and leaving Trinidad, that Brian's Hugh Wooding Law School credentials would not allow him to practice in the US. This thwarted our plans, which had involved a fairly short stay at Uncle Joe's house while Brian searched for a job in a law firm, but Mrs. Lin insisted that we were already too far along the path towards our departure to turn back.

We arrived in the United States on August tenth, two months to the day after Taiwo was born. I had wanted him to be born on US soil, to belong undeniably to the country that would likely be his home, but Mrs. Lin had decided it was more important for us to be in Trinidad for her only son's graduation from law school, and after that, it was too close to my delivery to risk traveling.

As a result, I found myself adjusting simultaneously to marriage, an infant, and life in the United States. While Brian and Mrs. Lin had been annual visitors to Uncle Joe in D.C., my migration was the first time in my memory that I had traveled to the United States. I held firm to that belief, even when the sight of ground provisions boiling in a large iron pot on the stove, its steam filling the small, dark kitchen, threw me into an unsettling and inexplicable sense of having been there before.

I had stepped off the plane with great trepidation, fearful to leave behind my last link to the Caribbean, to take my last breath of salt-filled air. Life was a narrow single-lane street; everything I left behind was left behind definitively, the path I walked dismantled like pitch-black asphalt crumbling into an equally dark abyss. All that was left was intermittent chunks of memory. I stood for a minute at the top of the plane's ramp stairs and pulled the baby close, as much to protect him as to provide a barrier between me and the world I was about to enter.

UNCLE JOE LIVED in the top half of a two-story brownstone flanked on either side by identical structures. I had never lived so close to a neighbor before and was equally fascinated by the idea that I could hear their conversations through the wall, and horrified that they might misinterpret some of the noises they heard from the small bedroom into which Brian, Taiwo, and I had squeezed all of our belongings. Uncle Joe's wife, Aunt Camilla, fit us into the two bedrooms left vacant by their now-adult son and daughter, and the four walls pressed against me constantly, not only because there was a mere foot of space around our bed, but because the windows were never opened and I was ever aware that Taiwo was breathing the same air that had been circulating from nostril to nostril of the five adults who occupied the house.

In those early days, I almost regretted my decision to flee the Caribbean. Before arriving, I had fantasized about freedom. Every time I closed my eyes, my mind had filled with thoughts of anonymity, of blank pages, and of putting one more step between me and my Jamaican past. But once Taiwo had been born, when I found my arms filled with a responsibility I could never shirk, fear had filled me so completely I had been almost paralyzed. I wanted to turn back, to return to Aunt Marjorie's garden. Aunt Marjorie would know what to do with the tiny creature who had crawled out of my body and curled his fingers around my heart so tightly, I was afraid one day it would disintegrate and I would have no more love to give to him. What I felt was so all-encompassing it was impossible to believe it would continue to bubble forth indefinitely, impossible to imagine that the gush I felt when he cried, when his lips tugged on my nipples, when anyone else tried to hold him, was endless. While I had buried details of my own early experiences with love, one thing I knew was that love always had boundaries.

I knew Aunt Marjorie would whisper the right words of assurance or boil the herbs that would stem the love-flood so I could bear it, but by the time Taiwo was born, I had stopped writing to Jamaica, had moved in with Brian, and had not left a forwarding address, effectively rendering the path back to Aunt Marjorie impassable. My arrival in the US destroyed the rest. I was alone to figure out how to navigate raising a child in an environment so foreign to me that even leaving the house seemed like opening a door into an alternate reality.

I did not share my worries with Brian. Frustrated but determined to recover quickly, he had taken a sharp breath—one day—to adjust before beginning his job search. He spent his mornings poring over the newspaper and his afternoons in the library, using the computer and printer to find and apply for jobs. He had also enrolled in night classes at a Washington, D.C., university. Classes began a few weeks after we arrived.

I played the role of cheerleader. One morning I found him standing over Taiwo's cradle. Taiwo had had a restless night, and I had spent much of it in the living room so my pacing and soft lullabies would not keep Brian awake. I had just put the baby down to sleep and when I returned from the bathroom, Brian was at the side of the crib. He wore a sleeveless white cotton undershirt and boxer shorts, his clothing of choice when we were closeted in the room we shared at Uncle Joe's. His expression was one of fear, a fear I understood.

"You're going to be a great dad," I whispered.

"Not if I can't get a job."

"It's only been a week."

"And he's gained half a pound," he said. I was surprised he had noticed. "He's going to need more clothes, more food . . . and my mother . . . and you."

I did not take offense at being placed at the end of his list of concerns. His mother had been needling him relentlessly like the tree frogs that provided constant background noise to the nights in the Caribbean, sounds you only noticed when they were out of place, like between the silences on a telephone call or in a strange land. In Trinidad, Mrs. Lin had been the driver in all of her affairs; now she had to wait to be driven, but she insisted on conducting from the back seat. Brian usually accepted her instructions quietly, noncommittally, but I could see the tension wearing on his edges.

"We just reach, Brian. You have to give yourself a chance," I said.

"There's no time for chances, Amaya. We have savings, but they not going to last more than a few months if we move out before I get a proper job. And we can't stay with Uncle Joe indefinitely. I thought . . ." He dropped his head into his hands. "I just don't know where to start. In Trinidad, is easy. I mean, tings hard. You have to know somebody who know somebody to get anything done, but I understand that system. Here people actually reading your paperwork, paying attention to what you write, what skills you have. I feel like I don't have enough to offer."

"That's not true. You have a degree, and you're going to be a great lawyer. Besides,"—I smiled, hoping to lighten the mood—"you have Uncle Joe here to get you the hookup. He already got one interview lined up for you and you didn't even have to apply."

Brian faced me directly. "Yeah. An interview. You know how I feel when I walk in a room of strangers here? All my life I live in this skin and never thought about it. Never noticed how my light skin gave me an up in Trinidad. Here when I walk in a room . . . anywhere, the library, the store, I only see white people. Looking down on me, already make up their mind about what I can do . . . what I might do." He lowered his head slightly, and his shoulders fell. "I walk into a room here and I wonder if they going to turn me out, or if someone going to stand up and walk out because they expected me to look different. I have to dress a particular how, make sure I don't smell—neither bad like they half-expect nor good like I covering something up. I have to open my mouth quick so they hear me speak, so they know I'm foreign and put me in a different box in their mind. Not the top box, I'll never be in the top, but not the bottom either."

Brian did not get that job or the next that Uncle Joe organized, and he ended up taking odd jobs while he went back to school to qualify to practice law in the US. Life was better for us than for many Caribbean immigrants. We were green card holders and because of Uncle Joe, we always had a roof over our heads and food on the table. After several months, we met Jamela and Geoffrey and joined forces in friendship and then in the law firm, but it was too late. Brian's optimism bowed with the slam of every door until he no longer expected life in the United States to give him any breaks, not even the ones he deserved.

Fairfax, Virginia - August 2003

Brian placed a hand over mine. "I understand what you're saying, Maya, but I have to figure how to handle this right."

I felt an urge to tell him the thing that had kept me unsettled all evening: *It's time to make a change because one is coming whether you like it or not.* But I said nothing. My premonition was simply a residual echo from a tumultuous day, like the unease I felt whenever it rained after a powerful storm. Like the rain, my uneasiness would pass and life would regain its footing in the morning. I released a deep breath and a wave of tiredness flowed over me so powerful I felt if I did not lie down immediately, I would sink to the floor right where I stood.

"I'm going to bed." I kissed him on the top of his head. He did not protest as I left the room, leaving him to unwind with the newspaper.

CHAPTER FIVE

When I awoke the next morning, the previous day's events pushed their way to the front of my mind, but as I anticipated, they were more subdued, dulled by the perspective of time and rest. Brian snored lightly next to me. Neither he nor Taiwo needed to rise until seven, and Aunt Marjorie usually slept in until at least eight, under the influence of the medicines doctors prescribed to manage her dementia. Brian's hair lay flat, slicked away from his face as if he had fallen asleep while posing for a portrait. The absence of hair on his face emphasized the widow's peak that had become increasingly noticeable over the twenty-two years I had known him. Apart from a sprinkling of stubble on his chin, his face appeared smooth and untroubled. He was coverless and shirtless, and the sunlight that slid through a slight opening between the curtains caused the light layer of perspiration visible on his arms and legs to shimmer like morning sun on a sandy beach.

I stared at him for a minute, wondering what it would be like to sleep so peacefully. Sleep came easily to him regardless of what was happening in his life. He often likened it to falling backwards and knowing his fall would be broken by a soft landing. I envied that. Since we had moved to the United States, I no longer suffered the nightmares that plagued me in my early adulthood, but I still faced nighttime with underlying trepidation. For me, sleep was never a true refuge.

I considered going into the garden. There was a lot of hard work to be done after my impetuous upheaval the day before. A current of excitement at the prospect of creating something new ran through my body, making me acutely aware of my skin and the weight of my coverings: a soft cotton-jersey mix I favored, a comforter, and an extra blanket that created a cocoon-like weight on my body. I had never adjusted to life in a temperature-controlled environment with the closed windows and continuously recirculating air, and Brian and I constantly competed for control of the thermostat. As if on cue, the air conditioning rumbled to a start. A metallic smell filled my nostrils, accompanied by a draft of cold air. I pulled all three layers of covers over my head, insulating myself from the outside world. I closed my eyes as I envisaged the next in the series of reincarnations of the garden.

When I finally roused myself from bed to prepare breakfast, the creative energy that had buoyed me while I lay thinking about my garden still coursed through my body. I hummed, my mind focused on the garden even as I combined the flour, eggs, and other ingredients for the bakes and rolled the doughy mix into symmetrical round balls.

I sliced, kneaded, and fried until the scent of salt fish and bakes—both Brian and Taiwo hated ackee—filled the kitchen. A hand snaked around my waist and I flinched as Brian's stomach pressed against my arm. He bent and kissed my cheek.

"Someone woke up in a good mood," he said.

I suppressed the annoyance that surged to the roof of my mouth, the instinct to sift out only the negative in his comment, the unspoken suggestion that I was usually surly. Instead I smiled and gave his hand a gentle smack as he reached around me, stole one of the fried bakes directly from the pan, and popped it into his mouth.

"Hot. Hot." He hopped and opened his mouth to exhale hot air onto my cheek.

"What you expect? They're still on the fire." There was rebuke in my words but laughter in my voice, a duality that had characterized much of our relationship. Brian liked to believe that he had evolved beyond believing in the traditional roles of men and women. When his work schedule allowed, he contributed to the household chores, and he encouraged me to study, to work, and to hire help. However, he relished when I cared for him by cooking, cleaning, and washing his clothes. One of my best friends, Lisa, called me a pushover. She had gotten divorced and survived—thrived even, but her situation was different in every way possible. Brian had been my first and only relationship; he had rescued me at nineteen, loved me unwaveringly and without question, and my caring for him was a small return. We had adjusted and adapted until our life rolled forward with the steadiness of a car maintaining the speed limit on a busy highway. That morning, even as we bantered, I felt the urge to put my foot on the accelerator to outrun whatever was coming next.

"Morning, Mom."

"Morning, Tai." Trapped in Brian's arms, I answered without turning around. "Come set the table. Your father's hungry."

"Yeah, Daddy's hungry," Brian murmured close to my ear, his breath, still hot from the bake, hitting a spot behind my ear. The desire rising in me surprised me almost as much as my response.

"Later, baby. Later."

Brian's expression mirrored my surprise, just fleetingly, before his cheeks flushed with pleasure.

"Whispering is rude," Taiwo said. His voice was almost indistinguishable from his father's, and for a moment it had seemed as if Brian had thrown his voice from across the room.

"So true, sweetheart. Sorry." I elbowed Brian, who dropped the arm at my waist, leaving a warm imprint in the spot where his fingers had made contact with my side. I fried the rest of the bakes then sat at the table between Brian and Taiwo and helped myself to breakfast.

"You look nice," I said to Taiwo. He was wearing a shirt and tie—I suspected the latter was one of Brian's—a contrast to the T-shirts he usually wore to his job handling stock in a grocery warehouse.

"Thanks, Mom," he replied.

"Special occasion?" I asked.

"I am getting an ID with my photo on it. Now that I'm on full staff. They are taking my photo today, so I wanted to look professional." He smiled at Brian, his eyes reflecting a question as he waited for Brian's approval.

I nudged Brian under the table with my knee. He looked at me, and I angled my head ever so slightly in Taiwo's direction.

He turned towards Taiwo. "Yes, you looking good, Tai. Like the next CEO."

I hid a frown at Brian's flippant response. Taiwo was clearly very serious about how he would appear for his first permanent job. But Taiwo's smile deepened. His skin was a few shades darker than Brian's, but I could see his cheeks redden slightly.

As I sat at the table, Brian and Taiwo happy on each side, I felt cushioned by their presence. I scolded myself for the apprehension I had felt about the future.

"We're still on for the outreach center at six?" I asked.

Taiwo nodded.

"Where's Auntie going to be?" Brian asked. His lips narrowed, tense. Ever since he had agreed to help me to bring Aunt Marjorie from Jamaica to live with us, Brian had held me to my promise that Auntie's presence would not impact his daily life. Both Lisa and Jamela had been sure that his stance on this would soften as time passed, but six years later, he still snapped to attention whenever he sensed that he might be left alone to care for the woman who occupied the space in the house that had been intended for his mother. Recently, as the number of days when Aunt Marjorie's behavior led the Ramus House to call asking us to pick her up early increased, he had been insisting that we hire live-in help, but I had resisted, reluctant to force strangers full time into Aunt Marjorie's life.

"We won't be long," I said, letting a soothing tone enter my voice. "We've been volunteering at the shelter twice a week for a month now, you know that.

I leave a snack and juice for her so she doesn't need to leave her room. We'll be back before her soaps finish. Victor and Phyllis are her best friends. She'll be fine." I laughed.

"Hmm," Brian responded. He put a final forkful of saltfish in his mouth and pushed back his chair. "Thanks for breakfast. I'll see you at the office?"

"I'm going too, Mom."

"Bye, sweethearts."

The kitchen sank into silence, the only sounds the muffled noises of the men moving around the house, making last-minute preparations: brushing teeth, donning shoes. Then there was complete stillness as the door closed behind them. I rose from my seat and stood at the sink, which Brian had filled with sudsy water before leaving. A large bubble floated up, and I followed its progress as the light from the ceiling fixture caught it and divided it into a spill of colors. The colors swirled and somehow made it look like there were people moving inside the bubble, fairy-tale lives in minute existence. I reached an open palm towards it but the displacement of air from my hand pushed it up and out of my reach.

CHAPTER SIX

After breakfast, I dressed then steeled myself as I approached Aunt Marjorie's room to get her ready for the seven hours she spent at the Ramus House each day. She opened her door on my first knock. She stood in the doorway, dressed for her day in one of the calf-length, short-sleeved cotton dresses she brought with her when she arrived from Jamaica. Stately, alert, and clear-eyed, Aunt Marjorie's expression was set with stern displeasure and for a moment, I relived the awe with which I held her when I was the one living in her house.

"Good morning, young lady," Aunt Marjorie said as she walked past me, her low-heeled shoes clicking on the wooden floor.

I followed her at a respectful distance, first through the living room, then the dining room, and into the kitchen. I was taken aback by her alertness and wondered what was in store that morning. Our mornings varied from easygoing events during which we exchanged pleasantries as peers, to combative experiences in which Aunt Marjorie resisted leaving her bedroom at all. Mornings that began like this one, with Aunt Marjorie fixated on a particular idea, could be especially unpredictable, so I was happy I had swapped the thick, chewy bakes for a couple of slices of bread she could eat without frustration.

She ate in silence and did not mention the sacrilege of being served salt-fish with neither ackee nor bakes. I was relieved by her compliance and shifted my attention back to my plans for the garden. I would plant herbs, of course, but I was also drawn to plants like chamomile and aloe vera, both known for their calming and healing properties. I would locate and replant the sage bush, the leaves of which I had been crushing and administering to Aunt Marjorie in small doses because of its purported effectiveness in righting the chemical imbalances that accompanied Alzheimer's. August was just about over, so I would focus on plants that would survive the upcoming winter like parsley, oregano, tarragon, broccoli, kale, and perhaps radishes to add some color to the garden. *Look how far you've come, girl*, I thought. When I first arrived in the United States, I had assumed I would not be able to garden during the winter months, but I had quickly discovered joy in the extra effort involved in tending plants so they survived in harsh conditions, the only activity that could entice me to stay outside for prolonged periods in the winter.

Washington, D.C. - September 1983

When we first moved in with Uncle Joe, I was sure I would suffocate within the walls of the cramped living space. Then, one afternoon, one month after our arrival, when Brian was at work and Taiwo slept, I slid the ever-closed bedroom shutters open and peeked out of the window. There I saw the back of another set of townhouses, a mirror of the building in which we lived, except for the intimate laundry hung out on a clothesline stretched across the width of the opposite balcony. I peered to the left of the clothes towards the window, half expecting to see a young woman staring back at me with the haunted eyes I saw in the mirror. The thought of another house with another young woman trapped in a life she had not quite expected disturbed me, and I cast my eyes away from the window and down to the ground. For the first time, I noticed a small area, weed-infested and dusty. The backyard was enclosed by a gray chain-link fence with a swing gate that hung a little lopsided and creaked loudly enough that later, when the night was still, I would hear it and imagine someone was sneaking in to plant a seed or two in the dry soil. When I nudged Brian awake to investigate the noise, he suggested it was just the wind, and I wondered what wind could find its way between the closely packed buildings.

I imagined watering the seeds the imaginary intruder planted, or building a garden myself. I would have to select the hardiest of herbs. At first, I could not bring myself to choose, because whenever I thought of individual herbs in the garden, their smell would fill my head so thoroughly I would lose all four other senses in my fight to suppress the memories of the garden I left behind at Aunt Marjorie's home in Jamaica. In those moments, I would close the window and try to fill my mind with other pursuits, entertaining Taiwo or perusing the books Brian brought home from school. But I could not stay away from the window, could not stop myself from looking down on the little garden and its potential, and eventually I began to choose plants for the imaginary planting. Then my prevailing fear became the impending winter that was anticipated with great anxiety by everyone in the household, and I despaired once more. If I planted, whatever I planted would die. I wondered if I would even survive.

Eventually I could no longer resist the urge to feel the soil between my fingers. I left the house, walked past the row of buildings on our block, and slipped into the alley behind. As I counted the houses I passed to ensure I entered the correct backyard, I wondered if perhaps the gate would be locked. It was not. I entered, and so began the first of many evenings spent in the back garden, with only Taiwo strapped to my front for company. I tilled the soil with pieces of discarded wood, a stolen spoon, and my fingers. I bought garlic, ginger, and rooted herbs from the farmers' market where Aunt Camilla took me on a Saturday morning, prepped them, and placed them in the soil. Over the next few weeks, I retreated further into a world that revolved around Taiwo and the garden, which yielded green sprouts then robust plants under my care.

Fairfax, Virginia - August 2003

Memories of that burgeoning garden filled my head as I made my way through my morning routine. I cleaned up the kitchen and got Aunt Marjorie into the car. I often discussed the garden with her when we rode to and from the Ramus House, or on other errands or trips. When Aunt Marjorie's mind had been clear, horticulture had been her main passion and even now, she often provided useful advice once I presented my concerns in an uncomplicated way. I knew the destruction of the garden would upset her, and I considered how best to prepare her for the discovery she was likely to make that afternoon. As I merged onto the 495 highway that circled the Northern Virginia, Maryland, and Washington, D.C., area, I glanced at her to gauge her state of mind. It was then that I noticed her straight back and tight lips.

"Something wrong, Auntie?"

She bit her lip. "I never thought I woulda have this trouble from you, but I hear voices this morning, Maya." She gave a meaningful pause. "Men's voices."

I hid my smile as I responded, "Yes, Auntie. Brian and Tai."

"You sneaking boys inna me house?"

"No, Auntie."

"So who name so? Brian? Tai?"

I thought quickly. "We were working on a project. They came to pick it up to take it to school." Lying to Aunt Marjorie had become routine once I gave up on trying to force her to remember reality. The latter approach had always led to irreconcilable conflict and sometimes to physical confrontations. The final straw had been when she had become convinced that the woman she saw reflected in her mirror was a stranger. Aunt Marjorie engaged in conversations with her new friend, made plans with her, then grew very agitated when the woman did not materialize at organized rendezvous points. During that phase, I had been forced to accept that the essence of the woman who had raised me had been whittled away by disease, locked into some cabinet her brain could no longer access. I was grateful Aunt Marjorie still remembered who I was, even though she often thought I was still the seventeen-year-old who had left her home almost twenty-four years before.

"Good. You know sey I don't abide by no boys in the house. Not one, and for God's sake not two. And what kind of name Tai is, anyway? Like you wear round your neck?"

My attempts to hide my laughter were visible on my face at this point, and I resorted to a fit of coughing to cover it up.

"One spoon of castor oil for that cough when we get home," Auntie prescribed.

Those words struck me with the force of a stinging clap across my cheek. Impossibly, the smoky musk that emerges when someone opens a long-shut jar of Jamaican castor oil filled my nostrils. My hands froze on the steering wheel and in my next conscious minute, the car was at a complete stop in the rightmost lane of the four-lane highway; Aunt Marjorie was screaming my name; and horns, seldom heard on Virginia roads, blared from the cars behind me.

CHAPTER SEVEN

Half an hour later, sitting outside our office building, I huddled over my mobile phone. No one was nearby; the few people arriving and leaving did not pay any attention to me, but I felt exposed without any walls to shield me from prying eyes and ears.

"Thanks for taking my call, Dr. Hinds. I'm fine, thank you," I responded to her inquiry. "Actually, not really fine. I blacked out today. On the 495."

"You blacked out?" Dr. Hinds echoed.

"Well, more like my mind went blank," I whispered. "My aunt said something, I don't remember what, then there was nothing. When I stopped, we were about a mile past our exit. I could have gotten us killed."

"Did you lose consciousness?" Dr. Hinds spoke with a precise professionalism underlain with warmth, just as I remembered from our family counseling sessions with Taiwo.

"I don't think so . . . not really. I didn't slump over or anything."

"Have you ever had a seizure?" The urgency in Dr. Hinds's voice was unnerving.

"I don't think it was anything like that. I continued driving . . . until I did not. It's like time warped or something."

"You should probably see your primary healthcare physician, Amaya. To rule out any underlying cause."

"I feel fine . . . physically, I mean. I feel fine. Besides, I had a checkup like a month ago. I think whatever it is, is more up your alley." I paused. "I don't know what to do. I'm afraid to drive again."

"Okay. I'll see you. I can try to help you get to the bottom of this." Dr.

Hinds spoke more slowly, and my heart rate slowed in response to the even cadence of her words. "Come into my office. I will run a basic physical evaluation as well. I think I can fit you in today." There was a pause on the phone, and I heard the soft rustle of a page turning. "I have a cancellation at noon, actually. Can you make that? Take a taxi. You don't have to drive."

My heart rate accelerated once more at the mention of driving and the possibility of losing control again. I focused on my breathing.

"Amaya? When can you come in?"

"When can I come in?" I echoed. "I haven't gone into my office yet. Can I check my schedule and get back to you?" I added, although I knew I had no meetings until three.

"Call soon. I have that spot that just opened up this afternoon, otherwise I may not be able to see you until next week."

I held the phone to my ear for several seconds after the call ended. The concrete wall on which I sat was cold through my cotton trousers. The flower-filled courtyard was on the west side of the high-rise in which the firm's offices were located, and so the sun had not yet heated the air. I was worried. I had not told Dr. Hinds that the morning's episode was not the first time I had blacked out recently. That first time, I had assumed dehydration or stress had been the cause. This time, I had been well-nourished and relaxed, laughing at Aunt Marjorie's accusations. I had to acknowledge that there was a problem.

I could have killed Auntie and me both, I thought again. The prospect that something was wrong with my brain frightened me, especially after witnessing Aunt Marjorie's mind deteriorate like a leftover helium party balloon, slowly deflating and falling closer and closer to rock bottom. Were these blackouts a sign of the diminishing of my own mind?

"Talking to the boyfriend?"

I started. I had not heard Jamela's approach. I put the phone away and smiled as I noticed that my best friend was wearing a blouse with red-and-white vertical stripes under her black suit, the colors matching the Trinidadian flag she sported on her lapel.

"Girl, please," I replied. "When would I have time to have another man?"

Jamela sat on the wall next to me.

"Hiding from the boss, then?"

I nodded, still smiling.

"You know how it is. I see him all day then all night. A girl has to get a break sometimes."

We laughed, and my mood lightened as if a corbeau had been nesting on my consciousness, darkening it, but subtly so I had not been aware of its presence until it launched itself into the air, freeing me. I considered telling Jamela about the blackouts, the lost time that worried me so. I knew she would keep my secret, but I also knew Jamela's pragmatic and calculated approach to life would kick in and she would push me to seek help, even if it meant driving me to the doctor and hauling me inside in a fireman's carry.

"I was just getting some fresh air. Winter is on its way, and you know I don't venture out here once it gets below sixty degrees."

"Yes, I know. I'm glad you're taking care of yourself." Jamela smiled, but her hazel eyes, their dark pupils rendered piercing by the surrounding light-brown and olive-green irises, remained serious.

I looked away from her searching stare. I hated that my mood was so transparent. I knew I would not be able to hide my worries from Jamela for long, and once she knew, the visit to Dr. Hinds would be inevitable. *I'll go. Just once to see if it helps*, I thought. My mind drifted and when I refocused, Jamela was still looking at me, her head tipped slightly to the right. Her lips parted, and I guessed she was going to press me about my state of mind. I preempted her.

"I like the pin . . . and the blouse."

A grin spread across her face. "You know I have to represent, even if Trinidad is only my adopted country. When we were growing up, my mom took two days off every Independence. It was almost like Christmas or a mini carnival. She stayed home and started decorating and cooking the day before: roti, dhal, curry chicken, the works. Then on the day, she played soca all day, had all her Caribbean friends over. People in and out all day until late."

"That sounds like fun. I'm sure Brian forgot Independence was this weekend. He's so caught up with this Sweden deal," I said.

"Geoff too," Jamela said, her smile fading. "Not on the Sweden deal, but work is all he talks about."

"They're at a pivotal point," I said.

"Yeah, but we have a fifteen-year-old boy at home who still talks to us. That's some kind of miracle. But he's gonna stop if his daddy can't ever be fully present to listen. I don't want him to end up like Ian. I swear that boy moved to France just so he could be as far away from us as possible." She laughed, but it came out as a short grunt.

"You really miss him."

"Yeah. Well, the truth is they are meant to become independent and move out. I guess we did too good a job." She breathed in sharply, remembering that I had a grown son who had not moved out and was unlikely to do so any time soon. "Not that you didn't do a good job . . . We all have our crosses to bear." She reached out and touched my hand.

"It's fine," I said, punctuating my words with a smile. Jamela had been an ever-present support during the early years after Taiwo's autism diagnosis, and her pride in his progress towards independence was second only to Brian's and mine.

"Well, I have a nine-thirty meeting with a client on an immigration case. Tough one." Jamela sighed and stood, dusting the back of her skirt. She switched her briefcase from her left hand to her right. "Come. I'll walk in with you. Maybe we can get lunch later? You look like you need to talk."

"Actually, I have to make another call, and I have an appointment at twelve," I said. "How about tomorrow?"

"Tomorrow is tough. How about a movie then dinner on the weekend?

We haven't done that in forever."

"As long as it's not scary."

Jamela laughed. "Nobody is taking you to a scary movie. You cover your eyes when something happens; you cover your eyes when something's about to happen, and then when you *think* something is about to happen, your hands are over your eyes again. It's a waste of money."

I smiled. "You're not wrong. I can't handle horror."

Jamela's expression softened. "Sometimes I feel like you've dealt with your fair share of monsters already." She did not wait for an answer, but headed towards the door that led inside our building.

I breathed a sigh of relief. From the day we met, Jamela had displayed an uncanny knack for figuring out my moods.

CHAPTER EIGHT

In our early days in the United States, I did not venture out on my own beyond the front steps that led up to Uncle Joe's house, the playground, and the garden I was tending in the back. Brian did not understand my reluctance to engage more in the new world we had entered. He worked hard to provide for us and he felt I had the easier job, caring for an agreeable baby.

"Between you and my mother, I don't know who is worse. Long face on your end, complaining and nagging on hers. You all lucky I'm not a drinking man." It was seven-thirty a.m. and he had just come home from a shift at the cemetery, his pores exuding the damp smell of newly-turned earth. Brian had started working as a stock assistant in an office equipment company and had also been taking on a few shifts as a security guard at a city-run cemetery on nights when he did not have classes. Mrs. Lin was unhappy about both jobs, mortified that her well-educated son who had graduated at the top of his law school class was reduced to hard and demeaning labor. The fact that he was working in a cemetery did not sit well with her Catholic sensibilities.

"This is hard on all of us," I said. Taiwo stirred in the cradle positioned next to our bed. Everything in the room touched and shook and shivered together. I stretched a hand out and gently rocked the cradle. Taiwo settled back into sleep.

"Really?" Brian's voice rattled the airwaves and Taiwo stirred again. "I don't see you working two jobs and studying. At least you could be pleasant when I get home. Dat's too much to ask?"

He wants to wake the baby, I thought. *Wants to make me as miserable as he is. Well, I am.*

Anger welled up inside me, rising from my stomach to my throat, stifling me, and I knew I had to escape. I was as stuck as Brian was. Why should I be required to pretend everything was great when it was not? I had fended for myself since becoming an adult, planning my next move, but since joining the Lin family I found myself in the backseat of my life, tasked only with sitting at home caring for Taiwo, who was an easy baby and took to my breast eagerly. I considered working, but having not completed my first degree, the jobs for which I was qualified were even less meaningful than Brian's, and leaving Taiwo with my mother-in-law to earn minimum wage was unthinkable.

When Brian left the room to take a shower, I bundled myself and Taiwo in the warmest clothes we had and left the house, the baby secured in the carrier. He was three months old, a long, lean, fourteen-pound weight strapped uncomplaining to my chest. I stepped out of the townhouse, descended the steps, and turned right to walk down our street. A light blustering of wind followed me, lifting leaves from the ground, which then whirled in concert with the angry thoughts in my head. *What more could Brian possibly want from me? Can't he see I am just as lost as he is?*

I considered going to the garden and releasing my frustrations there, but my mind rebelled against the thought of being confined again, even outdoors. Besides, October had just begun and the mornings were chilly in my estimation. I had not gotten used to gardening in gloves. The layers between my fingers and the earth were restrictive. The park was just three blocks from our house. I was drawn to it, in part because it reminded me of Queen's Park Savannah in Trinidad, with its undulating grassy terrain, walking paths, and flat areas for picnics and the playground. Like sections of the Savannah, this park was lightly wooded with tall trees, and it was an odd respite in the midst of an urban setting. Unlike the Savannah, it was small, only about an acre—not quite enough space to fully shield me from the D.C. bustle.

Absorbed in my thoughts and barely aware of where I was going, I found myself at the playground. Taiwo was too young to enjoy the playground activities, but he seemed to like watching the children at play; he turned to look whenever a sudden shriek or peal of laughter rang out. Although it was only about eight o'clock, there were already seven or eight children on the playground, seemingly in constant motion: chasing one another around the equipment; climbing the single, aging slide; and pumping their legs to make the creaking swings go higher and higher. Mothers and nannies sat on the surrounding benches, and I walked past three seats before I found one that was unoccupied. I sat, cradling Taiwo's neck and rocking my body back and forth. I looked down at him and he looked back at me. Although he didn't smile or coo, he seemed to know me and to understand that I was a place where he could feel safe.

As my mind slowed its angry pace and I became more aware of my surroundings, a wave of homesickness filled my body. The tree to which the bench was anchored was clearly a relation to a tamarind tree, with waxy leaves and fruit with a tough exterior and, I imagined, tender, delicious insides. Morning light filtered through the leaves, creating a spotted pattern on my jeans that shifted and swayed as the leaves moved in the breeze.

"He's so cute!" I barely restrained an eye roll as I heard the familiar reaction to Taiwo's wide-eyed serenity. This was another reason I kept to myself. Taiwo was fair-skinned, the dark brown on his ears the only indication that his skin would darken. The few white women I encountered in the park looked at Taiwo's complexion, pale like vanilla against my chocolate-hued skin, and assumed I was his nanny, not quite worthy of their time. Many Black women fawned over him, going as far as to reach out to touch his skin as if it were some sort of talisman. Me, on the other hand, they regarded with distrust, possibly assuming based on Taiwo's appearance that I was married to a white man.

I raised my eyes to find a Black woman looming over me. She wore her hair in a curly afro, a contrast to the chemically-straightened styles worn by most of the Black women I had seen in the neighborhood, and she only wore a padded vest over a long-sleeved T-shirt in spite of what I considered to be cold weather. She had an open face, warm, free from guile, with light lines around her nose and mouth, suggesting she was older than I was. Without asking permission, she sat next to me. I shifted to give her room.

"Thanks," she replied. "Mine is fifteen months old, Francine, she's over there." She pointed to a small child walking unsteadily on the graveled playground. I felt a stab of concern for the tiny body's safety in the midst of the older children on the swings and slides and spinning contraptions, but her mother seemed unperturbed. An older boy, about six years old, approached the little girl, picked her up, and swung her around before placing her on the ground and running off once more.

"That's her big brother, Ian. This one's my last." The woman patted her belly, and I noticed a slight bulge under her vest.

Later in our friendship, Jamela would confess that she saw me sitting alone on the bench wearing all my winter clothes like a lost lamb in need of rescuing. "You looked like if someone said 'Boo' you would break down crying. I decided not to give you a chance to escape." In quieter moments, Jamela admitted she might also have been in need of rescue.

"I'm Jamela Gil. What's this cutie pie's name?"

I hesitated, all the stories I had heard about strangers in the US being inherently dangerous coming to the front of my mind. Why did this woman want to know my child's name? Was she going to try to lure him away? I pulled him closer and he whimpered.

"I'm not going to steal him." Jamela laughed. "God knows I've got my hands full." She patted her belly again. "Our second surprise." She raised her fingers to signal quotation marks in the air around the word "surprise."

I smiled.

"His name is Taiwo," I said softly.

"Do you have an accent? Are you from the islands?" The words tumbled out of Jamela's mouth with as much excitement as the children screaming on the playground as they flew higher and higher on the swings. Since leaving Jamaica, I had worked hard to neutralize my accent and standardize my phrasing so their precise origin was undetectable, but the way I spoke still attracted questions. I normally responded viscerally to the Caribbean islands— each so individual they had been unable to successfully maintain an economic union—being referred to as if they were a single entity, a playground for Americans. But I forgave Jamela as soon as I heard her next words:

"My mother is a Trini."

I laughed. Jamela sang the word "Trini" the way she must have heard it said all her life. "You have an accent too," I said.

"In truth!" she quipped. "My mother raised me and my brothers as if she were still living in Trinidad. I tell people I am more a second-generation immigrant than a first-generation American."

"I'm from Jamaica," I said in a delayed response to her question. I was drawn to this woman with her wide smile and dimpled cheeks. "And my name's Amaya."

"Nice to meet you, Amaya." Jamela laughed again and I was not sure why, but I laughed too.

"How long you been here?" she asked.

"Almost two months," I replied.

"Ah, you just get off the boat," she replied. "How you settling in?"

"It's been okay." I patted Taiwo's back. "This one keeps me busy, so I haven't really done anything. But then everyone is just so busy." My thoughts ran on Brian and his claim that I was surly, and I tried to lighten my words. "It seems."

"True," she said, her expression suddenly serious. "It's the American dream."

"It's nothing like I expected." I bit my lip. I did not know why I was confiding in a stranger, but something about Jamela made me feel she could be trusted with my insecurities.

"How so?"

"It's going to sound silly."

"Try me."

"Everything I know about the US is from TV, shows like *Laverne and Shirley*, *One Day at a Time*, and *Little House on the Prairie*."

"I can imagine." Jamela's tone was serious, but it was obvious she was trying to hold back a laugh.

"What?" I said.

"I am just imagining, if *Little House on the Prairie* was your model, what you must have thought of life here! All of us riding around in horses and buggies." Her laughter erupted, and Taiwo shifted against me.

"I knew that wasn't today . . . wasn't current," I said stiffly, miffed at Jamela's mocking. "What I'm saying is that I watched *Sanford* and *The Jeffersons*, but most of the shows are with white people, so it didn't really prepare me for this." I waved a hand in front of me. "I expected to see white people and not to connect with them, you know? I never really met one before I came here. But I did not expect so many Black . . . I mean African Americans and . . ." I bit my lip, not sure how to express my feelings without being offensive.

"You thought you'd have more in common with them?"

"Yeah," I replied, grateful for Jamela's ability to put my thoughts into words. "It's weird, I look into their faces looking for something familiar. Like at home, people's faces belong, but nothing seems familiar here. It's like the geography and our different experiences marked us. They may as well be white!"

"I would keep that last part to myself if I were you," Jamela replied.

I felt my cheeks burn. "I didn't mean to offend you."

"Offend me?" She laughed. "I told you. I grew up with a woman who claimed any house we lived in as part of Trinidad. She bad-talked Black Americans every day. I guess present company was always excepted?"

I warmed to the topic, Jamela's openness making me feel more and more at ease. "I never thought I'd miss the salt in the air so much. When I was in Trinidad, I hardly went to the beach. You can't leave Jamaica and go Trinidad beach. But it's an island, so I guess the sea was always on the breeze. And I miss the rain. I so miss the rain." Sandwiched in the Lins' house where I was expected to be grateful for the opportunity to be in the US, I had not allowed myself to really think of all I longed for. "In Jamaica, moisture gets caught up in the Blue Mountains. Nowhere to go. So when it rain, it rain until the sky empty. Here, showers breeze past like an exam. Powerful but over quick quick. And as for visitors . . ." This last part was an echo of Mrs. Lin's complaints. She was withering in the solitude and sameness of our days.

"Do you regret coming?" Jamela interjected when I paused.

"I'm not sure," I said slowly, thoughts running through my mind of how the similarities to Jamaica had plagued and overwhelmed me and made me want to escape Trinidad. "I guess it's early and I still feel unmoored. I need something to anchor me to this place."

"I guess you miss family?"

"I have no family." I softened my tone when I saw her expression. "I only have an aunt and . . ." I bit my lip. "We aren't in touch."

"I get it," Jamela said. She looked at me, her hazel eyes soft with concern. "You've taken on a lot. Moving and with this little one. It must be overwhelming. But there's a lot of good here. And great opportunities for the babes." She gestured towards Taiwo. "You will find your way."

I nodded, relieved to have expressed my unhappiness without the guilt I felt back at Uncle Joe's house. We had so much, we were so lucky, and Brian was working so hard it felt unfair to complain, yet that did not make my discomfort any less real.

Our conversation took us from the playground to a nearby café, where Jamela wrangled with her six-year-old and her toddler, trying to settle them to eat, handling demands for ketchup, fries, and soda. I looked down at Taiwo, snuggled against my bosom, content in his own world, and tried to imagine a day when he would be so vocal and demanding.

"This place has the best cupcakes," Jamela said. "My husband works a couple of blocks from here. On the days when I have to drive him to work, I bring the children to the playground, then we come here for a treat." She took a bite of the cupcake she was holding. Creamy white filling oozed from the middle and coated her fingers.

"You should try it," she said, offering me the side of the cupcake she had not yet bitten.

I drew back from the invitation.

Jamela shook her head sharply. "I am so sorry! I spend so much time with children, I forget how to behave with adults." She laughed and pushed the box of cupcakes towards me. "Take your own, of course. Please, try one."

WE FELL INTO an unspoken plan to meet regularly at the playground. I looked forward to the meetings. When I was with Jamela, my laughter emanated from a place deep in my belly that I had only just discovered. Only a week had passed of daily meetings when I confided in Jamela about our situation at Uncle Joe's, now well into its second month, and the reason I had been looking so forlorn on the bench the day we met.

"Get out!" Jamela exclaimed. I was still getting used to her propensity for loud outbursts. "My husband's a lawyer too, and he's actively trying to grow his practice. I was supposed to pass the bar and be his partner in the firm, but . . ." She gestured towards the playground. "Someone has to raise these little people. Someday . . ." She focused on a spot above my head for a few seconds. Then she looked at me, her eyes opened wide. "We need to get our men together. Why don't you guys come for dinner tonight?"

I paused. With Brian's schedule, it was unlikely that he could be free on such short notice, but I would insist that he made the time. This is what he had wanted, for me to do something besides sit at home and mope.

"Mommy!" The yell attracted our attention. Across from us, on the playground, Francine stood, her hands straight out, as if she were a billboard, displaying a mud-splattered body. Jamela stood, a laugh shaking her body. "Maybe tomorrow night."

JAMELA'S HOME IN Falls Church, Virginia, was just as I had pictured it, tastefully decorated yet slightly chaotic in that way of homes where children are allowed to be children. I sat on the couch and a petulant "ma-ma" emanated from my seat. I laughed as I fished a baby doll from beneath me and handed it to Francine.

Jamela and I had agreed not to tell our husbands they were being set up. The two men hit it off immediately, and when they discovered their shared interest in law, the conversation became so animated they did not even notice when Jamela and I retired to another room. By the end of the evening, they were discussing plans to work together and to build a law firm once Brian was called to the bar.

"I haven't seen you laugh like that in . . . I don't think I have ever seen you so happy," Brian commented as we walked to the metro after dinner. He took my gloved hand in his, and I squeezed his slightly.

"I like Jamela a lot," I responded.

"I can tell. You don't laugh like that at my jokes."

I blushed. Brian laughed and I joined in.

"Did you like Geoffrey?" I asked.

"Yes, it's our first meeting, of course, but he seems like a good guy. We have a lot of ideas in common." He looked off into the distance, lost in thought for a beat or two. Then he smiled and swung my hand a little. "For the first time since we came to this place, I see a way out. I feel like I'm working towards something."

"We are working towards something, Brian."

AND WE HAD worked. Brian's outlook on life improved significantly after meeting Geoffrey. Because of his Caribbean roots, Geoffrey knew the rigorous nature of education in Trinidad and at the University of the West Indies, and so he was willing to give Brian a chance. Brian began work as a paralegal, work he could do in advance of passing the bar, with the promise of a promotion once he met the required qualifications. The pay was significantly better than what he had earned as a stock assistant, so he was able to stop working his night shifts at the cemetery and focus on his studies. Jamela and I remained in the background, our friendship firmer because our meeting had been the foundation on which all of their success had been constructed.

CHAPTER NINE

Fairfax, Virginia - August 2003

Although eight or nine years had passed since I last crossed the threshold into Dr. Hinds's office, it was just as I remembered: plainly decorated, with off-white walls bare except for a single painting of a tropical scene. The artist had painted a forest with flowers and leaves of bright greens, oranges, and yellows of every possible shade along a riverbed. The painting was obviously Caribbean-inspired and after seeing it on our first visit and then discovering that she was Black, I had decided that this doctor might work out. My instincts had been accurate. Taiwo loved Dr. Hinds, which felt like a miracle because at eight, he had been poked, probed, and questioned until he mistrusted most adults, and I feared that mistrust was slowly being transferred to Brian and me. Dr. Hinds understood Taiwo and knew how to help him find words to describe his thoughts and feelings. Now that I was alone sitting on one of the three armchairs Brian, Taiwo, and I once occupied, I hoped Dr. Hinds would understand me too.

She leafed through a folder containing a few sheets of paper.

"Your vitals look great. Your responses and reflexes are fine. I still want you to check in with your primary care doctor." She peered at the pages. "Dr. Patterson? She might want to order an MRI to rule out a more serious issue. Or refer you to a neurologist. But go ahead, tell me what's going on."

"I don't know." I twisted my hands in my lap.

"Okay." She drew the word out as she often had in Taiwo's sessions, giving him time to think and also modeling behavior he would later use to buy himself time to figure out tricky social interactions. I was not thrilled about being treated like a child, but I really did not know what to say. Dr. Hinds let the silence linger for a few more seconds, then she spoke, her voice soft. "Tell me about the blackouts."

I described the episode I had on the highway. When I was finished, Dr. Hinds looked at me expectantly as if somehow she discerned that there was more. As the silence grew once more, I found myself filling it with as much as I could recall about the minutes I lost when I encountered the woman in the parking lot.

"And you are sure you have never seen her before?"

A memory of the sense of familiarity I had felt when the woman pursed her lips swelled in my gut, a burning like after I ate over-spiced curry. My mouth filled with saliva and I swallowed hard, suppressing the thought.

"I am sure," I said.

"Okay," Dr. Hinds drawled again. "Have there been other instances where you've blacked out?"

I tried to recall. Was this really a new phenomenon? I could not think of anything in my recent past. I would have sought help if anything happened that could endanger Taiwo or impair my ability to care for him when he was young. I threw my mind further back, to leaving Jamaica, meeting Brian at university in Trinidad, moving in with him and his mother after getting pregnant, hearing that we won the visa lottery. A clear memory began to emerge.

Maracas, Trinidad - April 1983

In the last month and a half of my pregnancy, I kept the computer on the desk in our bedroom running all day, the low whirring of the CPU's fan a comforting backdrop as I struggled with how I felt about my future with this new family that was being built around me. Brian used the machine to study in the nights, but in the daytime, even as my protruding stomach made sitting increasingly uncomfortable, I spent hours in front of the screen, playing a game in which I stacked blocks. There was something satisfying about the process of building, even though my edifices were totally dismantled with every loss. In that respect, the game truly mirrored my life at that time.

Mrs. Lin hated the game.

"When las you read a book?" she asked one day.

I jumped. I had been so engrossed in directing the falling bricks, I had not heard her enter the bedroom. Retorts about the nicety of knocking and the peril of scaring pregnant women rose in my throat, but I kept my lips pressed together. Silence had become my armor, more effective than words at fending off Mrs. Lin's insults. I clicked on the mouse and a cluster of three blocks—two next to each other and one freeloading on the top—slid into an open spot in the pile accumulating at the bottom of the screen. Three more block batches drifted down, hypnotic, the way I imagined snow would fall from the sky when we experienced our first winter in the United States. I focused on another block of three and turned it so that the single block was on the bottom, hanging on as if at any moment it could fall or be crushed by the top two.

The screen went blank.

"What the . . ."

"Oh, so now you could talk, eh?" Mrs. Lin held the power cord for the monitor in her hand. The soft bleeping of the game continued, and I imagined my blocks falling, unmoored, crashing into the piles below. Mrs. Lin's face was red. I wondered, if I reached out and touched her cheek, if my fingers would singe on contact. I forced my own face into a façade of calm. Using the edge of the small computer desk as support, I pushed myself into a standing position and walked past Mrs. Lin. I walked out of the room and down the hallway towards the living room.

Mrs. Lin followed me. "You scrambling my grandson's brains with that chupidness. You should be reading, or listening to some classical music. Do something constructive for him, nah . . . for . . ."

I stopped in the narrow hallway but remained silent.

"What you going and name him?" she asked.

I placed a hand on my stomach and thought about the ultrasound, conducted at the upscale clinic Mrs. Lin had insisted I attend, which had confirmed the gender of the child growing inside me. I had not known until that moment how much I wanted him to be a boy, or rather, how much I did not want him to be a girl. Every time I thought of mothering a girl, I found myself engulfed by a series of images like a cinema reel. The one that came to me most frequently was of a girl I did not know sitting between her mother's legs, getting her hair combed. The snippets themselves were not unpleasant, but they left me with an intense sense of doom I could not explain.

I considered keeping my silence, or worse, continuing my journey through the sunken living room and into the kitchen, but that Caribbean upbringing that engendered an innate mixture of fear of and respect for older people overruled. I knew there was only so far I could and should push my mother-in-law, so I responded, "Taiwo."

She was silent for a moment, then she spoke. "Tai-wo? Like the Chinese town?"

A wave of exhaustion washed over me although it was only ten a.m. I could leave Mrs. Lin to believe that her grandson would carry a name that even vaguely reflected his Chinese heritage. And why not? I had spent a lot of time thinking about the name I would give to the baby moving in my belly. Alexander, defender of man; Patrick, noble; Eric, ruler. I discarded them all. I did not feel qualified to impose a characteristic or destiny on the child at any point, and certainly not while he was still in my womb, an unknown quantity apart from being human and male. Better to choose a name that described how he had come about, or to honor someone who had come before him.

"Is a Yoruban name."

"Yoruba?" Mrs. Lin said the word slowly like she could taste it, bitter on her tongue. "I thought Jamaican slaves came mainly from Nigeria?"

I repressed a sigh.

"Yoruba isn't a country, it's an ethnic group, a part of Nigerian culture."

Mrs. Lin looked at me, her eyes narrowed, her brow—ever-softened with a myriad of creams and lotions—furrowed, and her lips pursed as if she had just taken a swig of tamarind juice she had mistakenly thought was sweetened.

"You even know what the name mean?" she asked. "Suppose is a curse word or something."

I hesitated again, heat rising in my chest at her insolence. I had heard the name on the BBC World Service. The announcer was reporting on twin Nigerian athletes, Taiwo and Kehinde, who were breaking records in the Olympics' triple jump event. The announcer was fascinated by the athletes and their story, and repeated their names several times. Something in me stirred. I did not have the words to explain how, when I spoke the name "Taiwo" out loud, my whole being had responded with a sigh. The syllables, which I was sure I had never sounded out together before, felt natural on my tongue, as if the name was one I had spoken every day in a previous life. I felt certain this was the name I should give to my child. In that moment, I had mused that the name must have a profound meaning, but when the announcer—as if reading my mind—explained the significance of the twins' names, I was no closer to understanding the impact it had on me.

"It means 'the first twin to taste the world,'" I replied.

"Twin? Taste?" Mrs. Lin snapped. "What chupidness is that? Brian agree to that?"

"The baby is mine too," I replied. *And only one-quarter Chinese*, I thought but did not voice. I was not sure if that was how genealogy worked, but I assumed that if Brian's father had been half Black and I was mostly Black, then the offspring Brian and I produced would be more Black than Chinese. But what if he got a half of Brian's genes that had mainly Chinese influence? Or a half that had none at all? I wondered if that was possible.

Mrs. Lin's eyes narrowed even further until the blacks of her pupils were just barely visible.

"You so vex all the time. What happened to you?" She cocked her head slightly to the side as if to get a better look at my face. "When you were a child, who hurt you?"

A rush of sound filled my head. *The sound of the sea*, I thought. It grew louder until it was a pressure in my brain, a tidal wave threatening my stance. I stumbled into the kitchen, my eyesight blurred. I reached for the back of a chair and stood, hand propping my back, supporting my baby. I felt myself slipping downwards, falling—not physically, but falling away from my present into a black hole where memories should have caught me, strengthened me, supported me with the assurance that I had endured before and survived. But there was nothing to stop my fall.

Breathe, I repeated in my mind. *Breathe*. Slowly I began to feel more balanced, and I was able to move. I opened my eyes to find Mrs. Lin staring at me. My mother-in-law's head was still tilted to one side, but her lips, which had been pursed in exasperation, now turned slightly downward, and she dropped her hands from her hips. Genuine concern filled her face, and she reached out with a carefully manicured hand towards my nail-bitten one. I tensed and Mrs. Lin retracted her hand, using it instead to smooth her own hair. She leaned closer to me, although she did not attempt to touch me again. I stepped past my mother-in-law, opened the back door, and entered the garden.

The sun struck my face, fingering through the muted fog of my brain and clearing my mind. I looked around. The yard comprised mainly low-cropped grass; three fruit trees near the property line—lime, soursop, and mango; and a clothesline made from two T-shaped white metal poles about fifteen feet apart and connected by long vinyl ropes. Colorful pegs held five of Brian's white shirts on the line. They swung, flapping, carefree in the breeze.

"Can I plant something?" I did not look behind me. I knew Mrs. Lin was there. I hoped the concern she felt would translate into indulgence.

"We leaving in a few months, four at most. Why you want to plant now?"

"I won't take much space. How bout over there?" I pointed to the eastern corner of the backyard, partially shaded by the lime tree, the spot I saw while sitting at the computer in the bedroom and the spot in which, in my mind, I had already planted a scaled-down version of the garden I had left behind in Jamaica. "You want me to do something, don't? Something for the baby? This is what I want to do."

I heard a sharp exhalation and knew I had won.

I stood in Mrs. Lin's yard for several minutes, staring at the spot, moving plants in my mind, picturing them established, instinctively knowing where they would prefer to be placed, where they would flourish. The area was small, and I would have to choose the seeds carefully. I did not know where I would get the knowledge, but I wanted to grow the things I would need to help the baby, leaves to soothe stomachs, to entice milk production, and to naturally ease pain. Planning the garden reminded me of the computer game, choosing where to drop the blocks, but instead of sprouting a short-lived wall, these blocks would sprout new life.

"We'll have to give the soil a good soak first," Mrs. Lin said behind me. "The rainy season soon come, but these days dry like bone."

I looked up at her, but instead of the condescending expression I expected to accompany the advice, I saw on her face an unveiled plea for a truce, for companionship.

"You're right," I replied.

CHAPTER TEN

The memory cleared, and I found Dr. Hinds looking at me expectantly. It took me a few seconds to recall the question I was supposed to be answering. *Had I blacked out before?* It seemed I had, that day in the kitchen when Mrs. Lin asked about my childhood. I did not know where to begin explaining the scene to Dr. Hinds, the complicated relationship I had had with my mother-in-law, the unmooring I had felt, pregnant and trapped in her house.

"No, the parking lot and this morning are the only times I've really blacked out," I said.

"It could be that you're experiencing symptoms of stress. Are you in the midst of a difficult time at work? At home?"

"We're working on a crucial project," I said. "But it's challenging in a fun way, exhilarating more than stressful."

"Okay, but you're also taking care of your aunt. Caring for someone with Alzheimer's can be extremely taxing. That plus the pressures of work might be having an impact on you."

"I'm not sure." I thought about the last few weeks. I had been feeling unusually in control of my life despite all of the external demands on my time. "I don't know. I think . . . I feel like nothing was really wrong until I saw that woman on Monday. It's just the blackouts."

"Just the blackouts?" Dr. Hinds cocked her head slightly to the side but maintained contact with my stare as if she were searching past my eyes into the parts of my mind yet inaccessible to me, reaching beyond my consciousness for the answers to her questions. I broke the gaze.

"Well, Brian thinks . . ." I stopped speaking. I folded my arms, rubbing my hands back and forth on my forearms as if I were cold.

After a long pause, Dr. Hinds probed gently. "What does he think, Amaya?"

"That I'm running from something in my past."

"What makes him think that?"

"Well, it might be because I never talk about my childhood." I was aware of the throbbing of the blood in my wrist against my forearms.

"Never?"

"Not really." The pace of my heartbeat increased, pounding against the inside of my chest.

"Well, that is a bit unusual, Amaya. Why won't you talk about your past?"

"It's not that I won't." I took a deep breath then exhaled slowly. Some calm returned. "I can't. There are parts of my childhood before I left Jamaica that I remember . . . and parts . . . most of it . . . I don't."

"Okay." Dr. Hinds's brow was creased into deep washboard wrinkles. She leaned forward in her chair. "Can you give me an example?"

"I remember bits and pieces of growing up with my Aunt Marjorie. Nothing complete." I stopped and bit my lip. "My parents died in a fire when I was a baby."

I paused and Dr. Hinds filled in the obligatory "I'm sorry to hear that."

I acknowledged her condolence with a nod and continued. "I have images of being six, others of everyday activities: Aunt Marjorie cooking and combing my hair, the two of us gardening, and doing homework at the kitchen table." As I enumerated these memories, my body relaxed, and my heart rate slowed with each breath I took. "I have a photo of me and Aunt Marjorie and I remember the day it was taken, but I don't recall much more, not clearly anyway." I shrugged. "But I doubt that has much to do with anything. My life was pretty ordinary."

"People remember their childhood in varying levels of detail, but it is unusual to remember so little, especially into your early adolescent and teen years. Have you tried to find out? Visited Jamaica? Called someone you knew? Searched on the Internet?"

I shook my head. *Dr. Hinds must think I'm crazy,* I thought. I knew my story was strange, but I had never had any urge to explore the past I had left behind, especially when my present was so lush.

"It hasn't really affected my life," I said. "Until now, if that's even what this is . . . why this is happening."

"Okay," Dr. Hinds said. She stood and walked over to her desk. She picked up a prescription pad and pen. She turned away from me and scribbled on the pad as she spoke. "So I am actually going to give you a referral to a neurologist. They should do an MRI and also run neuropsychological testing." The tone of her voice shifted into a drone as if she were talking to herself, deep in thought as she considered her treatment approach. "Just from our chat today, your semantic and short-term memories seem to be intact. The testing will help give us a clearer picture of whether you have retrograde amnesia."

She turned slowly to face me as if suddenly remembering I was still in the room and did not understand the terms she was using. Her brow was furrowed into small wrinkles I did not recall having been there before. She returned to the chair opposite mine and leaned forward. When she spoke, her voice was almost a whisper, as if she were coaxing a skittish pet to come home. "Memories are a funny thing. They are fragile and inconsistent. We forget events then we rebuild them, something like how paleontologists rebuild dinosaurs they have never seen, inferring their shape and size using found bones, footprints, fossils, and so on. When it comes to memory, the mind uses items like photographs, mementos, and stories we hear. Sometimes the creatures we rebuild closely resemble reality. Sometimes . . ." She shrugged.

I nodded although she was not making a lot of sense. *How could memories change? And what did that have to do with me or my blackouts?* I did not remember details of my past, but I knew there had not been anything major to forget, just a simple, uneventful childhood with Aunt Marjorie.

Dr. Hinds continued before I could formulate my thoughts into a question.

"Sometimes we can convince ourselves not to rebuild the memories of painful events in our past, and if we do a really good job at that, it becomes near impossible to access the truth. Let me give you another analogy. I'm very squeamish about blood, especially my own. That's probably why I am a psychiatrist and not a surgeon." She laughed lightly, shaking her hair from her face.

I smiled.

"When I get a bad cut," she continued, "I immediately cover it with a bandage, and I don't uncover it until it is healed. The idea of pulling back the bandage and seeing the blood is so abhorrent that I don't do it. I can't. I pretend the cut's not there. It is possible that you have covered up something that happened to you with a mental bandage and every time you approach it you black out, which is your mind's way of turning away, afraid to pull it back and see the blood. The problem with trauma, though, is that it doesn't heal under cover."

Tears pricked at the back of my eyes. I forced them back. *Why was I crying?* I had nothing to hide.

"I'm sure there's nothing to uncover," I said to Dr. Hinds, forcing my voice to sound steady. I gripped the sides of the chair, ready to push myself up and out of the office, but I stopped myself. I breathed in, held the breath for the count of three, then released it quietly. "And even if there was. Even if you and Brian are right and I am hiding some big secret"—I raised my hands in mock quotation marks—"why would it resurface now? Why after all these years?"

"Only you can answer that. There may have been a trigger. You mentioned that Aunt Marjorie referred to castor oil." She wrinkled her nose and laughed. "That brings up unpleasant memories for me. Perhaps that stirred up a memory beneath the surface. Something you're not ready to face. And the woman in the parking lot. Was there anything unusual about her?"

"Not really. I mean, she wore these earrings . . . and her accent . . . I think she was from the Caribbean . . . but I meet people from the Caribbean fairly often and I'm fine, so I don't know why this woman would have had the impact she did."

"It could be that something about her reminded you of someone in your past."

"It could be." I tried to picture the woman, but the panic I had felt just moments before swelled again and I had to blank my mind. "What can we do? What can I do?"

Dr. Hinds did not answer right away. I sat back in my chair and waited as she thought. Finally she leaned forward again and clasped her hands in front of her. She twisted the gold band on her left index finger as she spoke. "If I may. I am going to make what might seem like an unorthodox suggestion."

I nodded.

"I am trained as a hypnotherapist. I use it to help my clients change destructive behavior or regain control in certain areas of their life. I work with people who want to stop smoking or gambling. I've also worked with victims of amnesia. In that case, forgetting is the destructive or, rather, unwanted behavior."

"So you're going to wave a watch in front of me? 'You're getting sleepy'?" I droned the last phrase.

Dr. Hinds smiled, and I sensed this was not the first time she had been mocked in this way. "It's not like what you see on TV," she said. "Your blackouts, as you call them, aren't associated with falling or loss of consciousness. They could be intense concentration, not unlike when someone calls your name while you're reading a book or watching a movie and you don't hear them because you're so engrossed. With my guidance, you may be able to channel this intense focus to explore what's going on in your head."

Hypnosis? I hoped my skepticism was not visible on my face. I looked at Dr. Hinds. There was something about the way she sat across from me, perfectly still, her face calm, exuding confidence through her straight back and long legs crossed at the ankles, unperturbed, so comfortable in the space, confident in her abilities. I longed to be her, to feel that calm, to feel that control again.

"What do you want to do, Amaya?"

"I want this to stop. I want to get to the bottom of whatever is happening so I can go back to normal."

"I believe hypnosis might help you get to the truth. I'm not making any promises. The idea of repressed and recoverable memories is controversial and the truth is, only about five percent of people can achieve a deep hypnotic state, but most people can enter a place where they are suggestible at some level. You have to want it, though. Right now, you aren't recalling anything after your trances. You will need to be intentional about it. You will have to want to remember."

The words hung in the air. I examined Dr. Hinds's face. *Does she see me as some sort of human guinea pig? A case study to boast about at some medical conference?* But I could not find a trace of insincerity. Instead I saw genuine concern. And if the hypnosis helped, if it stopped the blackouts, maybe it was worth a try.

Dr. Hinds broke our eye contact with a brief glance at the clock on the wall behind me. "I'm not going to force you, of course," she said. "Visit the neurologist and then, depending on how that goes, think about the hypnosis. Discuss it with Brian."

I stiffened so suddenly that Dr. Hinds noticed.

"Or with someone else you trust. Then let me know."

I TOOK THE rest of the day off from work. I drove seven miles from Dr. Hinds's Tysons Corner office to Great Falls Park. I showed my annual pass and entered the gates, feeling relief as soon as I drove along the tree-lined road that led to the Visitor Center. Normally, I would go to the furthest part of the park, as far as vehicles were allowed, walk along the bank of the Potomac, and relish the gentle rush of the waters before they reached the rocky rapids. But I wanted the roar of the water to fill my ears, and so, despite wearing my high-heeled leather work shoes, I braved the graveled path and climbed over rocks to get to Overlook 1, a spot that afforded a view of a series of rapids. I was alone on the edge except for the black vultures that circled and swooped overhead, their white-tip wings flashing against the gray sky. A slight drizzle sprinkled on me like spritz from the spray bottle Taiwo used to help me water the plants when he was very young.

The bad weather seemed to have dissuaded others from venturing out to what was a popular destination, even on weekdays. The rain did not bother me. I inhaled, breathing the waterlogged air in through my mouth, my ears, my eyes, my pores. The waterfall was swollen, cascading in sheets of water so heavy that the rocks were almost completely concealed. The surf was full and resembled waves crashing onto an ocean shoreline. The close approxima- tion of the ocean helped to calm me, but what really transported me was the sound of the water rushing, moving, constantly in flux, cleaning, removing waste, bringing clean new slates and blocking out the doubts and stories I told myself.

My mind felt clear for the first time that week. I chided myself for run- ning to Dr. Hinds who, by the nature of her profession, was programmed to see more in the blackouts than was probably warranted. I expected the sug- gestion of scans and referral to other doctors, but hypnosis? I laughed. In the unlikely event that there was some dark secret in my past, why would I want to know at this point in my life? Exploring it would be like strolling on a beach strewn with sea urchins, unpleasant surprises that were potentially treacherous unless you stopped to extract the spines one by one and toss them away before the needles poisoned your present. I had overreacted. A smarter woman would have discussed the blackouts with her girlfriends over a few glasses of wine. I should have gone to Jamela or Lisa, not Dr. Hinds. The most sensible solution to my situation was to keep moving forward and dismiss the two strange incidents as anomalies.

I leaned against the wooden railings and closed my eyes. I was tired. I wished I did not have to pick Auntie up or go to the shelter with Taiwo or meet anyone else's demands that day but my own. I longed to return home and spend my time tilling the soil in the garden, prepping it for its next reality. I exhaled, then rose and walked to my car.

CHAPTER ELEVEN

J osé got his ID photo taken today too."

"That's great," I replied, keeping my eyes on the road as I drove Taiwo to our hour-long biweekly shift at the Shepherd Center. I was driving almost due west and the sun, still two hours from setting, was directly in my line of sight. My focus was laser sharp. Even though I knew I had overreacted to my blackout that morning, I was still being careful. I had no intention of losing focus in the car again.

"He has been afraid he wouldn't get hired on permanent staff," Taiwo continued.

I was genuinely happy to hear that José was doing well. I had not met him, but Taiwo had talked about him with great regularity over several weeks, and I had conjured an image of the man: short, thickset, with serious but friendly eyes. The scent of powdered laundry detergent permeated Taiwo's clothes when he returned home each afternoon, and I often pictured the two men in the supermarket warehouse surrounded by large boxes that thwacked and thunked in a regular rhythm as they stacked them, providing a soothing backdrop for storytelling. Taiwo would be the perfect audience, blending into the background until José might even forget he was there.

Taiwo was fascinated by José and his stories of Hurricane Mitch, which had forced the Honduran man to seek refuge in the United States. Every afternoon after work, Taiwo sat in the kitchen and related José's stories to me, probably verbatim. Stories of the devastation José had witnessed in Honduras and of his panicked departure with his wife and their infant son, and every afternoon as I listened, I felt an inexplicably strong connection to this stranger and to the sort of events that could drive someone to abandon their home.

"Today he told me he's scared." Taiwo's words tumbled out with uncharacteristic urgency. "Every year the government has to renew his visa to stay here, and that's coming up soon. He says everyone is afraid of foreigners since 9-11. He thinks they might stop renewing his visa and he will have to go back."

I did not respond, and a silence settled in the car, the only sounds the murmur of the engine and the air conditioner. As we sat, I felt as if our heartbeats were synching until they beat in slow tandem. I was always amazed by how connected I felt to him, twenty-plus years after the umbilical cord had been cut and buried in Trinidad at his grandmother's insistence.

A full minute ticked by, and I chanced a glance from the road to observe him. He stared straight ahead, his chin, nose, and eyes pointing forward in a uniform line.

"I thought he would want to go back. The hurricane was years ago, and he told me he misses home." Taiwo paused again for a beat. "I think he got upset with me when I said that."

"I'm sure he understands that you mean well," I soothed.

"He told me he misses what Honduras was. That the economy and infrastructure are still really bad. It's not safe for him to return. He says everything he had was destroyed and his family there has either died or left." Taiwo paused and looked in my direction. "Just like you, Mom. Just like you don't want to go back to Jamaica." He paused again. "Is Jamaica still experiencing the problems that made you leave?"

"Not really," I responded after a pause of my own. My hands tightened around the steering wheel.

"I looked it up on the Internet. I read that there were a lot of political problems in the 1970s when you were growing up."

I forced myself to focus on the road, to keep my foot steady on the gas, not to cover my ears to stop the sound that had begun like a plaintive moan but was crescendoing into a roar.

"Yes," I said. My voice sounded robotic and distant beyond the noise in my head.

"And now?"

I could not respond. My head ached, and I just wanted him to stop questioning me. I had no idea why my body was responding so strangely to this discussion. True, I did not talk often about my past in Jamaica, but I had shared a few anecdotes with Taiwo over the years and never felt like this. I couldn't think.

I inhaled deeply and shook my head left and right slowly. The ache in my head and the roar in my ears retreated slightly.

"It's difficult to explain. There was a time when the political situation was so fractured that violence was completely out of control. Over the years, the government has changed back and forth . . . with politics it's sometimes hard to measure if one party is making a difference, but the changes have been mostly for the better, I guess."

"But if things *are* better, why don't we visit? Why won't you go?"

"Because, just like José, there's nothing there for me now." I stared straight ahead, concentrating on the road as if even a single moment of distraction would lead to disaster. I forced myself to loosen my grip on the steering wheel, repeatedly straightening and bending the fingers of one hand then the other.

"What about Ralph?" I asked, changing the subject. "Is he permanent now too?" I hoped not. Taiwo did not talk about this coworker often. In fact, I suspected that he avoided mentioning him. I did not complain. I had taken an immediate dislike to the little I had heard.

"He got his full-time assignment two weeks ago," Taiwo responded.

"Really?" I replied. Ralph, José, and Taiwo had begun work at the same time. I glanced at him. He was staring straight ahead, his face tense.

"Yeah. They asked each of us to review the other temporary workers. They said it was a very small part of our evaluation, but José thinks Ralph gave us a bad rating and that's why we got our permanent assignments later than the rest of our group."

I held my face still. I had not realized that Taiwo had been promoted after the others who were hired at the same time. It could not be a coincidence that the foreign guy and the autistic guy were the two whose promotions were delayed. Anger surged through me, and I considered then discarded the possible avenues for legal redress. I knew Taiwo would not want me to intervene.

"Sorry to hear that, Tai," I said, swallowing hard.

"It's okay. We got it now. Ralph has no real power over us. But he pisses José off."

"What sorts of things does he say?"

"He calls José lazy and a thief, and says he will prove it one day and get him deported." Taiwo was silent for a beat and when he spoke, he spoke slowly as if processing a complicated problem. "If they have to leave, maybe Auntie Jamela can help? Like she helped Auntie Marjorie."

I exhaled, only then aware of the tension I had been holding stiff in my shoulders and arms. I glanced over at Taiwo and held his eyes for a moment. "That's really complicated, Taiwo. Auntie was related to us."

"You told me she isn't my blood aunt."

I sighed. "True. As I said. Complicated. Listen, we're doing what we can to help, you know we are. Volunteering, here, right now." We pulled into the parking lot of the outreach center as I spoke.

"Yeah, but this won't help José stay if his Temporary Protected Status isn't extended."

"True, but we can bring some people some comfort for now, while the people who can do something about that work on it."

CHAPTER TWELVE

The parking lot at the Shepherd Center was full when we pulled in, so I circled then headed back out to park on the street. The shelter was in a mixed-use neighborhood shared by businesses and homes, and the two-lane road was flanked by parked cars, leaving only a narrow corridor for traffic to pass through. I finally parallel parked in a spot about two blocks away. Before we left the car, I pushed in the side-view mirror to its closed position. I was not afraid of intentional vandalism, but the dents in the neighborhood vehicles suggested that the narrow street was not always carefully navigated.

"I wonder who's the manager on duty tonight?" I asked as we approached the front door, steering past a few people milling around the entrance.

Taiwo shrugged. We never knew what to expect when we walked into the shelter. The atmosphere varied depending on who was in charge and who came in to eat. If there were lots of families, the noise level would be high. Children, energized by the meal, might run around the tables, their voices and laughter giving a lighthearted sheen to whatever challenges their families were facing. That evening when we stepped in, a tense quiet filled the room, and the sense of foreboding I had been suppressing all afternoon fought its way up from my gut. I inhaled and exhaled slowly, forcing all the air out of my diaphragm. The strained mood in the room was an almost sure indication that Gary was on duty. He was very strict about following the rules and made sure we served exactly the right quantities of food. If any guests raised their voices, he would shoot them stern looks and even shush them. He seemed to think that if the center was too welcoming, guests would use it as a crutch and not work towards improving their situation. *The food isn't that good*, I thought. I wondered why he did this work when he held people who were struggling in such disdain.

Gary was serving food when we entered, but as soon as we had washed our hands, he pulled his apron off over his head. With only a nod of acknowledgment, he headed to the front desk. Taiwo and I donned aprons and gloves and took our positions side by side behind the waist-high counter that separated the volunteers from the guests as if one group had something to fear from the other.

The six-to-seven o'clock shift was usually the busiest time. This was when shelter guests who had jobs stopped by after work or grabbed a bite before they headed out to a night job. But that night was a slow night. There were only about nine people at the earth-brown picnic-style tables and benches. Each seemed to have come in alone, and they hunched over their food as if afraid Gary would take it away before they finished.

When we first started volunteering, I longed to know the stories of the people who came to the shelter, but management, Gary in particular, discouraged fraternizing. We were not even issued name tags.

"Most people can't handle the guilt when they hear the sob stories. You end up making promises you can't keep. The problems these people have . . ." Gary shook his head, but there was no sympathy in his eyes. "They're a bottomless pit. Don't get sucked in."

I had not attempted to connect with any of the people who came in, not because of Gary's warning, but because I suspected many of the people who came here might not even want to share their stories, especially with someone who could not offer more than a sympathetic nod. That night as I looked around the room, it occurred to me that this was just the kind of place where the woman in the orange sweater—I could not bring myself to say her name—might frequent. The odds were very low that she would walk into this very shelter, of all the places she could get a meal in Northern Virginia, but my heart rate quickened at the possibility. I scanned the room. Six of the people were men, and the three women were Hispanic. She was not there—but that did not mean she might not arrive. I stiffened my expression. If that woman showed up here by some coinciding of fates, I would serve her like any other guest and ignore any attempts she made to interact with me. Hopefully, she would not make a scene in public. This plan did not quell my anxiety. As I stood behind the table of food, spoon in my gloved hand, I could not help looking towards the door every time I heard it open.

Next to me, Taiwo sported his biggest smile and greeted everyone he served. In contrast, I struggled to lift my smile to reach my eyes.

During a lull in the stream of customers, a Black woman with braided hair entered. I spotted her as she walked through the door, a flash of dark brown skin amidst lighter tones. Taiwo and I had been working for thirty-five minutes and I had let my guard down, but now my pores raised and I felt a tightening in my gut. She stopped at the main desk, as required by anyone coming to the shelter for the first time. I could not see her face. I wanted to flee. *I can take a bathroom break*, I thought, step away from the table until she was served. Then I would not have to stand before her and risk making eye contact that might send me spiraling into the black hole as it had the day before. I wanted to leave, but every cell in my body held firm. *It might not be her*, I thought. *What are the odds that she would show up here*, I reminded myself. *What were the odds that she was in the parking lot*, my inner voice countered. *Now I'm talking to myself*, I thought, *and answering! Perhaps I need psychological treatment after all.*

The woman finally turned and walked towards me, her head down, her braids hanging over her face. When she lifted her head, relief flooded my body. This face was angular, the eyes set wide apart. It was not the woman from the parking lot. I placed one hand on the table and lowered my head. She probably thought I was praying, and perhaps I was saying a thank-you to the Universe. I looked up to find her studying me with curiosity.

"Hi, Amaya," she said.

My eyes opened wide. *Another perfect stranger claiming to know me?* Assuming I could trust my short-term memory, I had never seen her before.

She must have noticed my reaction.

"Don't panic so," she said with a smile. Her voice had a Caribbean lilt, not Jamaican or Trinidadian but definitely not American. "The man at the front let your name slip."

I smiled in return, not trusting myself to speak. My heart was still racing. My hands shook as I spooned rice and vegetables onto the plate she proffered. After I served her, I tried to recapture some semblance of calm. I closed my eyes and attempted to conjure up an image of my garden, but all I saw was the upturned soil: turmoil and uncertainty.

"Mom?" Taiwo's gloved hand against my arm pulled me to my immediate reality. A man stood in front of me, a plate outstretched. I could not make my arms move to serve him. I knew my anxiety was unwarranted, but that did not make it any less impactful and paralyzing.

"I need to leave," I said to Taiwo. "Can you help him then come?"

"But we have another twenty minutes on our shift," he replied, glancing at his watch.

"I know. But I don't feel well, and it's not too busy."

"But if we both leave . . ."

He was right. We could not both abandon our posts.

"I'll wait for you in the car, then. I really need to sit down . . . somewhere else."

I saw worry settle on his face, but he focused his energies on being polite and attentive to the man in front of him. I made my apologies to Gary then slipped out into the hot evening air, past the people gathered outside, not looking at another face until I sank into the driver's seat of my car. I locked the door, reclined the seat, and closed my eyes.

CHAPTER THIRTEEN

The next day, I had little time to think about the shelter, the woman, blackouts, or anything except work. A pile of folders, each with a different demand, had grown on my desk during the time I had taken off to visit Dr. Hinds the previous day. The Framtiden deal had dominated my time for the last two months, but there were other tasks to be accomplished, checks to be signed, invoices to be approved, contracts to be vetted.

I sighed. Some days, my job felt overwhelming. It was invaluable to the firm to have an office manager who was family. I had almost unrestricted access to the company finances. Having someone in that role who had a vested interest in the firm's success meant that Geoffrey and Brian did not have to look over my shoulder to ensure I was not robbing them. The workload was heavy. I had an assistant, Ignatious, but he operated at my behest, so if I took off unplanned as I did yesterday, the machinery of our work slowed then ground to a halt. I knew I had to do a better job of delegating, but it was hard. I was so used to only being able to trust myself. I sighed again.

I pushed aside the documents related to the Swedish deal and got to work on the other items on my desk. Despite the pressure, one thing I enjoyed about my job was the variety of tasks I tackled on a daily basis. On any one day, I could be working on budget issues, preparing legal correspondence, scheduling court cases, dealing with staff, sitting in on client interviews, paying contractors, and more. Sometimes I felt like an ER doctor, triaging the information that came into the firm, then making decisions about what to send on, what to handle with my staff.

I had been working steadily for about an hour when the phone shrilled.

Ignatious's voice was almost a whisper. "Mrs. Lin, it's Ms. Lisa."

"Thanks, Ignatious," I replied. "I'll take this call, but please hold all other calls after this one."

"Sure thing," he replied.

"Hey, girl," I said after hearing the click of the call being transferred. "What's going on?"

"Hey, things are really crazy at work. I have to take a rain check on lunch today."

I inhaled sharply and glanced at my calendar. Sure enough, I had written Lisa's name in block letters under 12:30 p.m.

"You forgot, didn't you?" She laughed. "That worked out then. I thought you'd be disappointed, especially since you requested the lunch."

"I know. It seems like that was a lifetime ago. I don't even remember what I wanted to talk to you about."

"Sounds like you definitely need some girlfriend time."

"True. How about lunch on Friday?"

"Don't stand me up this time," she said.

"Me? It's you who stood me up."

"For a lunch you didn't even remember?"

We both laughed.

"Block off a couple of hours. I'll make us a reservation at a new restaurant I've been wanting to try. Come ready to spill whatever's going on with you."

As I put down the phone, I thought maybe I would tell her about the woman and Dr. Hinds's suggestion of hypnosis. Lisa's reaction would be different from Jamela's. Her life had been more tumultuous, and she tended to respond to things with more pragmatism than Jamela did. Or maybe all that had happened would be behind me by Friday. I had been fine for a full twenty-four hours, and the pile of work on my desk was already dwarfing any other concerns.

My mind wandered from the issues on my desk to the events of the week, to the garden. I had not had an opportunity to get in there since I dug it up on Monday night. *After I pick Aunt Marjorie up, I will drop by Dyfield's Garden Center and we'll select some plants together*, I thought. Aunt Marjorie would love that, and might even be up to helping me plant or, at the very least, sitting and watching me as I worked. I turned to a new leaf on the legal pad next to me and began making a list of the plants I would buy that afternoon. If I put it on paper, I might be able to stop the ideas from swirling in my head and focus on the work on my desk.

There was a light tap on the door. *I told Ignatious no calls. I guess I didn't specify no visitors*, I thought. The handle moved an inch or so before the lock caught. I heard a shuffling, then a sheet of printer paper appeared under the door.

I rose from my chair and picked up the note. The words were written in Brian's neat, rounded letters. He wanted a detailed analysis of my ideas for restructuring the Sweden deal by Friday. Two days. It was unlikely I would be in any state of mind to enjoy lunch with Lisa the day this was due.

Challenge on, I thought.

Before I returned to working, I shot an email to Lisa. "Something just came up. Maybe next week?"

CHAPTER FOURTEEN

Aunt Marjorie and I walked the rows of the garden center. She pushed the trolley, leaning on it for support. It occurred to me, as it had many times in the last few years, how small her body had become. Gravity had shrunk her tall frame so she barely had to bend over to place her elbows on the handlebar of the cart. Yet she did not look frail. Her expression was one of determination and anticipation of a difficult yet pleasant task.

I should bring her here more often, I thought.

She inhaled deeply, and I knew she was absorbing the scents of the herbs that surrounded us. She smiled, and although the smile was not directed at me, I smiled back.

"What should we get?" I asked.

"We haffe get the garden back in shape," she said. "I don't know what you was thinking about, digging the place up so." She frowned at me but a smile danced in her eyes. This was my Aunt Marjorie.

"Take up some of that thyme there. No, not that one! You cyan see how it mawga? Wait." She took her handbag from the basket of the trolley and tucked it under her arm before approaching the plants. "Not leaving it there for no tief," she muttered.

She picked out several herbs, picking some up herself, pointing to others for me to reach. The basket filled with many more plants than I needed, but I indulged her. This state felt precarious. I knew if I nudged in the wrong direction it would come to a precipitous end. I was not ready to lose the moment. I wanted to bask in her excited contentment.

After the cashier tallied our purchases, Aunt Marjorie moved to open her handbag. I put a hand on her upper arm to stop her. "I got this," I said.

"Well, I never thought I'd see the day. Amaya turn big woman."

As we pushed the trolley across the gravel towards the car, the scents of the garden center fading behind us, a shadow passed over her face like a large cloud obscuring a night of brilliant stars. "I miss my garden," she said. "It never was the same after you left."

I stopped in the middle of the parking lot. Up until then, Aunt Marjorie and I had been flip sides of the same coin. She had memories of the years before 1979 but not much else after that. My strongest memories were of the time after I left her house. If she had been able to articulate her early memories, we would have been the perfect whole. And there I stood in the midst of one of the few occasions when Aunt Marjorie encroached on my territory, expressing an understanding that she was no longer in Jamaica.

I let the silence settle between us. What was I supposed to say? That I regretted leaving? I did not. When I left for university in Trinidad, we had both known I would not return to Jamaica. But I had missed her. Sitting at my desk in the small room I shared with my roommate, I would imagine Aunt Marjorie at her kitchen table in front of a cup of hot tea. The remembered smell of the brewing herbs would force my eyes closed with a longing to be within reach of her garden.

I kept in touch that first year, knowing that if I did not, she would find a way to reach me, if not herself then through someone on the list of names she had slipped into my hand before I left. I wrote letter after letter, trying to excise every bit of my loneliness from the words. It was no use. I knew she would unearth some trace of unhappiness in between the lines. She never showed her concern but her newsy accounts of elections, Bob Marley's death, and other events close to home pulled me back towards the very darkness I had left Jamaica to avoid. After the letter in which I told her I would be staying in Trinidad for the vacation after the end of my first year, I stopped writing and stopped opening the many letters she sent.

Standing in the garden center parking lot, I fought against the swell of emotion that flooded my mind along with the memories of those days, the separation from Aunt Marjorie, when I missed her and the garden as much as she missed me.

"Maya?" Aunt Marjorie's voice startled me back to the present.

I found myself with one hand on the open trunk, the other holding a pot, my thumb deep in its soil, forcing it to spill, much like those memories had spilled from the past into my present. I grasped the trunk tightly, forcing myself to stay upright, to return to the present, to keep moving forward. How had I let that beautiful moment with Aunt Marjorie lead to those painful memories?

"Amaya?" Aunt Marjorie repeated, and I returned, fully present. The moment was not about me, it was never about me.

BY THE TIME Aunt Marjorie and I arrived home, it was late afternoon and we only had time to offload the plants into the backyard. I pulled out the hose, and Aunt Marjorie began watering our purchases. On my way inside to get dinner started, I stopped halfway between the back door and the spot where she stood, hose in hand, watching the water running onto the plants in a steady stream. Comforting was the only word I could conjure for the way the water flowed out, slow and unceasing, sounding like a full but calm river. I longed to stay, to water and plant, to feel the dirt warm on my fingers and under my nails, but duty called. Slowly I turned and headed towards the house.

CHAPTER FIFTEEN

The next night, Taiwo and I made our second trip to the center for the week. When we arrived, there were about seven or eight people hanging around outside as usual, leaning against the wall, smoking, talking, laughing. None of them paid any attention as Taiwo and I walked into the shelter. We arrived in the midst of peak activity and were immediately pulled into service, serving the people who had come in search of an evening meal. Samantha was the manager on duty, and the atmosphere in the center was vibrant and lively. I had no time to relive the anxiety I had felt on our previous visit. Taiwo and I worked side by side in constant motion for about half an hour before there was a lull and I had an opportunity to survey the room.

There were about thirty-five women, men, and children present. Everyone on the serving side of the table, except for Taiwo and me, was white; everyone on the other side was Black or Hispanic. I observed the children, six of them sitting across from one another in two rows of three, laughing, jostling, and kicking each other under the table, oblivious to the potent tension ricocheting among the adults in the room. I imagined that, if questioned, each individual would have a different description of the path that had led them to the point where they needed the support of a place like this, but on the surface, the adults looked evenly weary. Deep worry lines born of sleepless nights, dangerous journeys, and uncertain futures etched every face.

"Do we know that lady?"

I followed Taiwo's gaze and drew in a sharp breath. Shock reverberated through my body as if I had been hit from behind by a large and unexpected wave. I placed one hand on the counter to steady myself. Sitting at one of the tables was the woman from the parking lot—Angela. The same woman whose appearance had triggered a reaction so intense that I had lost my ability to function, the same woman who claimed to be my sister. My heart rate accelerated and my vision blurred as my body threatened to shut down again. I rallied against the urge. I focused on the trays of food in front of me, replaying the first thing that came to mind, the instructions we had received on our first day of service: "One spoon of macaroni and cheese, one piece of chicken—unless they get a drumstick, then they can have two. They help themselves to salad, except the children. No children in the salad. And no seconds, no exceptions." After one or two deep breaths, my heart rate decelerated and I felt collected enough to look up at the woman again.

There was something familiar about her face. She was young, perhaps in her late twenties I guessed. Too young to be someone I knew before I left Jamaica. It was more likely she reminded me of someone tied to the experience Dr. Hinds thought I was suppressing.

The woman did not seem to have noticed me. She had no plate in front of her, which was not unusual. When the shelter was full, as it was tonight, patrons often tried to secure a seat before coming to get their food. She might have been negotiating with the others at the table to hold her seat, because she smiled, revealing a slight triangular gap where one of her front teeth was distant from its neighbor on the right and twisted slightly towards its left companion. I cut off another sharp intake of breath just before a sound escaped my lips. The warm smile sent a shiver through my body. I thought of Dr. Hinds again and her offer to tease memories from the recesses of my mind.

"I don't know her," I replied to Taiwo when I had recovered enough to speak. "Why do you ask?"

He shrugged. "I don't know, she just looked familiar. Do you remember Dr. Hinds? She would have said she has a knowing face." He smiled, but I recoiled at his mention of Dr. Hinds.

"Well, we're not supposed to fraternize with the shelter visitors, so we'll never know," I said, keeping my voice as light as possible. I lowered my head and prayed that the woman would not notice me. We were too busy for me to leave for any prolonged period of time. Even Samantha had come from behind the desk to help with the steady flow of patrons. I had to stay, and a part of me was okay with that, the part of me that wanted to talk to Angela, to find out what she had meant by declaring she was my sister. Another, more dominant part of me feared the interaction. The fear was as intense as it was unreasonable. The woman was not my sister, so there could be no harm in clearing up the misunderstanding. But no matter how I pushed back against my fear, it remained like a sentry, unmoving, unblinking, unyielding.

I took opportunities to look over at her when there were customers obscuring my full gaze. I caught her looking over to the entrance. Her mouth moved, her lips forming the word "Shit."

She turned and looked directly at me, and in that moment I knew that she had known I was there all along but had been biding her time to approach. Now something had disrupted her plans. Her eyes widened as if she was trying to communicate with me. They were filled with fear.

I turned towards the door to see what had elicited that response.

A man stood just inside the doorway. Dressed in light-wash boot-cut jeans and a fitted dark brown cowboy shirt with the sleeves folded to his elbows and the neck open one button lower than would be accepted in a business setting, he seemed out of place in the center, neither like someone in need of food nor someone likely to volunteer or work at a shelter. He turned slowly, spinning on his heel, scanning the room from left to right until his eyes found Angela. He lifted his chin in her direction, then he followed it, picking his way through the tables, his head high as if he was afraid of catching something from the people around him.

"Hey babe," he said loudly, his voice rising above the murmurings of the other patrons. "I've been looking all over for you." He strung an arm around her waist. She smiled, but her eyes had dulled, as if her spirit had retreated into a dark place in her mind. Her body was rigid in the man's embrace.

"I lef you a note," she replied.

"You know reading's not my thing. You're not supposed to come *inside* this dump. I give you plenty to eat. Don't I, sweetheart." His words were benign and his smile wide, but there was an undercurrent to them, as if beneath the surface of his pleasant demeanor lay a crocodile waiting for the best moment to emerge and feast. He looked around the room as if ensuring none of those present harbored any doubt about his ability to care for Angela. His eyes met mine and he paused for longer than a beat. I stared back. His expression remained unchanged, a calm, almost pleasant facade, but behind the stillness in his eyes I could tell he was puzzling over something. Perhaps he read the defiance in my eyes, the fact that I saw through his sickly sweet charade. The hair on my skin quivered.

"Yes, you do, of course, Nate," Angela assured him. Her voice was soft, so I imagined more than heard her words.

He looked at her, breaking our gaze, and I felt as if I'd been caught and released. I exhaled.

"Good," he said. He slid his arm down Angela's hips then grabbed her hand. "Let's go, babe. This place is for losers. It's not on your block anyway." He guided her towards the door, but not before turning to look at me once more. My overactive imagination read a warning in his stare.

I became aware of a sharp intake of breath next to me. I looked to my left to where Taiwo stood, his eyes locked on the couple, a frown on his face. He looked as if he was contemplating jumping over the table and rushing over to Angela and Nate. I felt a similar urge, but I knew tangling with that man would be a bad idea. I had come across his type before: slick, thinking themselves above the law until they got in the kind of trouble that landed them in need of defense from the criminal division of a law firm.

"Let's go back to work, Taiwo. Lots of people to feed." I heard a lightness in my voice that belied my impulse to separate Angela from Nate's grasp and shelter her under the umbrella of protection usually reserved for Taiwo.

He dropped his shoulders, but I could see that he was still processing what had happened between Angela and Nate. He shifted from leg to leg and when he was not using his hands to handle the food, he moved them up and down as if he were playing an imaginary djembe. His gaze on the door through which Angela and Nate disappeared, he gave a particularly large gesture with his left hand and nudged the platter of salad, which in turn put the tray of chicken into motion. The energy seemed to double then triple as it moved from dish to dish, and the tray of macaroni and cheese slid towards the edge of the table like a skater on ice heading towards the edge of the rink, except it did not slow down but instead picked up speed as it dove off the metal table towards the floor.

"No!" I shouted, immediately regretting my exclamation as I saw through the corner of my eye—my mind's eye, that is, because my attention was fixed on stopping the collision of the macaroni and cheese and the ground—the shock on Taiwo's face in response to my exclamation.

I flung myself to the floor and caught the tray just before it splattered onto the white tiles. For a moment, I lay on the ground, the dish of macaroni pie in my outstretched hands, my breath coming in short gulps the only sounds in the room. Applause broke out around me, at first smattering, hesitant, and I imagined that the men and women who had come in to serve wondered why I had gone to such lengths to save a single tray of food when there was much more than enough to go around. As the applause built, someone reached over to help me up. It wasn't Taiwo. I looked for him, but he was nowhere in the room.

I resisted the urge to run out into the street, to find him where I knew he would be, on the sidewalk, his slim thighs drawn up against his chest, his body tightened into a ball as if he were trying to make himself small enough to squeeze back into my womb. I resisted the urge to follow him because at that moment, sheltering him was what I wanted most. To protect him, to always be the cushion on which he fell, the place where he found warmth, but in reality, no one was there for anyone forever. And so I waited, fists balled, my fingernails pressed into my palms, my eyes fixed in the direction of the double doors that had swung shut after he fled the room. Each time the doors opened I looked away, forcing my face into a relaxed expression as if it was the most natural thing in the world that he had walked back in. Each time the doors opened, a stranger entered.

Finally Taiwo returned. He held the door open and Angela appeared. She took his arm. I held my breath, waiting for Nate to follow but he did not. *How did they get away from him*, I thought as I watched them walk arm-in-arm towards the table at which she had been sitting. I searched for a sign of discomfort on Taiwo's face, his usual reaction to being forced into close proximity with a stranger, but I was disappointed. Instead, pleasure flooded his expression. There was no trace of the embarrassment that had caused him to flee the room.

CHAPTER SIXTEEN

That evening, the four of us—Brian, Taiwo, Aunt Marjorie, and I—sat around the dining table. We held hands, forming a circle around the table while Brian gave thanks for the food. He had long dropped the word "God" from the blessing, sending instead a generic expression of gratefulness out into the Universe. He also no longer lamented about the length of time that had passed since we had been to church. I did not disapprove of this shift in our life, despite having grown up in an environment where there was little room for independent thought on the relevance of God, much less his existence.

I inhaled deeply, taking in the scent of the curried chicken I had prepared for dinner. The dish was easy to make on long days like this had been, and the mindless ease with which I could prepare it was exactly what I had needed that evening with my mind, as it was, still continuously recapping the events at the shelter.

"How was your day?" Brian asked.

"Good." I smiled at him, and the smile he gave me in return filled me with warmth. He reached over and covered my right hand with his left. A wave of guilt flowed over me, guilt for not telling him about my visit to Dr. Hinds, for concealing my experiences with the blackout, and for second-guessing how he would respond. "How was yours?"

He ran one hand through his hair. "Long." He paused for a beat then sighed heavily. "Spent in discussions with Framtiden. And it's not like I don't have other clients to deal with."

I gave him a sympathetic smile but did not say more. We made it a point not to discuss work when Aunt Marjorie and Taiwo were in the room. Doing that would be like conversing in a foreign language no one else in the room understood.

"I'm going to try to get into the office early tomorrow. Probably around six."

I nodded. I turned my attention to Taiwo.

"How was your day?" I asked, even though I already knew. Checking in with each person at the table was part of our evening routine.

He looked at Brian. "We met a lady from Jamaica while we were at the shelter tonight."

Brian raised his eyebrows. "Jamaica? Really?"

"Yes. Her name is Angela and she seemed really nice," Taiwo continued.

At the word "Jamaica," Aunt Marjorie, who had been quietly chewing a mouthful of meat, swallowed and spoke. "Is who come from Jamaica, eh? They bring mangoes?"

"I don't think so, Auntie," I replied, shooting a sharp glance at Brian, who was stifling a laugh.

"She came from Jamaica to be a nanny for her friend's daughter, but it didn't work out and now she has nowhere to go."

"She's here illegally?" Brian directed his words at Taiwo, but his eyes were on me.

"I don't know . . ." I began.

"Yes, she is. She told me. After that nasty man left. He wanted her to leave too, but she promised to meet him in half an hour. I did not like him." Taiwo frowned then continued. "She said she came to Virginia because she thinks she has family here."

I looked down at my plate, remembering how she had said she was my sister. Had that been some sort of psychotic break? A reflection of her desperation to claim anyone as a relative?

Taiwo continued. "I told her about how you brought Auntie up here and got her a green card. I said . . ."

"What did you say to her?" Brian's voice took on an uncharacteristically menacing edge, like a mountain lion padding slowly towards a frightened deer. I wondered if Taiwo had heard it. I looked at him, but he was observing his father. I could almost see the thoughts processing in his mind: *He sounds upset . . . retreat, retreat, retreat.*

"I didn't say anything at all, Dad." He dropped his head and continued eating in silence, shoveling the food into his mouth as if to staunch the words he had originally planned to utter.

My heart tightened as it always did when my son was hurt. Brian's anger would dissipate as easily as it had surfaced, but Taiwo took his father's approval or disapproval and wore it like a coat of mail. Even at twenty, he still squared his shoulders, measuring against his father whenever they walked side by side. I wanted to reach out to him as I watched him hunch over his plate, but I did not intervene.

I thought of Angela instead. A memory neared the surface of my consciousness. I was on a ladder using a drill to hang a painting on a wall in a house. The ladder was being held by a man, but I could not tell who it was. I imagined it was a handyman Aunt Marjorie had hired, although it would have been odd for a handyman to let me up on the ladder and, worse, to allow the mistake that was about to happen. As I drilled, the metal drill bit touched a wire connecting the light switch below the photo to the fixture above it, sending a jolt of current through my body. I shuddered and the memory faded, leaving me only with the sensation of being deeply affected by both the drilling incident and my encounters with Angela.

I considered that my reaction to meeting her might have been a result of my not having encountered anyone from Jamaica in a while. When Brian and I left Trinidad, we settled in Virginia, in part because this was where Jamela and Geoffrey, the first real friends we made, lived and partly because that was where we got our first breaks after a challenging start. Caribbean people who came to the D.C. metro area tended to follow those who moved before them into the more diverse communities of D.C. and Maryland. We encountered relatively few Caribbean people in Northern Virginia. I did not seek them out either. I frequented the neighborhood farmers' market instead of traveling to the Caribbean markets in D.C. or Maryland, even on days when I craved tropical fruits and ground provision. The closest I got was the Asian supermarkets that carried close seconds, often disappointing in their tastes and textures. I preferred the anonymity of life away from the inevitable questions of "who you be?"—that compulsion Caribbean people had to place you on the social ladder and assess your worth.

LATER IN BED, after settling Auntie in for the night, I considered talking to Brian about the unsettling in my stomach I knew would keep me awake. Auntie would have attributed it to the curry and prescribed a dose of ginger tea, but I was sure my discomfort did not have a physical cause. I did not have to raise the topic with Brian. When I joined him in bed, he placed the legal journal he was reading face down on the side table on his left, making space between the lamp and the clock, cracking the spine. He rolled over to face me and propped himself up on one arm, the palm of his hand pressing the fleshy part of his cheek forward until it almost touched his nose. There was a time when this might have been sexy, not the cheek flab, but him putting away all other distractions and focusing entirely on me, but time and familiarity had dulled the power of his attention.

"So tell me about Miss Jamaica," he said.

A defensive wall rose within me.

"There's nothing to tell. I don't know anything about her."

"Tai seemed quite taken with her."

"Shouldn't be a surprise. He's always been an empathetic child . . . person."

"So you didn't share his desire to bring her home?" His smile was smug, as if he had watched me search for a treasure and had just revealed that he had known where it was all along.

It was one of his favorite dinner party dissertations, how I had received a single phone call from Jamaica and insisted that we initiate the process of getting my aunt a green card. I had never been able to explain to Brian the impact of the call from Jamaica, the impact of hearing Christine's voice unchanged from our days as high school friends, the impact of her accusation that I had abandoned the one person who had been there for me all my life. When Christine described the dilapidated state of my aunt's house in Black River, my heart had ached, but when she mentioned that the garden was overgrown and trampled by intruders, something had unhinged inside me.

I shook my head in response to Brian's question about my wanting to bring Angela here.

"Good," Brian said. "We don't need to bring any trouble in here."

"How you know she's trouble?" I sat up. The current I had felt when I saw Angela snaked through my body, igniting the synapses in my brain, readying me for a fight.

"She's here illegally. In this climate . . ." His voice trailed off. Two years after 9-11 he was still uncomfortable about his position as an immigrant.

"We were lucky. Literally lucky. Your mother won the visa lottery. But for the grace of God . . ."

"We'd be in Trinidad. Or back in Jamaica, where you refuse to go." He finished my sentence.

I flinched.

"Sorry, I should not have gone there," he said, "but I would never have come up here if we couldn't do it right. We can't take any chances, Maya. From the time we open we mouth and people hear we don't sound like them, we have a mark on we backs. We are citizens but not by birth. Don't be fooled by all that pomp and circumstance of the swearing-in ceremony. One mistake and they can take it away just so." He snapped his fingers. "And send you back to the only place that can't put you out, your birthing land. You to Jamaica and me to Trinidad and Tai trapped somewhere in between. You think I feel safe here? You think you are secure in that grace of God? God has no say in this. If they decide you gone, you gone." Brian pounded a fist on the bed between us.

"Perhaps," I replied. "But life was good for you back home. You could have stayed and thrived. We don't know what this woman has endured, what drove her here. Jamaica still rough these days. Suppose we raised Tai there. They would not have handled his autism in Jamaica or Trinidad like they did here: diagnosed him early, guided us so he would grow into the independent adult he is today. What would you have done to make sure he got what he needed? What would you have sacrificed, risked, to ensure his life was the best possible? I don't know about you, but if you think I would have sat in Trinidad and listen to them call him dunce and push him in the back of the class, you have another think coming." I dropped my voice. "But we were lucky. Pure dumb luck."

"That luck killed my mother."

"She died of a heart attack." I reached over and touched his cheek.

"She died of a broken heart . . . Do you even remember what it was like when we first got here?"

I was silent. In the twenty-two years I had known him, I had only once before seen Brian this angry.

"That's your answer for everything, isn't it? Clamming up. Disappearing into your head or wherever it is you go. Shutting me out." He threw his arms up in a gesture of disgust. I flinched as his hands neared my face, and Brian's body slackened, his shoulders slumped. He sighed. "Why do you stiffen at every sudden movement I make? Twenty-one years of marriage and you think I'd hurt you?" He steupsed, the sucking sound short, dismissive. "The bottom line is we can't afford to harbor criminals, not after everything we've built here. Don't get carried away, Amaya."

He rolled over, his shoulders high on the bed like an impassable mountain range. So I hadn't told him of the connection I felt with Angela. I hadn't reminded him of how each of us had felt when we first migrated, alone and isolated despite being surrounded by family.

CHAPTER SEVENTEEN

Washington, D.C. - August 1983

When we arrived in D.C., Aunt Camilla took a week and a half off work to help us settle in. She was a gracious host, filling the house with scents of Caribbean cooking, cooing over the baby, and ensuring we were as comfortable as we could be in the space. I was aware that our adopted family was making a great sacrifice adding three adults and a baby to their household for an indefinite time period. I could see it in the pools of weariness in my aunt-in-law's eyes even as she smiled and catered to us. As a result, I made my presence as innocuous as possible, spending most of my time in the room I shared with Brian and trying to disappear into the dark fabrics of the furniture when I ventured into the other parts of the house.

Mrs. Lin compensated for my quietness. She seemed unaware that her circumstances had changed, and stormed through the townhouse with as much bluster as if she still lived in the spacious bungalow she had owned in Trinidad. Aunt Camilla's nerves frayed with every interaction with her sister-in-law. The two women were about the same age; Aunt Camilla might have been older, but Mrs. Lin behaved as if she were the more . . . the more everything. When all three of us were together, I felt as if I were trapped between a mother dog and a hungry snake.

On our second day in the United States, Aunt Camilla took Mrs. Lin and me shopping at a mall just outside of Washington. Brian had declined the invitation to accompany us, and remained home to get started on his job search.

As Aunt Camilla, Mrs. Lin, and I drove through D.C., the landscape changed from the unkempt brownstones of the neighborhood in which the

Lins lived, into what was clearly a more affluent area, with colonial-style homes that reminded me of some of the buildings around the Queen's Park Savannah in Trinidad. We soon entered a business district with stores and restaurants. Driving on the right side of the road was disorienting; I found it difficult to overcome the sensation that we would run into the sidewalk, and so I distracted myself by reading the signs as we passed by—some, like McDonald's, familiar from television, and many I had never encountered before. I wondered if there would be a day when I would drive through these streets without the awe I felt now.

Preoccupied with the enormity of the task of fitting in and finding my way, I was unprepared for the sight of what Aunt Camilla called the Mall. The traffic was slow in this area, our progress thwarted by pedestrians and cars, and so I had an opportunity to take in the majesty of the long stretch of green flanked at one end by the Capitol and at the other by a tall cream structure just barely visible through my window. I wished I could turn the window down and lean out further to see the statue more clearly, but when we got into the car, Aunt Camilla had locked the doors and turned on the air conditioning as if driving with the windows down had never been an option. I had to content myself with admiring the height of the thin, pyramid-like Monument and wondering how much of the world one would be able to see from the top. I felt acutely aware of my insignificance in space and time, and for the first time I had a glimpse of how different Taiwo's life would be from mine. I looked down at him, asleep in my lap, lulled by the rumble of the engine. *How will I teach you to live in this world that I don't know or understand?* I thought.

Aunt Camilla overtook a slow-moving car, perhaps driven by someone like me, fascinated by the D.C. sights, then swerved suddenly to avoid an oncoming car as she returned to her side of the road. She drove with an aggressiveness that contradicted her calm exterior.

"Sorry about that," she said in response to a muted yelp from Mrs. Lin.

"We accustomed to this and worse," Mrs. Lin replied. She turned slightly in her seat. "Not so, Amaya?"

I did not respond. I hoped I could avoid getting caught in the middle of the women's rivalry.

"You been out of Trinidad too long," Mrs. Lin continued. "Traffic bad there. Real bad."

Aunt Camilla's shoulders stiffened and in the rearview, I saw her lips straighten like a shoelace pulled taut then tightened into a knot. "Good thing you here now, then," she replied.

A silence settled in the car so tense I feared it would wake Taiwo. Aunt Camilla looked into the rearview mirror, and her eyes caught mine. She sighed and smiled.

"I'm happy all you here," she said. "It was real boring in the house with the kids gone and Joe and I watching at each other every night." Both she and Mrs. Lin laughed, tentatively, as if the sound of their own laughter came as a surprise. Taiwo turned and sighed in his sleep, exhaling deeply, his breath moving through the car and dispersing the tension.

The rest of the outing passed without incident, but when we returned home that evening, Mrs. Lin retired to her room "exhausted," even going as far as to wipe imaginary perspiration off her brow with the back of her hand. She did not emerge until Aunt Camilla had prepared dinner and placed it on the table. I had offered to help Aunt Camilla but she refused, instructing me to "take care of that sweet baby," all the while humming an indefinable tune.

THAT DAY'S PATTERN repeated all week, with Mrs. Lin and Aunt Camilla in a cycle of one-upmanship then reconciliation. I begged off of going out on any subsequent outings, citing Taiwo as the excuse, even though I dreaded spending the long days in the small townhouse, where Brian paced like the lion I had seen in the Emperor Valley Zoo in Trinidad where he had taken me once during the vacation after my first year at university. The animal strode back and forth in its enclosure then stopped and looked at me with an expression I had interpreted as "I deserve more."

In the time Aunt Camilla spent home from work, she cooked every evening and Mrs. Lin ate, always offering profuse praise but never offering assistance. The day before Aunt Camilla was scheduled to return to work, the five of us sat in the dining room for the Sunday afternoon meal, a long, narrow, and windowless room furnished with an ornate mahogany table. The chairs fit underneath with barely enough room for guests to slide into their places. Uncle Joe sat at the head of the table nearest the door. Brian sat at the foot, Taiwo in his lap.

"You looking forward to going back to work?" I asked Aunt Camilla.

She pursed her lips and glanced at Uncle Joe, who smiled.

"Your aunt have a real love-hate relationship with that job."

Aunt Camilla smiled as well.

"Yeah, it's like an ex-boyfriend I can't ditch." She cast a saucy look in Uncle Joe's direction. He laughed. "Even while I been on vacation, they been calling me with questions. This was my first job when we got here in '67. Well, my first workplace. Providence Hospital. Back then I was a nurse, until my back gave out." She told us how the back trouble had forced her retirement after ten years and how she now worked managing the nurses. Her hours were regular, nine-to-five, but she revealed that dealing with staffing issues was almost as emotionally exhausting as dealing with the indigent patients that had frequented the hospital when she first arrived.

"Just stay home, then . . . if things that bad. You have a husband alive to support you," Mrs. Lin commented with a heavy sigh as if the conversation was making her exhausted as well.

Uncle Joe froze. His hand, holding a forkful of rice and peas, hovered in the air between his mouth and his plate. A few grains of rice fell off of the fork as his knuckles tightened around it, his only movement. The air in the room thickened and no one moved, as if we had all been encased in stone. Even Taiwo, often fidgety during mealtimes, remained still where he lay cradled in

Brian's arms.

"I'm needed there. Is a hospital. Not the kind of job where you could just pick up and leave on a whim." Aunt Camilla broke the spell, pushing her chair away from the table. She picked up a half-full bowl of stewed chicken.

"I going and get some more from the pot," she said, heading for the kitchen. Uncle Joe shoved the fork into his mouth and rose to follow her, leaving Brian, Mrs. Lin, and me to finish our meal in silence.

The next day, Aunt Camilla went back out to work as scheduled. She arrived home to a quiet kitchen. She stamped on the mat at the front door for an extra long time, as if trying to release her anger in the tiny puffs that rose like clouds of hot air around her feet. I immediately felt guilty. Almost three months old, Taiwo was awake for increasingly longer periods during the day, and when Mrs. Lin was around, he fussed more than usual, demanding my attention each time his grandmother's voice reached his ears. I spent my days moving around the house, talking and reading to him when he was awake, quieting him so Brian could work undisturbed, and worrying when he slept about my fitness to be someone's mother. I understood that I had an obligation to tether him to his Afro-Caribbean ancestry, but I had nothing to share beyond Aunt Marjorie, who was not even a blood relation. With all of these concerns on my mind and no one to share them with, I had not thought about preparing dinner until Aunt Camilla opened the door, and I realized how unfair it was that she should have a full day at work then return to cater to guests who had spent the day at home. Mrs. Lin realized her mistake as well.

"I am so sorry. I didn't know what you was planning for dinner. Didn't want to get in your business, you know?"

"Don't worry, Grace. I'll just toss together some fried rice with the leftovers." Aunt Camilla did not look in Mrs. Lin's direction as she walked into her bedroom.

I entered the kitchen, Taiwo cradled in my left arm. I sat on a stool facing the stove and waited. A feeling of great inadequacy came over me. Even if I had not been handicapped by the infant in my arms, I would not have known where to start with preparing a meal for a family. Aunt Marjorie had chased me from the kitchen in the last days of high school. "Your job is to study. That way you not relying on no man to support you. Cooking will come." I worried how I would manage a household when we moved out of Uncle Joe and Aunt Camilla's place.

Aunt Camilla entered the kitchen, her face scrubbed of the makeup she had applied for work. She had exchanged her work suit for loose-fitting shorts and a T-shirt that revealed surprisingly muscular forearms. She leaned close to Taiwo and whispered, "How's my darling grand-nephew today?" before moving on to the fridge to remove the makings of dinner. She did not speak to me; instead, she navigated the kitchen with quick, focused movements, chopping, tossing, mixing, and soon there was a meal in the wok, yesterday's leftover rice browned with soy sauce, sesame oil, and a colorful array of every vegetable Aunt Camilla found in the fridge: carrots, broccoli, green peppers, shiitake mushrooms, bok choy, onions.

Neither of us spoke and the silence, born out of companionship rather than any awkwardness, flowed between us on the warm stream of scents emanating from the pot. Being in the tiny kitchen unnerved me; the smells, the sounds of pots being knocked against each other and oil sizzling in the wok on the stove, stirred up a reaction in my stomach that I knew was not just hunger. I felt the specter of another presence watching, mocking me for my inability to perform this task that every woman I knew seemed to master with ease.

"You know how to cook?" Aunt Camilla asked.

Her question startled me out of my thoughts. I readjusted my position on the stool.

"Not really," I admitted.

"You want me teach you?"

"Would you?" Then I remembered how tired Aunt Camilla often looked. "If is not too much trouble," I added.

Before we could discuss how and when we would begin the lessons, I heard the scratch of a key in the front door. The door creaked as it swung open then clicked shut. Uncle Joe strode into the kitchen.

"Good night, ladies," he said. Aunt Camilla and I greeted him with smiles.

He kissed Aunt Camilla on the forehead then moved to the sink, where he began washing the dishes she had discarded in the course of her cooking.

Mrs. Lin followed Uncle Joe into the kitchen. She inhaled deeply, and I felt as if all of the positive energy was being sucked out of the room.

"Something smelling good," she said. She sniffed again. "Thyme, garlic. You put enough sesame oil? Eugene used to love that too bad. That's how they mother used to make it, you know. Plenty sesame oil. I sure Joe love it too, not so, Joe?"

Before anyone could respond, Brian entered the small kitchen.

"Mommy," he said, "Aunt Camilla is not your maid, you know. This is her kitchen and she know how to run it."

"I just trying to help." Mrs. Lin sniffed softly. "Sharing some advice."

"Nobody wants your advice. You wanted to come America? Here you are, but you have to listen and adapt," Brian replied.

"Maybe I too old to change." She sniffed again.

"You better change, because we not in Trinidad anymore." He raised his left hand and pointed to its pinky finger with his right index finger, counting finger to finger as he spoke. "There's no Bianca to cook and clean, no Frankie in the garden, no Mr. Carroll to call when any little thing break in the house. You keep telling me I'm the breadwinner now, I have to step up to the plate. Well, look in the mirror. You have to grow up too, Mommy." He looked at her face, which had crumpled into despair. I thought her pitiful expression would stop his assault, but he continued. "Yes, you have to grow up."

Uncle Joe had been drying his hands on a towel on the oven door while Brian was speaking. He turned to Brian now, his shoulders square and his usually kind eyes dark with anger. "Boy," he thundered, "don't talk to your mother like that."

Aunt Camilla nodded. "All of you need time to adapt. You self should understand."

Brian exhaled visibly, his anger leaving his eyes and body with the breath. "Mommy, I didn't . . ."

But Mrs. Lin rushed from the kitchen and locked herself in her bedroom, unresponsive to Brian's apologies. He eventually retired to our bedroom. I remained to eat dinner with my uncle- and aunt-in-law in tense silence.

CHAPTER EIGHTEEN

W e all had a fitful night, the atmosphere in the house tightly wound like a child's toy top that would whirl out of control when finally released. The next morning, I rolled onto my side to face Taiwo's cot. He appeared to be asleep, his breathing even. I sensed Brian behind me, could picture his body on its side, mirroring mine. Tension flowed from him in hot waves that spoke of his need for me. He took the hand that lay at my side in his and intertwined his fingers in mine. I grunted and shifted slightly, feigning sleep.

"I know you're awake." He sighed. "You haven't touched me since the baby came. Not since we married, as a matter of fact, not really. At first, I thought was because you pregnant, then because you had just had the baby. But now I wonder . . ." The words lingered, a steeple on top of our intertwined fingers, teetering on the brink of cruelty.

Tears pooled in my eyes and when I raised them to look at him, I knew they were filled with irrational fear. I did not believe that Brian would hurt me, but the full realization of the corner he formed behind me, both a shield and a prison, came to me all at once.

"You fraid me?" He dropped my hand. "Amaya? Maya? Darling, I'm frustrated and I'm tired, but I would leave you, abandon my child, before I would ever raise a hand towards you in anger. I don't know what happened to you. I know you don't want to talk about it, but it's affecting our family so I can't just leave it alone. Promise me we'll talk about it, dou dou. Promise me."

I dropped my head into my hands, nodding my assent as I did so, knowing it was a lie. How could I share with him memories I no longer owned? I vowed silently, not for the first time, to make the problem go away. I would work harder to be the affectionate wife he wanted and put an end to his questions. I thought of the easy banter between Uncle Joe and Aunt Camilla, and wondered if Brian and I would ever reach a point where we communicated that way.

"Breakfast is ready." Mrs. Lin knocked once then pushed on the door. I swiped the back of my hands across my face to dry my tears. I wondered how much of our conversation she had heard. Taiwo stirred, a slight frown crossed his brow, and he opened his mouth as if to cry but only released a sleepy whimper. I empathized with his response to the sound of Mrs. Lin's chirp. His grandmother's boisterous approach—cooing, shaking him, demanding his smiles, his voice, any response or sign of affection, often resulted in his tears. Unlike Uncle Joe and Aunt Camilla, Mrs. Lin seemed incapable of reading his cues and tempering her approach to him. I hoped she would work it out on her own. Brian was less tolerant, although his entreaty was gentle, an apology of sorts for his outburst the previous night.

"Softer, Mommy. Please. Tai sleeping."

She frowned then straightened her face into a smile. "Come eat. All yuh can't stay hole up in there all day. Amaya need to eat. Keep up her strength to feed my grandson."

I forced a smile. Mrs. Lin was trying to make amends for her behavior the night before, but I was not sure if I could trust it to last. Brian stared at his mother as if he too was trying to process her motives.

The three-way standoff was interrupted by the wail of a siren.

"What the heck is that?" Mrs. Lin exclaimed.

Taiwo woke and added his voice to the shrieking.

"Smoke detector," Brian shouted over the noise. "You left something on the stove?"

No one waited for her answer. I grabbed Taiwo from the crib before following Brian and his mother out of the room. Smoke rolled out of the kitchen, tinging the air with white fumes that quickly changed to gray. Brian grabbed a towel as he passed by the bathroom, and he shook it vigorously over his head, dispersing smoke as he entered the kitchen. A sweet yet woody smell floated on the smoke, mingling the scents of a fruit market and the forest fires I had experienced in the Maracas mountains in Trinidad.

"No fire. It's just smoke . . . and burnt plantain," he shouted. "Open the windows."

Mrs. Lin and I rushed from window to window, forcing them up on reluctant hinges, but the air remained cloudy, and the smoke detector continued its urgent warning.

"Get Tai out of here," Brian instructed and I did, leaving the front door open behind me as I sat on the steps. Taiwo's cries quieted, and he looked up at me as if asking me questions about life that I could not answer.

DESPITE HER FAILED attempt to prepare breakfast that morning, Mrs. Lin continued to try her hand at other chores. She seemed incapable of finding the balance between doing nothing and doing it all, and her adult life in Trinidad, surrounded by helpers, had left her ill-prepared for modern housework.

About mid-afternoon, she decided to vacuum, and when she was unable to get the machine to work, she decided to empty the bag that held the dirt. I heard her coughing uncontrollably and when I rushed out of my room to help, I found her surrounded by a cloud of dust and debris.

"Are you okay?" I asked. I patted her back gently, a gesture of comfort rather than an attempt to dislodge whatever was causing the coughing fit.

"I can't win!" she shouted. "I just can't win anything. Nothing, except for that damn visa lottery."

I stepped back, uncertain of what to say next. I had overheard enough of my mother-in-law's phone calls to Trinidad regaling her friends with exaggerated tales of her new life in the United States, shopping and apartment hunting, to be sure that she would not want me to witness this moment of vulnerability. I wished Brian were home, but he had already left for the library.

"I had it all plan out," Mrs. Lin continued. "Stay with Joe a few weeks, then we would be out of here. One happy family. Now we stuck. Brian won't get real work for months. My grandson hates me. Camilla hates me. You probably hate me too. So much for happy."

"We jus get here," I said. "Brian will get work. Or you . . . you and I could look for work."

"Who gon an hire a tough-back woman like me with no experience working up here? And if you go to work, who going take care of my grandson?" She shook her head. "I just didn't think it would take this much time. It could be months before Brian pass the bar. I can't spend months in this shoebox."

"We could go back . . ." I ventured.

"And look like a failure? Sweetheart, no one goes back."

Mrs. Lin straightened herself, she shrugged her shoulders slightly, and I caught a glimpse of the woman I had first met in Trinidad. "It will be fine," she said. "I had a moment. This conversation never happened, you hear?"

Washington, D.C. - The Final Chapter

Three months later, we had met Jamela and Geoffrey, Brian was working at Geoffrey's firm, and by December, we had signed a lease on an apartment of our own in Virginia. Contrasting emotions competed for space in my heart. I was sure the Lins were longing to have their space back after hosting three extra people for five months. I also longed for space in which I could grow into our new life in the United States. On the other hand, I had grown to love Uncle Joe and Aunt Camilla. I would miss the Saturday-afternoon sessions in which Aunt Camilla and I had bonded as she taught me to cook, and my evening chats with Uncle Joe on the front steps when he came home from work, although those had become less frequent as the weather cooled then chilled.

About seven p.m. one mid-December evening, I had waited on the front steps for Uncle Joe's arrival, shivering in spite of the thick winter coat I had borrowed from Aunt Camilla.

"I know you happy to get rid of us," I quipped to Uncle Joe on his arrival.

"You not moving that far, you know. I may be getting rid of you, but you won't get rid of me that easy." He pulled me into a hug. "Come. It freezing out here. Leh we go inside."

Once we entered the warmth of the indoors, Uncle Joe pointed towards the back of the house. "What you going and do about out there?"

My face got hot. I had not realized that he had noticed my attempts to coax life from the dirt that filled the small area outside my window. In hindsight, I recalled that on some mornings, the soil had seemed a little moister than could be expected from the dew, or a little lighter, more tilled than I remembered leaving it, but I had dismissed these observations as tricks of my memory.

"Don't worry, I go keep an eye on it for you," he said. "It'll be real winter soon. Not a lot more you could do. But I was thinking I could plant a palm tree in the spring and maybe a banana tree, who knows."

IN THE MIDDLE of our first February in the United States, Brian passed the bar on his first try. Geoffrey took the two families out to dinner to celebrate Brian's success and the formation of Gil, Lin and Associates, although there were no associates yet. *We've survived the worst*, I thought as I sat listening to the animated conversation around the restaurant's table.

The reality turned out to be much more complicated. Brian and Geoffrey went on to develop a successful law practice. Jamela transitioned from full-time mother to practicing law once her youngest was old enough for daycare. I stayed at home to help Taiwo navigate his challenges. Mrs. Lin withered every winter, and by the time the ink dried on the contract on our three-bedroom, three-bathroom house in 1990, she had died of a heart attack.

CHAPTER NINETEEN

I sat up in bed after the fight Brian and I had about Angela, watching the tension in Brian's body relax into sleep. As I thought about the path of luck, triumphs, and losses that had led to our being in this particular space and circumstance, I tried to see his point of view, to understand his reluctance to help her. He was not wrong. She had broken the law, she was in the country illegally, but I understood what it meant to need to flee a place at all costs. I had left everything Jamaican behind when I moved to Trinidad. I had not even glanced over my shoulder until Auntie had needed me, and even then, I had only ventured as far as Miami, as if touching the waters between the United States and the Caribbean would manifest a tsunami that would pull me under and flush me out onto the shores of my old home.

I lowered my head. It felt too heavy for my neck to carry. I had told Brian I had no plans to help Angela, but that was not true. My decision would lead to a difficult battle with him, but battle I would. Something about the woman had gotten under my skin and penetrated so deeply that if it came to a choice between her and Brian, the decision would be a difficult one.

And that man, Nate, Angela had called him. He was clearly bad news. I wondered what hold he had over Angela and how dangerous he was. I sat up in bed and quietly swung my feet to the ground. Silently, I made my way out of the bedroom and into the study across the hall.

A glow emanated from the desk. The computer had been left on with a browser window open to a news article on immigration. *Oh, Tai.* I sighed. Had his search been prompted by José's situation, or had he been as taken with Angela as I had been? Had he found anything? I made a mental note to ask Jamela about Temporary Protected Status. The desk was uncluttered save a pen holder, a stationery tray with stamps, paperclips, and a larger tray with a few bills waiting to be paid. A single manila folder with my notes for the Swedish deal sat on the right. I looked at it, but the importance it had held just a few hours before had faded. I opened my email and composed a message to Daven, asking him to finish the proposal I had started for the changes to the deal. I was shafting him since it was due tomorrow, but he was very ambitious; he would rise to the challenge.

I clicked Send then switched back to the browser window and searched for "Nate Fairfax Virginia." A few seconds later, a list of websites appeared on the screen. I clicked on the White Pages link. Another long list unfolded. I took a notepad from the top desk drawer and wrote the names of all the Nates listed who were in the thirty-to-thirty-five age range. On a hunch, I left out those who were married or living with an adult relative. Then I ran the same search again with the name Nathaniel, then with Nathan, tapping my pen on the pad while I waited for the web page to load. I cleared the cache on my browser, shut down the computer, then tore the sheet from the notepad and placed it in my briefcase. I wasn't sure if the fifteen names I had written down would be enough to help me find him, but I would try.

Back in the bedroom, I considered the other half of my problem. My first encounter with Angela had begun an unlocking of thoughts I had suppressed for twenty-four years. Twenty-four years since I fled Jamaica. *Perhaps it's time to stop running from those memories.* Dr. Hinds's hypnosis could help me deal with my inability to recall the past. It could help me and give me something to offer Brian when I presented him with my plan to help Angela.

I lifted my eyes to the mirror on the dressing table at the end of our bed. Red-rimmed eyes stared back at me from a face that appeared to have developed new lines foretelling the start of a new path in my life.

CHAPTER TWENTY

I awoke the next morning with a course of energy racing through my body. Brian left early for work as promised, so by the time I awoke he was gone, having left a heart-signed note on my nightstand. I understood it as the beginning of an apology for his part in our argument about intertwining our lives with Angela's, but it did not mean that he was on board with the idea. I would have to act on my own, and I had already decided that the first step would be to continue my investigation of Nate once I got into the office. The second step was to set up the hypnosis appointment. If it worked, the stories I could finally tell Brian about my childhood would smooth the path to his accepting Angela.

The morning at home inched by. Every step, from dealing with Aunt Marjorie to getting myself ready for work, seemed to take longer than it should, and I was surprised that when I finally sat at my desk it was only nine a.m.

I placed my hand on the receiver of my desk phone. Lawyers in the firm contacted law enforcement for information on defendants and plaintiffs as a matter of course, but I knew I should not be abusing the privilege for a personal matter. *It could be life-or-death*, I thought, and when I picked up the phone for the third time, I made the call. I dialed the McLean District Police Station and asked to speak to Detective Bryant. While I waited for the call to be transferred, I folded and unfolded the list of Nates.

"Detective Bryant." The voice on the other end of the line was crisp and professional.

"Hi Detective, it's Amaya Lin from Gil, Lin and Associates."

"Mrs. Lin. Good to hear from you. How can I help?"

"I have a case. Need to check up on a client's associate."

Detective Bryant paused. I heard the creak of a chair moving. While I had spoken to him many times, I had only ever met him once, maybe twice, at the firm's Christmas dinners. I imagined his tall, full body folded into a wheeled office chair, his elbows on his desk, his face contorted into a puzzled expression.

"You sent in the authorization for the background check," he stated rather than asked.

"No," I said. "This one is different." I paused then plunged forward. "I need a favor."

"Are you working criminal cases now?"

I flustered. I was silent for a beat, a pause Detective Bryant would read as guilt. "I just need to find out about him. I suspect domestic abuse."

"She should file a restraining order, then. Is it the husband?"

"No . . . it's . . . it's complicated. Listen . . . Can you run a name in NCIC for me?"

There was a pause on the line, and I pictured his bright blue eyes drawing closer together as he frowned. He was a good man, principled, and I regretted putting him in this position. I was about to tell him not to worry when he surprised me by agreeing.

"What's the name?"

"That's the thing. I'm not sure. Can I fax you a list of possibilities?"

"What's really going on, Mrs. Lin?" His tone shifted, layered with formality.

"I don't want to put her in more danger by asking questions. Please trust me." Then I added, "I can describe him to you."

I heard a loud exhale on the other end of the line.

"Okay. Send me the list."

I did my best to describe Nate to Detective Bryant and faxed him my list.

A few minutes later, he called me back. His voice was deeper than before, as if the gravity of the information he had uncovered was weighing it down. "If this is your guy, he's bad news. That's the only reason I'm sharing this information. Tell your friend to stay far away from him. Check your fax machine. And regards to Mr. Lin."

I stood over the fax machine as a sheet appeared with an image of Nate. He was younger with longer hair, but it was definitely him, the same dark, deep-set eyes and thin lips. He was smirking, just as he had when he said "Don't I, sweetheart" to Angela. Nathaniel Boyle was his name. He was on parole and had been involved in robbery, drug trafficking, and promoting prostitution.

I sucked in a deep breath. The address on the rap sheet was about a block away from the shelter, which might explain, in part, why Angela had been there. *But why go to a shelter at all?* I wondered. The visit had obviously been a risk. What desperation had driven the young woman inside? I shuddered.

Nate's face stared up at me from the faxed sheet all morning. I should have put it in my desk drawer or shredded it, but I wanted to keep him in my sight, as if that would somehow prevent him from perpetrating any crimes. I tried to deal with the papers in front of me, and I succeeded for a while, working by rote, signing checks and checking client bills, but by twelve I was exhausted. The challenge of keeping my mind on work while pushing Nate from my consciousness was causing my brain to overheat.

There was a knock on my door and Jamela's reddish-brown hair appeared in my doorway, followed by the rest of her body. "What are you doing for lunch? I really need to get out of here."

I considered saying no. I had not yet decided what to do about Nate now that I had more information on him. But Jamela's expression changed my mind. She looked tired. Her eyes were dulled and her lips made a halfhearted attempt at a smile.

We walked to a small deli, where we ordered sandwiches, and sat on a bench on the sidewalk. A cool breeze blustered by, kicking up leaves only to deposit them just a few feet down the road.

"Déjà vu," Jamela said.

I smiled, thinking back to that day twenty years ago when we met. We had been so young then, unaware of how precious the years ahead would be.

"Geoff is talking about retiring once Jeremy is done with college."

I caught my breath. Images of life without Jamela, the firm without the Gil name, filled my mind like a reel of scenarios projected in slow motion. I swallowed hard.

"It's so weird," she continued. "Work is his life. I complain that he lets it consume him, but I can't imagine who he would be if he wasn't a lawyer."

"How do you feel about that?" I asked.

"I don't know." Jamela stomped her feet, and clouds of dust rose from the sidewalk beneath her black heeled boots. "I mean, it's a few years off. And he may change his mind . . . He just dropped it on me this morning. Maybe he wanted to see how I would respond."

"And?"

"I don't know how to respond. The work I do is important. I don't want to just stop."

I nodded, trying to stay focused on Jamela's issues, but the mention of immigrants sent my mind reeling towards Angela and Nate.

"Maybe you could continue working even if he retires?"

"He wants to travel. Maybe live abroad."

"Oh."

Jamela sighed. "It seems wrong to stress about a privileged opportunity to lie on a beach when the people I work for are faced with life-and-death situations every day. Then they come here to have strangers argue over whether they have suffered enough to stay."

I put a hand on Jamela's. "Give yourself a break. You deserve to do what makes you happy."

She smiled. "It's okay. Worrying over little things is how I deal with the big ones." She laughed, a throaty sound. "You know any good shrinks?"

I smiled back, wondering if she had any idea how intuitive her words were. "He won't want to live far from the kids and he knows you don't want to either."

"You're probably right." She shuffled her feet on the pavement again. "How are things with you? We haven't really talked in a while. That Swedish case still keeping you busy?"

"Yeah. We're close to closing. It's all Brian can think about."

"So no loving?"

I blushed.

"And what's with all these 'things' you keep having to take care of?"

I did not respond, and we sat in silence for several minutes, watching the cars and people pass by, listening to the hum of car engines, the edges of conversations, the sounds of the city. Sunlight crept across the sidewalk and shone on the tips of my heeled pumps, casting them half in light and half in darkness. I pushed my feet forward, fully into the sun, and sighed as they warmed.

I could have lingered there indefinitely, blotting out the worries of my day. The things that busied me seemed insignificant, drops of water in an ocean. There were so many women in situations similar to Angela's, women trapped in arrangements they entered out of necessity, and with every effort to dig themselves out, they made the hole deeper. I could help Angela or I could not, and it would have the same impact on the world.

"You okay?"

I had not closed my eyes, but a glaze lifted off of them as I turned towards Jamela's voice.

"How do you keep going? Helping your clients even when their cases seem hopeless?" I asked.

Jamela shrugged. "I don't know. I guess I see my grandmother in each of the women. She came here as an illegal immigrant, running from a life of poverty and an abusive husband. I don't even know if she knew she was here to stay when she stepped on the plane. She had a hard life here, hiding, working, being cheated because of her status, and she died a silent, bitter woman. Her anger filtered through to my father and his sister and affected how they raised their children." She sighed. "I guess each woman I help, I'm not just helping her. I hope that I'm helping the next generation. At least a little." Jamela smiled, an unusual shyness visible in her expression.

I reached over and covered her hand with mine. "You do good," I said. "And you'll do good wherever you are. That's why you went back to school slogging all those nights."

"I couldn't have done it without you helping with the kids."

"And I would do it again in a heartbeat. I love you."

Jamela's full smile returned. "Enough of the mushfest. You and I have a world to save." She laughed. She stood and brushed her skirt.

I remained seated. "Actually, I have an errand to run."

I DROVE THE twenty minutes to Nate's street. As I neared my destination, I wondered what I would do when I arrived. When I passed the shelter, my lack of a plan loomed large on me and I almost turned back. *I'll just drive by*, I convinced myself. Maybe I would catch a glimpse of Angela and get an idea of what was going on. I turned into the neighborhood. The houses near the main road were small with well-kept yards, but as I made one turn after another, following the directions I had printed out, the number of cars parked on the street increased and the facade of prosperity sagged into broken fences and overgrown lots.

Once on Nate's street, I slowed below the speed limit. I counted the house numbers. His was 3467, so it would be on my left. My heart beat faster as I neared the number. Looking ahead I saw a tall, slim person dressed in black swing one leg over the body of a motorbike. It was a big bike, probably as expensive as a small car, a fact I knew because I had looked at prices once when

Taiwo had expressed an interest in getting one. I had been surprised and relieved that the price was high enough to dissuade him from the investment.

The person—I could see that it was Nate—straightened the bike but paused, looking in my direction as if he sensed my approach. While my 2001 Camry was not a luxury vehicle and not new, it stood out in the neighborhood of relics. I could not think of a way to avoid him, so I pressed on the gas, hoping to move past him as quickly as possible without calling any further attention to myself. *Look straight ahead*, I admonished, but I could not. I glanced in his direction as I passed. My foot rose from the accelerator and the car slowed as our eyes locked. Recognition lit his eyes. His thin lips rose in a half smile and he raised his right hand, pointing his index and middle finger at me as if they were a double-barreled shotgun. I gasped. My foot found the accelerator and did not let up until I was blocks away.

When I was sure he had not followed me, I pulled to the side of the road, double-checked that the doors were locked, then dropped my head to the steering wheel. My heart pounded. *What was I thinking? What did I expect? That I'd burst in and rescue Angela?* Once the thought entered my mind, I knew that was exactly what I had to do.

I was too shaken to go back the way I had come. The suggestion of a gun in his hands had touched something deep inside of me I had not known was there, and the touch had caused it to burst into flames. I breathed in deeply, but my heart would not slow its tempo until I resolved I would not return to the house. I decided instead that I would go to the shelter that evening in the hope that I would run into Angela there.

CHAPTER TWENTY-ONE

It was six p.m. when Taiwo and I arrived at the shelter, but the shadows were just beginning to lengthen. I scanned the people hanging out at the front of the building, looking for Angela. She was not among them.

"We aren't expecting you tonight," Gary said as we entered the dining hall. He smiled, but there was a wariness in his eyes concealing his real question—*what are you doing here?* He stood between us and the expanse of the room as if defending his territory.

"I know," I said. "We were free tonight and thought maybe you might need some extra help." Taiwo fidgeted at my side. He had not been free. He did karate on Friday evenings, and I had had to beg him to come with me. I had been determined to come to the shelter to complete my mission, but lingering anxiety made me hesitant to come alone. Taiwo and Angela seemed to have bonded. His presence would be helpful convincing the woman to . . . to what? I was not sure what I would offer Angela if she agreed to leave Nate. Would I take her in? How would I get that past Brian? What if Nate came looking for her? I had never been this impulsive before, and the drive I felt to act scared me.

I scanned the room over Gary's shoulder. It was not yet full, just a few men hunched over their plates and one family with two children sharing a video game while they waited for their adults to finish eating. There was no sign of Angela.

Gary frowned, and I tried to reassure him that we did not have an ulterior agenda. I smiled. "We just wanted to help, but we can see you aren't busy at all so we'll go."

Gary lowered his shoulders an inch. "Thanks for stopping by," he said. He moved forward, forcing Taiwo and I to step back towards the door to keep a reasonable personal distance between us. "We have your number, so we can call if we need extra help."

I smiled again. "Great. We'll see you next week." I gestured towards him, pointing my index fingers then dropping them just as quickly as I recalled Nate's gun-shaped gesture earlier that day.

As we left the center, I turned to survey the people outside once more. One man and one woman leaned against the wall under a No Solicitation sign, young and white with drawn faces as if they had just sucked on a cigarette. There was a charge in the air, an unsettling feeling, a jitteriness. I had never noticed it before, but now that I had, it was all I could sense. Fear crept into my veins like a cold liquid injected into my bloodstream. *Drugs*, I thought. *They are buying and selling drugs.* I wondered at their proximity to the shelter. Was the staff involved? If not, why not enforce the "no solicitation" ordered on the sign? Were drugs why Angela was there? Why Nate hung around? I shook my head slightly and sighed. There were too many questions, but the one clear idea was the direct connection between illegal drugs and danger, warranted because I had sensed and seen the potential threat Nate posed. Being in the country illegally was one thing, but I could not bring Angela into our home if she was involved in selling or taking drugs.

I continued walking towards the car and, for the first time since encountering Angela, I was able to consider the young woman with clarity. Her story did not ring true. Why would someone, a friend, bring her to the US then abandon her to the streets for no reason? She would have to have committed some egregious crime, stolen from them, slept with the husband, hurt the child, or worse, although I could not imagine what could be worse than hurting a child. But a disgruntled friend was more likely to put her on the first available plane, more likely to send her home in disgrace than to turn her out with nowhere to go, no place to eat, and undocumented. And what did she want with me? My instincts screamed that Angela was in trouble, but even more loudly that she was trouble itself.

I glanced at Taiwo paused beside me and tugged at his elbow, hurrying him towards the car. *What was I thinking?* I thought. I wondered if my need to protect him would ever recede. Perhaps, but not that evening. Bringing Angela closer meant bringing this dangerous world closer as well, a world where a man could threaten to shoot you without provocation. I could not do that to Taiwo, Auntie, or Brian. I would have to leave Angela behind.

"I think he thought we wanted dinner," Taiwo said when we were back in the car.

I looked over at him and laughed. "You might be right," I said. The laugh felt like an outpouring from my soul, and I laughed harder than Taiwo's comment warranted, my body shaking and my breath coming in gusts. Taiwo looked at me out of the corner of his eyes and raised his left eyebrow. I fought to control myself. I put the key in the ignition and turned on the car engine. "If we hurry, you can still make karate," I said.

THAT WEEKEND, I refocused on my own life. Aunt Marjorie and I worked in the garden, little by little finding homes for the plants we had purchased. The feel of the soil, the planning, the creation of order where there was none before was therapeutic. As Aunt Marjorie and I worked, I often stopped and breathed. Deep inhales, filling my lungs with the scent of the herbs. When I was in the garden I could pretend there was nothing else to worry about, no nightmares, no memories, no Angela. Unfortunately, I could not spend all of my time in the garden, and when I was not there, when I performed other tasks, and when I relaxed, thoughts of Angela encroached. I had decided to abandon her, yet I was unable to move on. I kept picturing the youthful innocence in her eyes and found it impossible to reconcile that with someone who was willingly involved in drug trafficking or prostitution. On the other hand, I knew from my work that people's capacity for crime could not be determined from their appearance. I had come across thuggish-looking young men who turned out to be thoughtful and honest human beings. I had also met many people with all the external trappings of respectability whose moral compasses were irremediably skewed.

On Sunday afternoon, I went to a matinee with Jamela as I had promised but begged off of hanging out afterwards. There was no room in my mind for small talk. Instead, I snuck out to the garden that evening and began digging a hole. At first, I dug it to accommodate one of the larger plants we had bought, but as it widened and deepened, I became increasingly unsure of what I would plant there, the possibilities evolving the deeper the hole became and in the end, I left it there, unfilled and gaping.

CHAPTER TWENTY-TWO

"A untie?" I allowed a light lilt to enter my voice as I knocked on Aunt Marjorie's bedroom door that Monday morning. The door was slightly ajar, but I entered slowly, like a trainer entering the cage of a baby lion held in captivity, never sure of when its true nature would emerge.

"Auntie Marj?" I repeated, pushing the door open a little wider until I could see the six-drawer mahogany dressing table we had shipped from Jamaica and squeezed into the guest room in an effort to recreate the spaces she knew best. Reflected in the mirror, I could see the bottom half of the queen-sized bed, and it was empty.

"Auntie?" I did not control the edge of urgency that entered my voice. Pushing the door all the way open, I stepped inside.

I was met with the ammoniac smell of pee. Aunt Marjorie was curled up at the top of the bed, hugging her legs as if she were on the water's edge, avoiding an approaching wave. Her nightgown covered the top of her shins, and I was struck as always by the boniness of her once-full-and-firm calves and arms. They looked as if the slightest jolt would snap them into pieces.

"I didn't make it." In spite of her cowering pose, her voice was strong, a challenge almost, to anyone who might dare to suggest she was any less of a woman because her bladder had failed her. I knew better than to respond as if I were accepting an apology.

"It happens to the best of us," I said. "Come. Get up." I moved forward to help her from the bed, but she swung her arms as if chasing away a swarm of flies.

"Leave me. Leave me." She gathered the damp back of her nightgown into a ball in one hand and slid her legs off the bed, still careful not to come into contact with the wet parts of the sheets.

I stepped back, my arms raised in a sign of surrender, with what I hoped was a neutral expression on my face. I backed up against the dressing table and Aunt Marjorie turned sideways as she inched forward, careful to touch neither the offending bed nor me as she made her way to the bedroom door.

As soon as I was alone, I stripped the bed and shoved the sheets into the hamper, along with the blue-and-white incontinence pad I had hidden between the mattress and the sheets for just such accidents. I sniffed the mattress then touched it with two fingers. *Dry.*

I took a step towards the door and listened. The shower was running. Even if Aunt Marjorie had not got under the water—one of the latest manifestations of her dementia—at least she was likely to remain in the bathroom for a while. Plus, had she decided to take a bath, I would have had to keep a careful watch, but a shower was safe. Brian had added a bench and a strong metal bar, and had retiled the shower floor with the most skid-proof tiles he could find.

Tossing the dirty sheets on the floor, I continued with my job. I took a new waterproof pad and sheets from the cupboard and quickly made the bed. I spritzed it with Febreze to remove any errant odors and was on my way out the door, the pile of soiled laundry in my arms, when Aunt Marjorie emerged from the bathroom wrapped in a yellow housedress.

I kissed her cheek.

"Good morning, Auntie," I said. "Had a good night?" I did not wait for an answer. "I'm doing laundry so I grabbed yours. Hope you don't mind. And I cooked cornmeal porridge, so come eat quick so you aren't late for Bingo at the center."

I ignored the bewildered look on Aunt Marjorie's face as I walked away, dragging the laundry basket and adding a casual bounce to my step. I hated confusing her that way, but once I had given up on pressing her to remember the things that had escaped her mind, the step to planting false short-term memories was a short one. I convinced myself that helping her to forget incidents like wetting the bed was actually good for her, helped her maintain the dignity she so treasured. The treachery filled me with guilt. I knew that in her heyday, she would not have approved of being taken for a pappyshow, as she would likely have called it.

There were days when I envied Aunt Marjorie's ability to enter each day, sometimes each room, with little recollection of what had come before and the absolute freedom to reinvent herself in what was to come. In the beginning, I had wondered if her memory loss felt anything like my own inability to recall my early past—like entering a room and finding it pitch dark, echoing with emptiness. I wondered if this had been the source of Aunt Marjorie's extreme agitation at the beginning of her dementia and if, as time passed, she thought less frequently of the abandoned rooms, had managed to close those doors completely, or had filled them with newly created ideas.

A few minutes after I had started the load of laundry and returned to the kitchen, Aunt Marjorie entered and sat at the table. She had donned one of her favorite dresses, a blue-and-white vertically striped button dress falling just below the knees, belted at her waist, and modestly highlighting a bosom which remained surprisingly upright considering the ravages time had inflicted on her mind.

"Good morning, Amaya," she said.

"Good morning, Auntie. Had a good night?" *Third time's the charm*, I thought.

"Thank God, yes, my dear. I woke to see another day."

I sat with Aunt Marjorie in companionable silence. The scents of nutmeg, cinnamon, and vanilla swirled around us, reminiscent of earlier times in her kitchen in Jamaica. I struggled to stay in the moment, not to be swept away into the past that I was slowly opening myself up to accepting and embracing. My heart swelled as I looked across the round table at the elderly face, eyes unsteady as she guided her spoon of cornmeal porridge towards her slackening jaw and failing teeth.

"Is who picture you have there?" Aunt Marjorie's voice penetrated my reverie. I followed her gaze to a photograph I had placed on the windowsill of Taiwo and me on a beach in the Outer Banks. The photograph had been taken two years before, but I had only recently mounted it in a black frame with gold trim and placed it on display.

Aunt Marjorie leaned closer to the photograph and steupsed. "Oh, is Amaryllis and Dave. What a way Dave handsome! You daddy never like him. I remember that clear like the blue sky. Thought him was wutless because him daddy was PNP."

I felt what was becoming a familiar sensation. The sound of rushing water filled my ears, and I was overcome by an overwhelming urge to close my eyes. I must have succumbed to what Dr. Hinds would have characterized as a deep trance, because when I was aware of my surroundings again, Aunt Marjorie was gone and so was the photo.

I went through the motions of getting ready for work and getting Aunt Marjorie into the car. Fortunately, she maintained her good mood and went to the Ramus House without a fuss. When I returned to the parking lot, I sat in the car with my head against the steering wheel and allowed myself to think about what had happened in the kitchen. I could not recall the names Aunt Marjorie had uttered and each time I tried, my heart rate increased and nausea threatened to send my breakfast up from my stomach and out of my mouth. The phenomenon was new. In the early days when Aunt Marjorie came to stay with us, we talked often of the last year before I left Jamaica, reminiscing about people in Black River. The doctors had encouraged these discussions as a way to prolong her recall as long as possible. During those times, I had never responded so viscerally.

This is getting ridiculous, I thought. *I can't keep blacking out every time Aunt Marjorie speaks.* I sighed. I had a mountain of work to take care of on my desk; however, I needed to get some answers about my episodes, and Dr. Hinds was the only recourse. I battled the traffic to Tysons Corner and stormed into her waiting room. I pleaded with the secretary who guarded the door to Dr. Hinds's office.

"I'll wait. Doesn't matter how long."

DR. HINDS'S WAITING room was just large enough for four chairs, a water fountain, and a table with a coffeepot and an assortment of teas. I made myself a lukewarm cup of tea, my hands shaking slightly as I positioned the cup under the water dispenser. The warm liquid slid down into my stomach, doing little to calm the intense jitters I felt at the thought of what I was about to do.

Despite my nervous energy, I sat still in the waiting room, head lowered to avoid eye contact with the patients who came and went into the inner office. I did not want anything to interrupt the beginnings of remembering, which sat at the edge of my mind like butterflies that had landed on my finger. Any sudden moves and they might disappear.

One and a half hours later, some of my anxiety had diminished. The door to Dr. Hinds's office opened, and a woman stepped out. She smiled at me, a serene smile that filled me with hope. It was finally my turn.

"Did she have hypnosis?" I asked as I stepped into Dr. Hinds's inner office.

"You know I can't discuss another patient with you." Dr. Hinds reached over and held my hand. "It's going to be okay." She pressed her fingers around my palm. "You're going to be okay."

"Okay," I echoed. "Should I sit or should I lie down?" I looked around and was embarrassed when I realized there was no couch. I giggled. "I guess I'll sit."

Dr. Hinds's voice was soft and even-toned.

"This is going to be easy, Amaya. Like taking a nap. You're just going to sit right where you are, and all you're going to do is listen to my voice. Make yourself comfortable. We'll start with something easy."

I settled into the chair. It was bowl-shaped, the color of a cloudless sky, and curved like a hug around my body. I gripped the arms of the chair and closed my eyes.

"I want you to think about a place where you feel safe and secure."

I nodded and focused. I exhaled slowly, willing my tense body to relax.

"Tell me where you are."

"I'm at home. In my garden. Under the palm trees. I've dug up everything else."

"Okay, let's focus on those trees. You're sitting on the ground. The temperature is perfect. The trees are swaying in the breeze above you, moving back and forth, back and forth."

I sighed and relaxed my grip on the arms of the chair.

"Is the gate to the garden on your right or your left?" she asked.

"On the right."

"Okay. You hear the gate open. Look over to the right, Amaya."

Eyes closed, I turned my head towards my right shoulder. Dr. Hinds continued her drone.

"You see me. I am walking through the gate. I am handing you a package. Take it. You've been expecting this package, Amaya. You are happy to receive the package."

I smiled and relaxed further into the chair.

"It's filled with memories, one of the earliest memories you have of your adulthood. Open it, Amaya. Open it and tell me all you see."

I focused on what had happened in the kitchen. I remembered Aunt Marjorie commenting on the photo then finding myself alone in the room. I recalled nothing in between, and nothing even just before the blackout. I knew I was supposed to be letting my mind go, but I made one last attempt to remember the name Aunt Marjorie had said.

Dave. That was the name, Dave.

CHAPTER TWENTY-THREE

St. Augustine, Trinidad - October 1982

I n my hypnotic state, everything seemed sharper, brighter, like the first time I heard Roberta Flack's voice digitally remastered on a CD and wondered if I had only imagined hearing her sing before. I saw myself standing under the red-roofed bus stand along the Eastern Main Road. I felt as if I were stepping forward and into the version of myself in the scene and as I did, the image blurred. The heat haze distorted my vision, the hot air hovering over the pavement, shimmering in layers of murky blue and brown. I shifted my head back and forth. The mirage shifted beneath my gaze.

My presence at the Curepe bus stop that day was a part of my normal Saturday-afternoon routine. I had recreated myself in Trinidad and part of that re-creation had led me to cut off my hair, which I had previously kept in shoulder-length, chemically-relaxed tresses. I experimented weekly at the hairdresser, trying to decide how to wear the short, soft curls that grew untreated from my head.

Brian drove me most places I needed to go. We had met during my Intro to Sociology class, in which he had been the teaching assistant. The material had been dense and the professor near incomprehensible. Many of my classmates formed study groups but I had not felt comfortable engaging in the kinds of relationships that might lead to expectations that I share information about my life before university. And so I sought help from the teaching assistant, thinking that interaction would be safe. After the year-long course had ended, we had stayed in touch and developed a relationship that teetered on the divide between friendship and something more. We spent much of our free time together, but on Saturdays, he was unavailable because his mother expected him to spend that time running errands for her.

And so it was that I was on my weekly trek to the hairdresser when I saw him . . . Dave.

We stood on opposite sides of the bus shelter, and were not the only people waiting there. A large woman, impossibly squeezed into a horizontally striped yellow and white top and thigh-gripping jeans, stood next to me, close enough that I felt gusts of hot air as she fanned herself with a copy of that day's *Trinidad Express*. She occasionally bent to share her vain attempts to cool down with the child who stood next to her, and when she did, the smell of coconut oil wafted from the girl's hair into my nostrils.

An elderly Indian man sat on the bench behind me, his smooth, straight hair spread over his head in thinning gray strands like the threads on a loom. Next to him stood a bent old lady with a surprisingly powerful voice that she had used to make many failed attempts to engage the elderly man in a litany of complaints about the weather, the tardiness of the bus, and the fact that the little girl was kicking at stones with her slippered feet. He ignored her.

I had dropped my head so she would not attempt to direct her frustrations at me, so I was not sure what drew my eyes to the young man leaning against the edge of the bus stand, one foot bent under him, a large black boot planted on the wall. But I saw him, then I recognized him, then the me I had carefully reconstructed over the past two years teetered on the brink of a precipice. I clenched my fists and held on.

I had time to escape. He had not yet recognized me, possibly had not even seen me. I swallowed but my mouth was suddenly dry. I dared not move to sip the bottle of water I held in my hand, for fear that any movement would call attention to my presence.

He had gone fully dread since I had last seen him. At least sort of. His hair was long, loced, but in neat rows clearly maintained by a hairdresser or some caring female. His body was taut beneath his white shirt, buttoned low to reveal the dark skin of his chest, which had the close-to-the-bone tightness of someone who ate sparingly. It was disorienting to see him in Trinidad, silhouetted against the urban bustle of the Eastern Main Road instead of the quiet streets of Black River. He wore dark blue jeans that hung close to his frame, and I had the overwhelming urge to grab the cheeks of his buttocks and pull him as close as possible to my body. The surge of desire stunned me. I had never acknowledged my attraction to him. He had been unattainable from the day we first met.

I shook my head to clear it. I did not want to remember the events surrounding the history I had with Dave. I had gone to great lengths to leave Jamaica and put everything related to that part of my life in a steel-encased box buried in the deepest corner of my subconscious. His presence acted like an excavator, probing and digging up that past. I fought against its efforts, and there, standing at the bus stop, struggling to remain in the present, I was easy to spot.

"Maya? Amaya Gordon?"

Despite the history we shared, I was surprised he remembered my name and even more surprised that he would choose to acknowledge me. Perhaps that compulsion that causes mere acquaintances to greet each other with long-lost enthusiasm when they meet in a foreign land was more powerful than any reluctance to dredge up memories of a traumatic past.

"Dave." I kept the question from my voice, keeping my tone flat to disguise the tightness in my chest. Only three years had passed since I last saw him, but it might as well have been ten, for all the growing up I had done. I was no longer the naive seventeen-year-old he had known.

I felt his eyes on my neck where I was sure my carotid artery was visible, revealing the pace of my pulse, still galloping through my veins, keeping pace with the memories.

I waited for the corners of his mouth to lift into that all-too-familiar bemused smile I hated. The smile had said "You're a youngster to be tolerated."

Beyond that I had been invisible to him and the less he saw me, the more I had desired him. Remembering that smile stirred an anger in me, anger that could defeat my desire.

I was disappointed. His expression held something close to tenderness and he moved towards me, closing the space between us with such fluidity I was not convinced he had not floated.

"Wha gwan?" He didn't touch me, but I felt his presence as powerfully as if he had. His pores emitted a sweet, barely-perceptible-but-definitely-there smell of weed, which I knew more from my days on Trinidad's St. Augustine campus than from my sheltered life in Jamaica. But his scent was not only ganja but a strong smell of man, testosterone mixed with the sweat brought on from walking the shadeless sidewalks of Curepe.

His question was loaded. I knew he wasn't asking how I was in a way that warranted a casual lie: "Me good, man." He was asking how had I survived.

I raised my eyes to his in answer. All the defenses I had piled up to shield myself from his allure crumbled in a useless pile.

He reached for my hand.

"Come," he said. He turned to the right and headed east along the main road, away from the bus stop. He dropped my hand and guided me as if we were connected by an invisible rope; I did not know where he was going, yet I abandoned my plans for the hairdresser and followed.

We walked for about ten minutes, at first through the busiest part of St. Augustine, shops on either side spilling out in the streets with baskets of goods we sidestepped to avoid. He walked quickly with long, even, purposeful strides, and I had to trot to keep up. As we left the main shopping area be-hind, the streets quieted and we had more space to walk. The buildings were single- or two-storied with wide balconies as their entrance and neat gardens enclosed by wall fences, residential in appearance although I knew many of them housed professional businesses, doctors' and lawyers' offices. The side-walks were no longer cluttered, so we walked side by side easily but did not converse. I looked ahead to each house we approached, wondering which of the wrought iron gates he would push against and turn into. In the silence, I asked myself the question I wanted to pose to him but could not: *What do you want with me?*

Finally, he stopped in front of a house almost identical to the ones on either side, two-storied with a balcony on the upper floor, facing the street. He held open the gate and looked at me for the first time since we had begun walking. *You ready?* his eyes seemed to ask. I entered the property and he latched the gate behind us before leading me along the side of the building and around to the back. He opened a door.

"This belongs to my bredren. He let me kotch here a few days while him away."

The apartment was small, a studio, the kitchen, living area, and bedroom all visible with one sweep of the eye. A suitcase lay open on the floor next to the bed, clothes tossed on the top, but otherwise the room seemed clean. I breathed in, having instinctively held my breath, expecting the room to have an unpleasant smell. It did not.

"Sit down." He waved at the couch, and when I sank into its worn springs, he sat beside me.

"How long it been? Three years?" he began.

I nodded. I didn't tell him that the image of the last time I saw him, eyes bloodshot and red-rimmed as he stood ramrod straight, trembling hands jammed into his back pockets, shoulders thrown back as he fought for control over his emotions, still reverberated in my dreams.

"You look different," he said.

"Well. Yeah." I shrugged, wondering how he could expect me not to have been irreversibly changed, but then he appeared very much the same. He had maintained the strong gaze that seemed to look right through me with a powerful, unnerving Lion-of-Judah vibe that would come off as aggressive were it not for the faintest hint in his eyes of a vulnerability so elusive he would probably deny it was there. I knew I appeared more confident than I had been three years before, even though in his presence that mask threatened to slip any minute.

I had many questions for him, questions I had considered on our walk, but now that we were together in this very much too-small room, chitchat about his family and what brought him to Trinidad seemed trite . . . impossible.

"You look more like . . . like her." He moved closer and caressed my face. His eyes held a question.

I could have said, should have said, *But I'm not her.* In fact, the words approached my lips, but the truth was that after Amaryllis died, I had channeled her energy and her spunk, growing bolder until I was no longer the shrinking violet Dave had barely acknowledged, an unshakable chaperone, his girlfriend's baby twin sister. When he lowered his lips, his eyes closed, I knew he wasn't kissing me, that he was seeing, smelling, touching, biting, remembering my sister. I could have stopped him, startled him from his waking dream into a cruelly disappointing reality in which he could only view me with hate instead of the love I craved. I should have stopped him, but I didn't.

When it was over, I rose from the bed where he lay, an unreadable expression so still on his face that I wondered if he was breathing. He rolled to the left, away from my stare, and then his long, lean body was still once more, like a fallen log against the floral sheets. I searched to find my hastily discarded jeans and, holding them against my body in a belated attempt at modesty, I guessed the location of the bathroom, dressed, then left the house without saying a word.

BACK IN MY room I stood in front of my mirror, examining my face for the traces of Amaryllis that Dave had seen, but instead, I made another discovery. In his passion, Dave had left bruises on my neck and arms. Brian and I had arranged to meet at a fete in the Student Union that evening. My heart rate quickened at the thought of his reaction to seeing the bruises, the disappointment that would flash across his face before he recovered and feigned indifference. I questioned why sex with Dave felt like an indiscretion, challenged that assessment, rationalized it. Brian and I were not a couple, had never declared any feelings for each other beyond friendship, had never even come close to consummating our relationship, yet at that moment, I knew I had made a big mistake. I had betrayed him. I cared what Brian thought of me, and there was no way I could explain why I let Dave enter my body, how I had thought that being with Dave would be like having Amaryllis with me once more, that it would prove that she still lived within me somehow. Brian did not know about Amaryllis, did not know any details of the life that had died behind me in Jamaica, and so there was no point from which to start explaining. That moment of passion had diminished none of my longing for a connection with Amaryllis and had put me in danger of losing someone I needed in my life.

I considered feigning illness and not going to the fete, but I was responsible for two shifts at the Student Union bar, and it was too late to back out. I observed my neck where one paint-splatter-shaped bruise was already beginning to turn reddish brown, barely visible in the dim light of my dorm room. I touched the mark and felt a stab of pain shooting from my fingers deep into my abdomen, pain too sharp to be the result of the surface bruise, referred pain from the memories being with Dave had brought to the forefront of my mind. Almost unbidden, my mind filled with an image of Brian's lips covering the bruise. I picked up the phone by my bedside and when he answered, I invited him over. Later, between the thrusts, I imagined my encounter with Dave swirling, slurping, then disappearing into a descending vortex.

CHAPTER TWENTY-FOUR

Fairfax, Virginia - September 2003

I left Dr. Hinds's office as quickly as I could after the session and returned to my office. She offered to schedule an appointment to talk about what I had uncovered, but I refused. I had already resolved never to return. The revelations had shaken my core. Before entering her office I had not recalled that meeting with Dave, had not remembered him or the existence of a sister. What did it mean that Aunt Marjorie mistook Taiwo for Dave in the photograph? Was Taiwo's parentage unclear? I had always seen Brian in him, imagined a tilt of the eyes, slimness of the nose, oval of the face. I tried to remember what Dave looked like, if there was a gesture or a tug of his mouth that reminded me of Taiwo, but I could not bring the details of his face to mind. A dam had opened, but the roar of the water was too loud and too fast to allow me to know anything clearly.

One memory filtered through, bobbing like a flashing beacon:

St. Augustine, Trinidad - January 1983

I was sitting in a light-filled room, enough sunlight streaming in to do what sunlight does: disinfect all sins.

I had asked Brian to meet me in the Student Union lounge because of that light and because it was the last place memories could hide, the stark-white walls and mottled-gray terrazzo-tiled floors too bland to provide fertile ground for the unforgettable. Those were the spaces in which I operated best, spaces where memories disappeared like wet chalk on a blackboard.

I had practiced my announcement in front of the mirror while my room-

mate was asleep. I whispered the words in the early morning after the lingering chatter from late-night study groups dissipated and the only remaining
sounds were the incessant songs of the tree frogs and crickets. The room was
dark except for the light from the street, which leaked between the metal-lou-
vered windows and splintered over my left shoulder. None of the rays reached
the right side of my face, leaving such a sharp blackness that it was easy to
imagine half of my face had been consumed by something unspeakably terrible. I imagined Brian in front of me, receiving my news. I would sit up straight
and look him directly in the eye with an expression that was a convincing I-
dare-you-to-reject-me and I-could-not-care-less-if-you-do. But even in my
imaginings, he sat staring at this half-face I saw in the mirror, seeing beyond
my poised expression, demanding to know what I was hiding.

"I'm pregnant."

Despite my resolve to make a bold take-it-or-leave-it declaration about
my situation, I had lowered my head at the last second, and my announcement slipped from my lips and landed in my lap so softly I was not sure I had
made a sound at all. I raised my head.

Brian seemed to be in the middle of a struggle for his life. One hand held
his beer bottle, and liquid leaked between his fingers and onto the table. The
other hand cupped his mouth, pressing his lips closed. His eyes had widened, making them seem insectile, bulging behind his large-framed glasses.
He looked like someone who had examined a cut they thought was minor and
realized they had in fact been fatally wounded.

When he recovered enough to swallow, he said, "You can't tell a fella that
sort of thing just as he knock back a beer. You almost kill me, girl." Using his
dry left hand, he fished a packet of tissues from his backpack and wiped up
the beer spill on his right.

I tugged at a dark brown twist of my hair, newly styled for this encounter,
from my forehead and leaned back in my chair, awaiting his response.

"You sure?"

I nodded. I did not trust my voice not to quiver and reveal my nervousness. I was three months along.

I was not ready to be a mother. Had I access to the garden I had cultivated in Aunt Marjorie's backyard in Jamaica, I might have been able to combine the right herbs to resolve the situation as soon as I discovered my pregnancy. But I didn't have that. I had no love for doctors, and my only other options were too physical to fully conceptualize. I rationalized that there was no need to spill any blood, convinced as I was that the darkness inside me could not provide fertile ground for life, and the pregnancy would end naturally.

So I waited. The weeks between seeing the double lines on the pregnancy test and the date of my best guess of the three-month mark had been stressful at best. In spite of my decision to let nature make the choice, I had felt as if I were carrying a small fishbowl in my belly filled with the precise amount of water the bowl's occupant needed to survive, and any sudden movements would send the water sloshing over the sides, leaving the occupant dead at the bottom. The more time that passed without any sign of a miscarriage, the more I visualized the life growing inside of me, and I found myself counting and recounting the weeks, longing for the arrival of the date when I could admit that I wanted to keep this baby.

I had considered not saying anything, leaving Trinidad, school, and never telling Brian he had fathered a child. But I did not want to raise a child alone, and alone I would be. I had no one but Aunt Marjorie to turn to, and turning to her would mean returning to Jamaica. A college dropout, I would have few prospects to make a living and support a child. Marrying a man who seemed to have fewer demons than most was not the worst possible outcome for my life.

"Are you sure?" Brian asked again, shifting the stress of the sentence to the last syllable. His voice was softer now. He pushed his glasses further up on the bridge of his nose then reached across the table, his long, tapered fingers with nails that never seemed to grow beyond the hyponychium. I had never seen him bite his nails, but as I contemplated our life together, which I knew would be the inevitable conclusion of my announcement, I wondered how many habits I would discover and have to adjust to in order to ensure the baby had the right father.

"Amaya?" He pressed his fingers into my forearm gently, always gentle. His voice was filled with concern rather than impatience as he awaited my answer.

I knew the real question on his mind, the one he was too well-brought-up, perhaps too afraid, to ask. Not "are you sure you're pregnant" but "are you sure it's mine?"

It was a fair question. Our relationship occupied a mercurial space between friendship and romance. We had never discussed monogamy.

Remembering this should be a happy announcement, I smiled as I answered his question, ignoring all the implications I had ascribed to it, all the insecurities I had built around it. "Yes, Brian, I am sure. We are having a baby!"

He rose slowly to his full height, throwing his shoulders back and towering over me. He blocked the cafeteria doorway, and the light, fighting to find me, spilled around his body, causing a glow between the spaces of his arms and his legs and for a moment, all I could see was his silhouette. I could not discern his features, couldn't tell if I was looking at his back or his front, and I told myself he was walking away. I sucked in a deep breath and blinked, a slow blink I hoped would change my reality, and it did. When my eyes reopened, he was kneeling before me on both knees. He leaned forward until his lips found mine, and he kissed me. Somewhere in my mind, I realized this was our first kiss outside the throes of sex. I considered pushing him away, suddenly conscious of the other students lunching and studying in the room. Instead I forced myself to stay in the moment, to let him lead. He pulled away, his hands still holding my forearms.

"You want to get married?"

Marrying Brian would fill the darkness in my mind with light.

"Yes," I replied. "Yes."

Fairfax, Virginia - September 2003

The memory faded, but the tension of the scene stayed with me. Brian had been the best choice, the only choice. "He's all Brian," I told myself, speaking the words out loud as I drove from Dr. Hinds's office. "Even if it's only by nurture, he is Brian's child."

CHAPTER TWENTY-FIVE

Despite the lectures I gave myself, the possibility that Brian was not Taiwo's father plagued my mind, and back at my desk after lunch, I was unable to focus on any of the work awaiting my attention on my desk. I kept recapping the new information I had uncovered. I had a sister, a twin sister. I had once been one of two. So often in my life I had imagined the presence of another, imagined that I was being observed, sometimes judged.

I remembered a waking nightmare I had once just before I married Brian. Dissatisfied with the vague details I presented to him about my family history, he had pushed me to tell him more about my childhood. I had squeezed my eyes shut and focused on the stark-white flakes of residual light that danced under my eyelids, trying to recall details of growing up with Aunt Marjorie. Behind them a character formed, slowly taking the form of a human, arms outstretched and twirling in the midst of what looked like a snowstorm, although I had only ever seen snow in souvenir globes and movies. She—I knew it was a she—seemed happy, and in the moment, I had wondered if the mirage reflected me or someone I could be, in a place I would be happy. I reached out towards her and my hand connected with Brian's body. The moment we touched, a loud bang sounded between my ears and a small drop of red appeared where the figure's head would have been. The blot spread downwards, darkening the white of her clothes. The figure kept dancing, but instead of swirling, she stretched her reddening arms out in macabre gestures, reaching out towards me in grabbing and scratching movements.

"This? This is what you want to remember?" A voice had filled my head with a vicious hiss. That was the last time I had tried to recall my past . . . until now.

"Amaryllis, Mari." I said the name out loud, trying to recreate the ease with which it had rolled off my tongue in my hypnotic state. What had happened to my sister? Why had I buried that memory so deep it had taken over twenty years to make its way to the surface? How did her existence as an almost-adult mesh with the fact that I was raised an only child by Aunt Marjorie? I was equally disturbed by my tryst with Dave. *What did that mean?* A part of me was terrified at the prospect of uncovering more unsettling details. But another part of me needed to know more, wanted to illuminate the dark places inside me.

I had not used a condom when I had sex with Dave, I was sure of it. But then again, Brian and I hadn't always used a condom either. Perhaps my idea that Taiwo had been conceived on my first coupling with Brian had just been a romantic notion. I could have become pregnant on another occasion when we had been less careful.

There were easy ways to answer the more factual questions. An Internet search might reveal news reports of my twin's fate, depending on how she ... I still struggled to acknowledge that she must be dead. The image of Dave's face, tear-stained and angry at what must have been Amaryllis's funeral, flashed in my mind. *I can call Christine*, I thought. Christine had kept in touch with the occasional phone call since reaching out about Aunt Marjorie's early dementia six years before. But what would I ask? How could I explain that there were giant holes of nothingness where my past memories should be? I thought about the way my past had been revealed to me so far, unfolding in real time as if I were watching it on a movie screen. The images were so clear that I recalled not only the details, but my reactions and emotions. It was difficult to experience, but gave me a much more complete picture than I could ever derive from being told the story by someone else.

"You have to want it," Dr. Hinds had said, and I did. But I was terrified. There was only one explanation for the thoroughness with which I had buried my past. *The truth must be horrific, but maybe now,* I thought, *maybe with time between me and the events, and with maturity, I can face it.*

The sessions with Dr. Hinds were risky. She was prevented by doctor-patient confidentiality laws from revealing details of our sessions, but there were limitations to the protection the laws provided. *What if I killed my sister?* The thought popped unbidden into my mind. When I thought of Amaryllis, my overwhelming emotion was frustration and anger. I compared that with my love for Jamela and Lisa. Which one was what having a sister was supposed to be like?

And what about Dave? Was my recollection of our meeting even accurate? Or something my wishful mind had concocted to fill in the memories I could no longer access. I discarded that idea as well. It had felt much too real, too normal, his motions too fluid to be something I had created. Which left the bigger question. Should I tell Brian about my indiscretion or not? He had lost so much—his father, then his mother, then Uncle Joe. Taiwo and I were all he had. By not telling him, I would protect him from further grief. But perhaps that was not my decision to make. That left me with a new question: how would I tell him? How would I form the words? How could I tell Brian I had a twin sister who had disappeared, but I could not remember how or why. And that "by the way, I had sex with another man the same day you and I had sex the first time, so Taiwo may not be your child." What would I say to reassure him of my love? The guilt threatened to overpower me and, for just a moment, I wished I could go back to a time when I was not aware of these details from my past.

I put my head on my desk, touching my forehead directly to the mahogany desktop. The material felt cold under my skin, and the cold jolted me into some semblance of clarity. *I need my garden,* I thought. The hole I had started digging over the weekend was still waiting to be filled. Perhaps after the holes in my memories were filled, I would know what I was doing in the garden as well.

I stood and walked to my door, the four walls of my office suddenly overwhelming in their density. Then I thought of walking past Ignatious and needing to explain my departure yet again. I stopped, returned to my desk, and called Lisa. "Can we do lunch?"

"Sure," she said. "Let me look at my calendar."

"Not your calendar," I said, "your clock. Can we meet now?"

"Now? What's going on?" I heard concern in her voice.

"I just need to talk."

"Okay. I'll meet you at Poets and Prose in Shirlington. How's half an hour?

LISA WAS ALREADY at the restaurant when I arrived. I stood across the street and observed her sitting in the window. She was still, her face perfectly made up in this way I envied, her look a curation of put-together pieces, carefully crafted, her image to the world. I had watched her get ready on a few occasions, so I knew it took time, but the final effect was of something just tossed on. Jewelry, makeup, suit. She was climbing the corporate ladder at an investment firm and playing the game, as she called it, just until she had climbed high enough to set her own rules.

I had met Lisa because her husband—now ex-husband—was a lawyer Brian and Geoffrey had worked with. They had seemed the perfect couple; he was quiet and unassuming, and Lisa a firebrand, loud and brash but with such a forthright nature that she never turned me off the way cocky people usually did. They were obviously great friends and in conversation traded insults and compliments, finished each other's sentences, boosting each other when they were overly modest: the ideal match. Then Lisa called a conference with Jamela and I at her apartment one day and in a torrent of tears and profanity told us that Lance was in love with someone else . . . a man, and he wanted to be free to pursue that relationship. She blamed him, blamed herself, but in the end, the strength of their friendship won through and they ended the marriage amicably. We took our cue from that and shifted our circle of friendship to make room for the new reality. I still marveled at how she came to terms with it so easily. Back then, in 1992, I had had little exposure to homosexuality, except from the perspective of religious tenets. I thought about the ramifications if Brian met someone else. Would it be worse if he wanted to be with another woman or a man? Was it easier to rationalize if the problem "really wasn't me, I just did not have what it took to make him happy," as Lisa often quipped?

At any rate, Lisa had emerged from the ashes of the relationship and rebuilt her life. She did not date much, which I thought was a shame, and I wondered if she was hesitant because of her experience with Lance.

Those experiences were the reason I chose to confide in her rather than Jamela. Jamela's parents had been amicably married all her life, and at some point, when several women came forward to present Jamela's uncle with children he had fathered, Jamela's mother had pulled her aside and assured her that "your father don't have no other children except the ones I give him." Jamela believed that. She believed in the purity of marital vows. She had been scandalized by Lisa and Lance's breakup, and I was afraid of what she would think if she knew that I once was the sort of person who had entrapped Brian into raising a son that might not be his.

"I hate to rush you," Lisa began. "But I only have an hour. Tell me." She looked more closely at me and lowered her voice. "Tell Mama Lisa what's wrong."

At first I was lost for words. At first. Then I poured it all out. Not about the woman in the parking lot or even about Amaryllis, but about the memory of having sex with Dave. Lisa listened, then after I lamented about the awfulness of what I had done, she asked a single question.

"How long ago was this, Maya?"

I dropped my eyes.

"Exactly," Lisa continued. "Over twenty years ago you slept with another guy. You were barely twenty, sweetheart. That's the age when we're supposed to make mistakes. And look how this one turned out. You have a wonderful relationship with both your husband and your son. This guy was just a sperm donor . . . and he may not even have been that." She paused and looked at me. Her eyes narrowed. "You aren't thinking of telling Brian, are you?"

I wrung my hands in my lap. "I don't know," I replied. "How can I keep something so monumental from him?"

"What would it change if he knew? You think he would choose not to be with you or Taiwo? You think he'd abandon you? Not the man I know."

"I just feel like I'm taking something from him by not letting him know they might not be father and son. And what if it comes out another way? What if Brian needs a transfusion or a transplant and it's discovered because Tai's not a match?"

Lisa shook her head. "There are some secrets you share, like 'I want to sleep with someone else.'" She smiled wryly. "And others that have no bearing on anything material, and those you can keep to yourself. Keeping things to ourselves is how women have survived marriage for the last forty-four centuries."

LISA WAS RIGHT. There was no benefit in telling Brian any of what I had discovered. Our marriage was in a good place because we gave each other space. It had not always been like that. In the early days in Trinidad, after I got pregnant but before we married, Brian had often pressed me to open up to him, and I had responded by playing the part of an open book even as I struggled to anchor myself in my new life, letting go of all that had happened before. When Brian was home, I was engaging, witty, supportive, all the qualities he said drew me to him when we first met. Most of our conversations were about our future: after he graduated law school, after he got a full-time job, after I had the baby. I pretended I could envisage our future and that it made me happy. I pretended I was doing more than just existing from day to day.

"You ever imagine yourself pregnant and about to be married at this moment?" he asked one hot Trinidad afternoon, catching me in the middle of a reverie about the blank page of life that lay before me. We were lying in bed, a rare moment of daylight when he was neither at work nor at school nor working at the computer that sat in the corner of the bedroom. The casement windows were open wide to a view of a retaining wall covered by flowering vines that made me think of thick green cords of a tangled past. We lay on our backs, our arms at our sides, our legs parted—his longer ones touching the foot of the bed, our bodies about a foot apart like two islands separated after a seismic event.

Brian stretched his right hand towards me. He laced his fingers through the spaces in mine, gently embracing my hand. Unbidden, my fingers folded to welcome his. He squeezed my hand.

A tear balanced on the edge of my left eye. I blinked, willing it not to spill over and call attention to the emotions that had surfaced at his touch. Until that moment, I had not known I needed that touch, and I considered that maybe I could risk sharing some of the burden I was carrying, some of the weight of the baby and my fears for my future—our future. I was about to speak but he began first.

"I know this has been challenging. I've been distant, and you've been cooped up here with my mother. I wish I could be here more," he continued, "but I'm barely keeping it together with work and studying—getting through my last exams so I can graduate and start our lives for real." He smiled and rubbed his thumb against my knuckles. "And here you are, never complaining. Never pressuring me. Just a brilliant light at the end of my day. I don't know what I'd do without you."

I bit my lip and blinked again, this time squeezing my eyes closed for a beat so that the tears threatening to fall dissipated, perhaps reabsorbed into the tear ducts or banished to a part of my brain where useless emotion turned to stone. I looked at him and smiled.

Fairfax, Virginia - September 2003

Back in my office, I reviewed Daven's proposal for the Framtiden deal, adding a few comments. The decision not to tell Brian about Dave kept resurfacing in my mind, forcing me to convince myself repeatedly that it was the right path, that I could rebury the memory of Dave and Amaryllis and all that I had remembered. I evaluated my choice over and over until I finally accepted the truth: I was no longer a twenty-year-old in a new relationship. Brian and I had shared so much in the intervening years that it was impossible not to share this transformative experience with him. I could not imagine sitting with him and laughing as if there were not a layer of deceit between us. I had to tell him.

From the moment of that decision onwards, every synapse of my mind was focused on the news I was going to deliver to him. I left the office without acknowledging Taylor at the front desk. I snapped at Aunt Marjorie and was dismissive towards Taiwo. I ordered takeout, unable to trust myself to focus on cooking dinner. Brian had called to say he would be late, which was a blessing since it meant I would not have to sit through a family dinner pretending that I was not about to deliver news that would shatter his world. I left Aunt Marjorie and Taiwo to eat together and retreated to my room to await Brian's arrival.

The garage door opened at about nine p.m. I counted slowly to two hundred, then waited for him to close the garage door after his nightly inspection of the exterior of the house. The kitchen door closed. If he had arrived earlier, he would have called out, "I'm home," but this late, he would not, for fear of waking Aunt Marjorie.

A few minutes of silence passed. My heart quickened in anticipation of the opening of the bedroom door. Instead I heard the toilet flush in the powder room, followed by the rush of water from the sink faucet. My empty stomach tightened and I felt ill.

When he entered the bedroom, I was sitting on the edge of the bed, facing the door. He looked at me, then his eyes shifted behind me to my reflection in the mirror above our chest of drawers. I wondered if he noticed the slump in my shoulders.

"Good night, sweetheart," he said. His brow furrowed slightly. "Everything okay?"

I shook my head, and he lowered himself to his knees in front of me. He held my hands.

"What's wrong, darling?" he said.

Tears welled in my eyes. I looked directly at him before I spoke. "Remember when we first came to the US, we had an argument and you said I would have to go to counseling if I did not pull things together?"

"I don't recall the exact incident, but I remember those early days. You changed, though." He paused as if recapping our lives in his mind. "You definitely changed."

"Yeah. I didn't deal with anything, though. I just buried everything even deeper. Now I have had an . . . an experience."

"What do you mean? What experience?"

"Hypnosis."

"Hypnosis? What? You're kidding, right?" Brian raised one eyebrow and laughed softly. He straightened and drew away from me slightly. He studied my face and his smile faded. "You're serious."

"Yes. I've been going to Dr. Hinds. Remember her?"

"No . . . not really."

"We took Tai to her. Early '90s. Just after he was diagnosed."

"Oh yes, sure. I remember. She was from the Caribbean, right? Barbados?"

"Guyana," I replied.

"Yes, I remember. But why go to her now? Hypnosis?" Brian ran his hand through his hair. He sat back on his heels. I tried to read his expression. I expected him to be skeptical, but he just looked tired, and my guilt tightened in my throat.

"I . . . I was trying to remember my past. The things I don't tell you. Can't tell you. About my . . . my family." Tears threatened my eyes and Brian leaned forward and grasped my hands once more.

"That's a good thing, right? I'm proud of you for trying."

There was a part of me that really wanted him to be dismissive, to give me a sign that he was not worthy of my confession. Instead, his kindness made me feel worse about my subterfuge. Guilt was sewn into my DNA; it controlled so many of my choices, and I was powerless to stop the road it was leading me down now. Brian looked at me expectantly. He would not let me back down.

Sweat formed in my palms.

"I remembered something under hypnosis. Something important. It seems I have . . . I mean had a sister."

"A sister? But how? Your parents died when you were so young."

"I think we were twins. Her name was Amaryllis."

"Amaya and Amaryllis," Brian said, rolling the names in his mouth as if he were taste-testing a bottle of wine. "Are you sure?"

"It felt so real. Not like a dream. I relived the moments in vivid detail. Vivid detail," I repeated.

Brian looked at me, his expression an open invitation to me to talk. "What else do you remember about her?"

"Not much about her," I said. I changed the position of our entwined hands so that I was now gripping his. I inhaled deeply then let my words out in one long gush. "I don't know how to tell you this, but I was . . . I was intimate with someone else before you."

Brian frowned. "You were intimate . . . you mean you had sex with someone else? Before me?" He shrugged. "Why is that a big deal if it was before you and I were an item?"

But was it? I thought. When had we really crossed that line from friends to a committed couple? And that was not even the point. I had deceived him, deceived us all about Taiwo's origins.

"It was around the time Tai was conceived," I said.

He became so still I wondered if he had stopped breathing. When he spoke, he spit the words out in a slow staccato. "What are you saying, Amaya?" His jaw continued moving after he spoke, clenching and unclenching as if he was fighting for control.

"I don't know, Brian." I heard the panic in my voice and fought to control it. I was just seconds from throwing up the nothingness in my stomach.

He raised his voice. "Oh, you know, Amaya. What are you saying?"

"I don't know. Maybe nothing. Maybe nothing at all." I felt a deep pang of regret for creating this wound I knew would permanently scar our relationship.

Brian stood. He stepped away from the bed, towering over me where I sat.

"Are you saying Taiwo might not be my child?"

"He's yours, Brian. You raised him. He'll always be yours."

"But you're saying he might not be." His face was red, his shoulders shaking. I shrank back where I sat. I pulled my arms close to my body then hugged them around my belly.

"I remember that afternoon, now," he said. "In Uncle Joe's house. That afternoon when I told you to go to counseling. I remember saying I would leave before I hurt you. I am leaving now, Amaya, and don't follow me. I really cannot trust my reactions right now."

He walked to the door, then stopped and turned. He looked at me, his face filled with scorn, anger, and other emotions I could not read. He turned and left the room, slamming the door shut behind him. I listened as the kitchen door slammed and the garage door unfolded before I ran to our bathroom and retched.

CHAPTER TWENTY-SIX

I did not sleep that night. The sounds of the house stretching and relaxing as the night cooled, sounds that normally comforted me, kept me on edge, forming jarring reminders that Brian was not at home. The next morning, I told Taiwo that his father had left early for work, and tried to get through our morning routine with as little disruption as possible.

"We're going to the shelter this evening, right?" Taiwo asked. His eyes bored into mine, and I imagined he was trying to convey much more than his voiced question carried. "*Where is Dad?*" his eyes seemed to ask. "*When will things go back to normal?*" And perhaps it was those perceived questions that caused me to smile and nod.

"I'll pick you up at six."

What were you thinking? I asked myself after he left the kitchen. The image of the scene I had noticed outside the shelter the last time came back to mind. *We have been going for so many weeks and never had any trouble,* I thought. *Angela isn't likely to show up again after Nate dragged her off. I can't let those fears dictate my actions.*

Aunt Marjorie seemed to sense that something was wrong.

"You okay?" she asked me more than once.

"I'm fine, Auntie," I responded each time.

"I know you, child. Don't try and hide. Tell me. Maybe I can help."

My eyes filled with tears. There was nothing I wanted more than to lay the mess that was my life on the table and have Aunt Marjorie sift through and organize the pieces of the mangled jigsaw into a clear picture. I stepped into the arms she stretched towards me. I melted into her hug, sniffing back the tears.

"Rest home today," she said into my hair. "I'll call school. We could spend the day in the garden."

"We should, Aunt Marjorie, we sure should," I replied when I was able to speak. "But today we have to go, okay?"

"De world nah stop turn if you step off for a breath, you know."

I held back a sob. Aunt Marjorie sounded so much like her former self, reliable and safe.

"Just make sure to get back on," she continued. She patted my back and placed a kiss on my forehead.

WHEN I ARRIVED at the office, I sat in the car for a few minutes, classical music at full volume, trying to collect myself before going into the building. I did not know what to expect. Brian had not responded to the texts I had sent that morning. I was fearful of how he would interact with me in the office. There were three different meetings scheduled to discuss various aspects of the Framtiden deal, and I wondered if he would be able to tolerate being in the same room with me. I could not help recalling the anger on his face and in his body language the night before.

I need not have worried. When I exited the elevator and entered the suite where our offices were housed, Taylor, the receptionist, looked up.

"Good morning, Mrs. Lin."

"Good morning, Taylor," I answered.

"Mr. Lin asked me to let you know that he had to postpone the meetings today because"—she looked down at the note on her desk—"we aren't quite ready to discuss the items on the agenda." She shrugged her shoulders quickly, then turned to answer a call. "Gil, Lin and Associates, how can I help you?"

I mouthed a thank-you, walked past Brian's closed door, and entered my office. I wondered if he was in, or if he had called to leave the message. At least I knew he was alive and not in an overturned car at the bottom of a ditch, which was just one of many possibilities I had considered when he had not come home. I sat behind my desk and tried to refocus on the Framtiden proposal. A lifetime ago, that deal had been my entire world, but now, it felt almost meaningless. After a few minutes I gave up. The weight of Brian's anger, plus everything I had learned about myself and my past, left no room for me to bear anything else.

A knock on my door interrupted my thoughts. The door opened, and Jamela's face appeared in the crack. "Can I come in?" she asked.

"Sure," I replied.

"You need to talk?"

I hesitated then shook my head. Jamela was my best friend. I had never kept anything significant from her since we met that day on a park bench twenty years ago. I was not ready to reveal the uncovered memories that had moved from the recesses to the forefront of my mind. I had not told anyone the full story of what was going on, and not knowing what was in my head, what new detail would come to the fore and spill from my lips before I had a chance to process or censure it, terrified me. And this was a definite possibility in a conversation with Jamela, whose legal training had turned her into somewhat of a hound dog for uncovering evidence.

Jamela frowned. She tilted her head, and her hazel eyes darkened with concern. "Really?" she said. "Because Brian came to our house last night. He and Geoff were up all night, and I don't think they were talking about work. Now you're in here looking like hell."

My hands went to my hair as I realized I had neither combed it nor put on any makeup before leaving the house that morning.

Jamela's voice softened to a more soothing tone. "You sure you don't want to talk about what's going on?"

"I was just in a rush. You know how it is with Auntie some mornings." I shrugged and gave a smile I hoped looked genuine.

She was not fooled. "Brian wouldn't sleep in the guest room. Said he felt too grimy. Did he cheat on you?" She placed her hands on her hips, and her body exuded indignation. A rush of emotions flowed up and out of me: love, gratitude, guilt.

"No. No," I replied. "He hasn't done anything at all."

Jamela stared at me as if she might read the truth on my face. I fought to keep a neutral smile as I held her gaze.

"How long have I known you?" she asked after a few seconds had passed.

I did not respond.

"Well, if it helps, I overheard Brian telling Geoff how much he loves you. So, whatever it is, you guys can work it out. And if you aren't ready to talk, that's okay too. Just know I'm here for you. Always have been."

THAT EVENING, I picked Taiwo up at work as we had planned. As he loped across the parking lot towards the car, I pulled down the driver's-side mirror to ensure that I was composed, with no sign of exhaustion or concern on my face. Years of coaching on reading nonverbal cues had left him ultra-sensitive to changes in facial expressions and body language, especially mine.

"How was your day?" I asked.

"Good . . . great . . . I did some work on the computer."

"Cool, what did you do?"

"I had to enter the stock count. A new responsibility." Taiwo smiled widely. "I surfed the net too."

"What did you look for?"

"Nothing much." He hesitated for a beat. "Just things . . . things I didn't understand."

"You sure you should be using the work computer for your personal research? We have a computer home, you know."

"I think it's okay. Ralph does it. I've seen him."

"Yes, but we've talked about this. Ralph is a neurotypical white guy. He can get away with things you can't." I glanced over at him. His smile was gone and he was biting his lip. My heart broke, and I purposely lowered my voice when I spoke again. "Maybe I can help? We can look together. At home," I emphasized.

"I want to figure it out on my own."

"Okay. You know where to find me." I smiled, my eyes back on the road. I was confident he would come to me for help if he needed me.

"What did you do today?" Taiwo asked.

"Nothing much," I echoed. I smiled. "I chatted with Aunt Jamela. She sent this." I blew a kiss in his direction. He pretended to grab it out of the air and wipe it onto his cheek.

"Thanks. She's okay?"

"Yes."

"And Francine?"

I smiled. Taiwo had a crush on Jamela's older daughter but while the two were very close, Francine saw him as a brother and nothing more.

"I guess she's okay. We didn't talk about her."

We drove the remaining fifteen minutes to the Shepherd Center in silence. Taiwo turned up the volume on the radio and an orchestral suite by Bach drifted out of the speakers, filling the car and allowing me space to think.

"Where are you going, Mom?"

I snapped to attention and found that I was just about to drive past the entrance to the shelter. I wrung the steering wheel left and made a sharp turn into the parking lot. As usual, most of the parking spots were taken, and orange cones reserved the ones that were free for the center's staff. I sighed. There were no spaces on the street, and I contemplated telling Taiwo to get out of the car and move one of the cones. I knew, even as I considered it, that he would never agree to do anything even mildly against the rules. I sighed again and shifted the car into reverse.

Just before I turned to move off, I saw a man in leather-like pants and a black button-down shirt approach the shelter doors. It was Nate. He moved to the left, several yards from the other men hanging around outside the shelter, and stopped, bending his head to shield his cigarette as he tried to light it.

"Figures he'd be stupid enough to smoke," I mumbled. I turned down the volume on the radio as I tried to decide on my next move. I did not want to be anywhere near Nate.

His cigarette now lit, he straightened and blew a long, slow mouthful of smoke into the air. He stared straight in my direction. I held my breath, but he gave no indication of having seen me.

"I don't like that guy," Taiwo said, his voice flat.

"Neither do I," I replied. I made no move to reverse.

A woman emerged from the shelter. Taiwo and I sat in silence and watched as Angela looked to her left then her right before approaching Nate, arms tightly folded across her chest. When Nate looked up at her, she pushed her shoulders back with great effort, as if shucking off a heavy coat. She released her arms and smiled.

Nate did not return the smile, and it was clear from the way he grabbed Angela's hand, yanking it roughly towards him, that he was angry.

"He's hurting her," Taiwo said. He unbuckled his seatbelt.

I whipped an arm across his body and stayed his hand on the passenger door handle.

"Wait," I said. "This guy is dangerous." I thought about the rap sheet emerging from the fax machine, and the gesture he had made towards me on his street.

"She needs help. We have to help her," Taiwo said, and before I could stop him, he opened the car door, twisted from beneath my arm, and swung his six-foot-two-inch frame out of the car.

"Wait," I shouted, yanking my door open and trying to jump out, only to find myself restrained by my seatbelt. Extricating myself from the belt cost valuable seconds, giving Taiwo enough time to make steady progress towards Angela and Nate.

As Taiwo approached, Nate turned to watch him as if assessing him as a threat. Taiwo was larger than Nate, but not even vaguely intimidating, due in large part to the time I had invested in coaching him so that he never moved in a way that strangers misinterpreted as dangerous.

Angela placed a hand on Taiwo's shoulder, clearly attempting to calm him. Nate shifted his stance, pushing one hip forward and looping a finger in his belt so that his hand pushed his jacket slightly backwards, hinting at the possibility that he was carrying a concealed weapon.

A gun. I froze, immobilized by equal and opposite primal forces. I had to protect my son, yet the prospect of Nate pulling out an actual gun clouded my vision with a dark, overwhelming desire to flee. Afraid I might succumb to a blackout, I dug my fingernails into my palms, hoping the pain would keep me in the present. The idea that there existed a fear powerful enough to challenge my instinct to protect my child shocked me. I closed my eyes and counted to three, each breath forcing me towards calm. I stepped out of the car.

I walked over to the threesome, slowing my pace while lengthening my stride so I appeared to be approaching calmly while crossing the parking lot in less than a minute.

I stopped when I was just a few feet away. Nate still had a hand on Angela's forearm and Angela's hand rested on Taiwo's shoulder as if the three were engaged in a séance, except the tension in the air emanated from emotions of the still-living.

Nate looked up, and there was no mistaking the menace in the glare he shot in my direction.

I focused my attention on Taiwo. His body was tense with his determination to rescue Angela. I would never get him to leave her behind without a fight. Any solution to the current standoff would have to involve either Nate leaving or Angela leaving with us. I reminded myself of the reasons that associating with Angela was a bad idea, even while I decided to take my chances with getting Angela to accompany us.

"Hey, Angela," I said. "You ready to go?"

Taiwo looked at me when I spoke. Our plan had been to come to the shelter, serve food, and return home, just the two of us. I could imagine the questions running through his brain. His lips opened, his bottom lip slightly protruded as he prepared to speak. I smiled, not daring even to shake my head slightly to tell him "no." Instead, I pressed my fingers just below my right ear with my second finger and thumb encircled, a signal Taiwo and I had developed for times where I needed him to just go with the flow and postpone his questions. I had used it on occasions when I had to tell white lies like the universal "sorry we're late, there was standstill traffic on the 495," but never before had I lied in such a high-stakes situation.

His eyes shifted to my right ear, and his mouth rounded into the beginnings of an "o" before he pressed his lips together. I turned to look at Angela, who had done a visible double-take, swinging her head towards me in response to my question.

"Remember I said I would take you to get some real winter clothes before it gets cold?" I gestured casually towards the short, light jacket Angela wore.

Nate stared at me, and even though I was not looking in his direction, I knew his cold blue eyes were laser-focused on my face, trying to read my intentions. I forced myself to relax, controlling each muscle, drawing energy from meetings at work when I had to listen to a guilty client's professions of innocence with a straight face.

I spoke again, filling the tense silence. "We have to hustle if we are going to catch the mall open." I smiled brightly at Nate.

"I forget to tell you. Amaya want to take me shopping. Don't bother make a fuss." Angela pouted playfully. "I'll be back."

How did she know my name? My body froze. I held my breath as my mind raced through possibilities, until I rationalized that Taiwo must have told her when they spoke last Thursday. I exhaled.

"We're just going to be about an hour, and I'll bring her right back to you."

I kept my voice light.

I took Angela's fleshy right arm in mine, and for a minute it seemed that Nate and I would have a tug-of-war over her body. I was not sure what I would do if he did not let go, but I was determined at the very least to leave the parking lot with Angela in tow.

Nate loosened his grip on Angela's arm.

"Okay," he said with a sneer. "You got two hours. I get antsy if she's away too long."

"We'll be right back." I commandeered Taiwo and Angela, steering them towards the car, making sure I shielded them from Nate's line of sight before I turned my back completely on the menacing man.

NO ONE SPOKE a word as I drove out of the parking lot. Once we were out of sight of the shelter, I pulled over and sat staring ahead, gripping the steering wheel.

Angela was the first to speak. "Where you a carry me?"

"Honestly?" I replied. "I don't know. I just had to get us all out of there." I looked up to find Angela staring at me, fists clenched, her ample body shaking as if she was fighting a battle for control. The composure and attitude she had displayed in Nate's presence was gone.

"We haffe get a coat. If Nate thinks you trying something, he going kill both of we."

"Kill?" Taiwo repeated.

"She's exaggerating," I snapped. "He gave us two hours, so let me do what I said. We'll go to the mall, I'll buy you a coat." I pulled back onto the road and made my way towards Tysons Corner. The radio was still tuned to the classical station. I reached for the knob to turn up the volume. Angela put her hand on mine.

"Doh take me back by him." Her voice trembled as she spoke.

"Does he hurt you?"

She shook her head.

"What's the problem then?" I wanted to add "Are you selling drugs for him?" But my instincts told me a direct approach would scare her off.

Angela dropped her head towards her chest.

"You can trust me." I lowered my voice. My assurance was met with more silence.

I sighed. Angela's refusal to talk was frustrating. I had to take her somewhere. I could not take her to my home and add yet another layer of complication to my already-tense home situation. Perhaps someone at the shelter could find her somewhere else to stay.

"We could go to the police," I said.

"No!" Her response was so intense that I almost accelerated into the car in front of us. Everything about Angela's situation stank like Jamaica's Riverton City dump, and every one of my senses screamed that I should protect my family, walk away from this woman, and leave her to dig her way out of a mess she no doubt had created for herself. But I could not bring myself to abandon her when I had been saved despite my own murky past.

"Are you here legally?" I looked over at my passenger.

She shook her head so slightly I read more from her silence than the brief acknowledgment.

"Do you have somewhere else to stay?"

She shook her head again.

"He have me passport, all me documents. He holding them until me pay off the money me promise. But it don't matter how much me give him, him want more."

"Tai said you came to look after somebody's kids."

"Me aunt help me get visa to come here and she get me the job. When me visa finish, the husband start to show me bad face. Me left, but me can't find work, seeing that me don't have no papers."

"Why not go home?"

Angela looked at me as if I had asked her why she breathed. "It don't have nothing for me in Jamaica. Me friend dem just a work, drink, and make pickney. Me want more, so me come to New York. Then things turn sour and me no have nowhere to go." Her eyes shone with a hint of tears. She looked young and vulnerable, and I longed to solve all of her problems, even as I had a myriad of questions.

"But why come to Virginia?" I asked.

Angela's expression became guarded, and the openness that had been growing between us narrowed again. My mobile phone rang. "Stick a pin there," I said. The newly formed tension between Angela and me hovered in the car and expanded in the silence that ensued as I fumbled in my bag to find the phone.

"You're coming to stay with us," I said, although I did not recall making this decision.

"Dad specifically said don't bring anyone home," Taiwo interjected.

I sighed. Bringing a stranger home would be the second strike in my already precarious situation, but I did not know what else to do. I could not deliver Angela back into what appeared to be an abusive living arrangement.

The phone buzzed again just as I found it. I took my eyes off the road to glance at the caller ID. It was Brian. My heart rate quickened. This was the first time he had reached out since our argument the night before. I was relieved he had called. Jamela's words, "He loves you," echoed in my mind. The timing was all wrong, however. I did not want this first conversation to happen while I was driving or in front of an audience, and especially not after having made perhaps the rashest decision of my adult life. The caller ID screen went blank as the call ended. I put my phone back into my bag, my fingers still curled around it. The ringing began again, insistent. I glanced in the rearview mirror and raised a finger to preemptively silence any further comment from Taiwo about Angela's sleeping arrangements.

I flipped the phone open. "Hey, Brian, what's up?"

"Where are you? Wait. It doesn't matter. Your aunt . . ." Brian began, stressing the word "aunt" the way he did when he was most upset about the addition to our household. "The police just called."

CHAPTER TWENTY-SEVEN

On hearing Aunt Marjorie's name and the police in the same sentence, my chest tightened, and I did not trust myself to maintain control unless the car was safely on the side of the road. I pulled over once more. I placed the phone to my ear again. Brian was still speaking, his tone clipped, undertones of anger heavy in his voice.

"She's okay. They need us—you—to get her. Then we need to talk. She needs round-the-clock care, Amaya, and we can't give it. It'll be expensive but we've got to discuss it." The tips of my ears felt hot as anger filled my body. This was not a new suggestion. He had even gone as far as to bring home brochures, glossy and bright with pictures of elderly people happily engaging in activities, assisted by smiling nurses. I could not help but notice that all the residents in the photos were white and most of the helpers Black.

Brian had shrugged. "It's Northern Virginia, what do you expect?"

But no flashy pamphlets could erase my memory of the Eventide Home fire, in which 153 women were burnt to a crisp on May 21, 1980, in Jamaica. Police said that the building for the old and indigent was torched by men from a rival constituency. I had heard about the fire a year after it occurred, and the image of women helpless in the building had scarred me.

At least Brian had not said "I told you so," and his mention of a discussion about decisions we would make as a couple filled me with hope.

"Got it," I said after Brian gave me the address of the precinct where Aunt Marjorie was being held.

"You okay, Mom?"

I looked in the rearview mirror, my eyes meeting Taiwo's saucer-shaped ones.

"I'm okay," I said, forcing my face to relax into the "everything is fine" facade I kept for the people in my life.

"Take deep breaths," he said, returning my smile.

I smiled, a real one this time, and followed his instructions with an exaggerated inhale and exhale. The dread that had filled me dissipated slightly and by the time I was ready to think about pulling back onto the highway, I had formulated the beginnings of a plan.

"Do you need a job?" I asked Angela.

"A job? Yeah. But me nah have no papers."

"I'll figure that out. But you have to cut ties with Rambo back there."

She bit her lip.

"You on drugs?" I asked her.

Her eyes widened. "No. Me only help him move them; me nah take them." She rolled up her sleeves to her shoulders to reveal smooth, fleshy arms unblemished by needle tracks.

"Ganja?"

"Likkle bit."

"Okay, I'm going to pick up my aunt. She's getting senile and needs looking after. If she likes you, and you like her, I'll take you in to take care of her. But no drugs, not even weed, no boyfriends in the house, and definitely no Nate. You want the job?"

"Yeah."

We drove to the police station in silence. I was deep in thought, cycling through approaches for how I would present this idea of moving Angela into the house to Brian. It was his idea, technically. And she could stay in the guest studio in the backyard, so she wouldn't really be living with us. Normally I would be able to conjure up a way to persuade him, even with such a major decision as bringing home a woman I had just met. I had spent a lot of time in our marriage selling Brian on ideas and had developed a strategy in which he would think the idea was his own. Even when he saw through my ploys, he generally gave in if only to keep the peace or to maintain his image of himself as a man who kept his woman happy. Under normal circumstances, the most difficult hurdle would be Angela's legal status, but with his anger towards me still simmering, I had no idea how he would respond or how to proceed.

I had been so caught up in my planning, I had not noticed that Angela was in the middle of some sort of panic attack.

"Is police station you bring me? Me thought you was going help me," she spluttered as she fumbled with the door, trying to figure out how to unlock it.

I held down the master lock on the driver's side with my left hand and placed my right hand on Angela's shoulder.

"I'm not turning you in. This is where my aunt is right now." I lowered my voice. "I'm going to go inside and get her out. You and Tai will sit here in the car until I come back. If you want a safe place to sleep tonight, be here when I return."

Angela nodded and took her hands off the door. She held them together in her lap as if trying to still their shaking.

I got out of the car and walked towards the station. I knew the area well. There was a public playground on the adjoining property where I had brought Taiwo to play when he was a child, but I had never realized that the nondescript neighboring building was a police station. I swallowed hard, pushing back on the memories that clamored for space in my head, shaking and shouting like caged monsters, the results of failed experiments. I pushed my shoulders back and stepped into the cool of the air-conditioned room.

A uniformed officer, a white woman, dark-haired with sunken cheeks, looked up. She did not look happy to be disturbed.

"Can I help you?"

"I'm looking for my aunt? Marjorie James?"

The woman looked puzzled. My patience began to thin. It was a small station. How many people could they have in holding?

"An elderly woman?" I continued. "Someone found her wandering and brought her here. I'm Amaya Lin. Her guardian."

I fished in my bag and produced my driver's license.

"Oh. Yes," the officer replied. Her demeanor did not change. "I need you to sign some paperwork before we release her to you. She was quite disoriented when we found her. She seemed dehydrated." The woman looked at me with a frown. "We may contact social services to check in on her living situation."

Just what I need, I thought as I signed the release forms, *more complications.*

The woman motioned me towards a closed door at the end of the sterile waiting room. She met me there and opened the door from the other side. I entered and suppressed a shudder when the door clicked shut behind me, leaving me in a relatively dim corridor. I hurried behind the police officer, who had walked forward wordlessly, passing a few shut doors. Anxiety welled up in me as I pictured Aunt Marjorie alone and frightened in this hostile environment, locked in a room like a criminal, misunderstood, and possibly suspected of being undocumented. I was so deep in my thoughts I almost ran into the officer, who had stopped in front of a door. She opened it without knocking and leaned in.

"You have a visitor."

"Maya!" Aunt Marjorie's voice was strong. "Come in," she said. "Dis nice man here bring nuf food for de whole of Black River, but im say is just fi me."

The room was what I expected in a police station, undecorated, a single rectangle table, four chairs, one on the side facing the door and three on the other side. A uniformed officer sat across from Aunt Marjorie, but the table, instead of being covered by papers or photographic evidence like in the detective shows Taiwo loved, was laden with food. The smell of deep-fried chicken filled the air. I stopped in the doorway, shocked by the sight.

"Auntie, we haffe go home," I said, slipping into Jamaican patois, which usually coaxed Aunt Marjorie into compliance. She had been an enforcer of the Jamaican version of Standard English when I was growing up, but as her dementia progressed her speech patterns had become more relaxed.

The officer looked up and smiled. "No, seriously," he said. "Eat something. We can't let this little lady leave without finishing her dinner." He smiled and patted Aunt Marjorie's arm.

"This one sweet, ee," she said to me. Then to him, "I too old for yuh, but me niece here is single." Aunt Marjorie winked and laughed. The smile enveloped her entire face. I longed to sit in this moment with her, to eat and laugh, but thoughts of Angela nervously waiting in the car kept me on task.

"Auntie, we need to go. We've been worried about you. Why did you leave the house?"

"Me not a grown woman? Why me caan leave me ouse when me want? Me just get turn round likkle bit. Me woulda find me way home. Orchid Drive caan be but round de corner there so."

The officer smiled, raising his eyebrows slightly in my direction. I did not respond. Explaining to Aunt Marjorie that she was no longer in Black River, no longer living on Orchid Drive, would only increase her confusion and distress her unnecessarily.

"Yes, Auntie, and it's time to head there. Come. Let's tell the officer thank you and go home now."

Aunt Marjorie complied and allowed me to lead her out of the police station and to the car. Angela sat slouched in the front seat, her head down.

I settled Aunt Marjorie in the back seat next to Taiwo then got into the driver's seat and drove off.

Curiosity must have eclipsed Angela's fear of the police, because she straightened in her seat and looked back at Aunt Marjorie.

"Amaryllis?" Auntie said.

WHEN I BECAME aware of the present once more, my head was on the steering wheel. Angela and Taiwo were staring at me, their faces mirror images of consternation.

"Mom! Mom! Are you okay?" Taiwo asked, panic obvious in his voice. "We were just going to call 911."

"I'm fine," I replied, shooting him the most reassuring smile I could muster. "I promise. I was just lost in deep thought." I forced myself to start the car and begin the drive home, even as my mind churned. *How much time passed? Why did I black out again? Why did Auntie mistake Angela for Amaryllis?* I thought about Angela's original assertion that she was my sister. Neither of us had raised it again. It was not possible. She was at least fifteen years my junior, maybe more. She would have been born long after my parents had died.

I pulled back onto the road and began my drive home. When we arrived, the house was ablaze with lights as if Brian were trying to scare away spirits. I pulled into the driveway.

"Tai, take Auntie inside and help her get ready for bed," I said. "Angela, you wait here in the car." I pulled into the garage and entered the house through the garage door. Brian stood in the kitchen, both hands behind his back.

Trepidation filled my body. The air around him seemed to vibrate with nervous tension. He had something to tell me. I feared it was about our relationship, that he had come to a decision on how to handle my revelation about Taiwo's uncertain parentage. I mirrored his stance, holding my hands behind my back to hide their shaking.

"You got her?" His voice was filled with concern and urgency.

"Yeah, Tai took her in through the front."

"Great." His face relaxed into a smile. "Then we have two reasons to celebrate." He paused. "We won the Framtiden contract. They sent over the signed paperwork just after I called you, with the investment option. We did it!"

He pulled a bottle of champagne from behind his back in his left hand and produced two champagne flutes in his right. His face was bright with childlike enthusiasm. I wanted to savor his excitement, to put my concerns aside and dredge up a level of emotion to match his, but all I could think of was the rift between us, and when and how I would explain Angela's presence. My world had been cleaved in two: life before and after Angela, with life after feeling much more complex, cloudy, and rudderless.

I was happy, though, and somehow I unearthed a smile, then a laugh. I threw my arms around Brian's neck.

"That's wonderful, darling. We did it!"

Still holding the bottle and glasses, he put his arms under my armpits, lifted me, and swung me around slowly. Never comfortable being lifted, I returned my feet to the ground, halting the spin.

"I . . . we . . . the firm could not have done this without you, Amaya," Brian said. He put down the bottle and glasses and put his hands on my shoulders. He had stopped smiling. My heart sank as he looked directly into my eyes. "I've been thinking a lot about what you told me about Tai, about us. I believe if I had known and understood the circumstances, I would have made the same decision to marry you and be Tai's dad . . . if you needed me. I don't need to know if the sperm was mine. I just wish you had trusted me with the truth. It feels like a betrayal, and I still need time to figure it all out." He paused and inhaled deeply. "I signed the documents for the Swedish deal, but they want to meet me and suggested I deliver them in person." He looked at his watch. "I've decided to go. I leave for Dulles airport in an hour. Perhaps this time apart will allow me to think about 'us' more clearly."

Tears pressed against my eyelids. Since our wedding twenty-one years before, Brian and I had never been apart for more than a few days at a time. The thought that I had hurt him so deeply that he was choosing to leave, even temporarily, filled me with despair. I nodded, unable to trust myself with a verbal reply.

"I left something in the car," I mumbled, and rushed out of the kitchen. Out of his sight, I leaned on the garage door, my thoughts torn between anxiety about what his leaving meant for our relationship and hope at what it meant for my situation with Angela. With Brian's impending departure, I could deposit Angela in the guest house, get Auntie to bed, get Brian on a plane, and maybe then I would be able to release the breath that felt more like water pressing into my lungs than air.

AFTER BRIAN LEFT for Sweden, Angela settled into the guest studio and into our lives. She took care of Aunt Marjorie in the mornings and evenings but otherwise kept to herself.

That her parents had died when she was young and she had grown up with an aunt was the only information I had retrieved. "We have that in common," I had responded when Angela mentioned these details. I hoped this revelation would encourage her to divulge more, but apart from a slight widening of her eyes, she did not respond and did not offer any additional information. She seemed to understand the precarious nature of her situation with Brian's return looming, but she retreated into an impenetrable shell whenever I pressed her. My frustration mounted like a pot of elbow pasta boiling up but never over, kept under control by a spot of oil in the form of Aunt Marjorie.

Aunt Marjorie loved Angela. While I often had to coax her out of bed in the morning, Aunt Marjorie would spring up at the sound of Angela's voice. She also had not had a bed-wetting incident since Angela had been with us, and she seemed more coherent. Even the staff at the adult day care center, where I continued to take Aunt Marjorie for half of the day, noticed the change.

One Sunday evening, a week and a half after Angela's arrival at the house, I walked into Aunt Marjorie's bedroom to find Angela combing her hair. Angela had released the thin gray tresses from the black netting Aunt Marjorie wore over her hair and was combing through them as carefully as a fisherman would untangle his net, one precious strand at a time, knowing that his livelihood depended on keeping the net unbroken. As Angela combed, she listened, her head bent close to Aunt Marjorie's to catch every word.

"Me hair used to be long, you know, and black and tick. Good hair. Come

Sunday, I would press it wid de hot iron, and it woulda stay straight de whole week. I used to ave it in all sort of style: curl under, in a bun, but let de rain ketch me?" She laughed, and Angela had to stop combing while Aunt Marjorie threw her head back. "Lord, how ah would run from de rain."

I could only see her back, but I pictured the animation of her face, each crease around her eyes a path for the laughter and tears that must develop during a long life.

"Foolishness that was, though." Aunt Marjorie's voice dropped in volume, and mirth left her demeanor as suddenly as the thunderclap of an imminent storm. "Foolishness. Look at me now." She put her hand to her head. "Maybe if I had left things alone it woulda be different. Not Maya though. I glad me take her in. I needed her. She was so young . . . like me when I was seventeen, starting out in the world. Those were the days. Jamaica seems so different now."

I slowly closed the door and backed away.

BRIAN CALLED THAT night to say he was extending his trip by a week.

"Plenty more deals to be made here. Your instincts were right. I would love your input. I'll email you some information tomorrow. Well, it's already tomorrow here." He chuckled.

As I listened to him speak and encouraged him to stay, I wondered if he was still deciding on whether to forgive my indiscretion or not. I did not dare ask, but once again, his references to a future that involved me gave me hope. Besides, the extension of his trip meant I had more time to find a solution to Angela's situation.

CHAPTER TWENTY-EIGHT

B rian's extra time away did not bring me any closer to resolving Angela's situation. Since I had already broken the law by taking her into our house, I did not want to involve any of the firm's lawyers, or to let anyone in the tight-knit world of Northern Virginia lawyers know the position I, and by extension Brian, was in. Instead, I searched the office files for ideas in immigration cases the firm had handled. This was against the firm's policies. As the variety of cases the firm took on had expanded, Brian had insisted on so-called Chinese walls, separating the sectors of clients so that we could avoid potential conflicts of interest. I worked exclusively on business deals, whereas Jamela dealt with immigration cases. Even when the firm had handled Aunt Marjorie's immigration, I was not allowed any more access to the process than a regular paying client would have had. I was breaking the firm's rules and several ethical ones as well. It had not mattered; after reading file after file of Jamela's careful notes, I had not found anything useful in paving a path for Angela to become documented.

And so, Monday morning, five days before Brian was due to return from Sweden, I stood outside the door to Jamela's office for a full minute before raising my hand to knock. The door opened before my hand made contact with the smooth, dark wood.

"I wondered when you would show up in here." Jamela ushered me in. "You've been moping around for over a week now. Last time I saw you looking so worried was Tai's first day at school."

I laughed, and all of my reluctance to talk to her about Angela vanished. I chastened myself for doubting that I could trust this woman who knew me so well. The laughter overwhelmed me and soon turned to tears. The relief saturated then weakened my muscles, and I slid into a huddle on the carpet. Jamela lowered herself to the floor next to me and took my hands.

"That bad, huh," she said.

I nodded, even as I acknowledged that I did not quite understand why. Angela was young, yes, but an adult, and old enough to take responsibility for her decision to leave her home in Jamaica and enter the United States under uncertain conditions. Yet I felt a responsibility for her, as if I had been the one who had promised her a life in the US then yanked it away. Angela's refusal to cooperate with her own defense would normally have led me to dismiss her case, but instead, I sheltered her. I sensed a deep level of vulnerability in her, a kindred spirit, perhaps because we shared the experience of having lost a lot. I raised my head, deliberately disrupting the train of thought before it led me through a dark tunnel that would open up into equally dark caverns from which escape was impossible.

"You ready to talk?" Jamela's hazel eyes were fixed on mine. A caring softness replaced the laughter that had been in her eyes.

I told Jamela the story of picking Angela up outside the center, right up to my impulsive decision to take her into my home.

"What does Brian think about all this?" Jamela asked. "Is this why he was so upset?"

I folded my lips inwards.

"You haven't told him?" she guessed.

I nodded.

"Okay." She was in full attorney mode now. I recognized the furrow of her brow and the sharp glint in her eye, and I wanted to hug her for simply accepting the fact that I had been harboring an undocumented immigrant and keeping her secret from my husband.

"What do you want to happen?" she asked.

"I want to help her stay. She's good with Auntie, Tai likes her, and, and ..."

I threw up my hands.

"Why do you care so much? This won't be easy. Immigrants are under extra scrutiny since 9-11. It's not a good time to be here illegally. Even immigrants here legally are catching hell to get simple things done." Jamela unfolded herself from her position on the floor with a groan. "Remind me not to do that again." She walked to her desk and sat down. "If we're doing this, you have to be in it for real."

I nodded, hoping she would not sense all the questions circling in my mind, wearing on my defenses, gnawing at the walls I had erected, trying to bloody my eyes so I would have nowhere to look but within.

"Send her to me. I'll get her to talk," Jamela said.

"She won't leave the house."

"Jesus, Amaya. You sure don't make things easy. Okay. I'm really busy right now, but I should be able to come over on the weekend or early next week." She pulled out her diary and began to flip through the pages.

I bit my lip. "Brian's coming back in a few days."

Jamela sighed. "Okay, I'll come over now. But don't be sneaking through my files anymore. I don't know what you were hoping to find, but you are now my client. No special access."

"Okay." I dropped my head. I wanted to say more. The burden I was carrying was much heavier than just Angela's status.

Jamela must have sensed that. "What else?"

"I have been having some disturbing memories." I finally told her everything, about the hypnosis, Dave, Amaryllis.

"I know Amaryllis was my sister. Even closer."

"Closer than a sister?"

"Yes, a twin. And then Aunt Marjorie mistook Tai for Dave and Angela for Amaryllis. I feel like there's been an alternate reality all along and it's merging with the life I know. I don't know what to think."

"Are you really ready to find answers?"

"I need answers, Jamela. This is driving me insane."

"Why not search the Internet?"

"I don't think there is a lot of information on the Internet about Jamaica, especially things that happened twenty plus years ago. Besides, what do I look for?"

"You have your sister's name. You could search for news of her death, or you could call up that woman who helped you bring Aunt Marjorie over. Christine?"

"I could. But what would I say to her? 'By the way, can you tell me if I have a sister and how she died?' And . . ." I did not know how to speak the words aloud, to hear my voice say the real reason I would not ask anyone or look up anything online. "Suppose I killed her?" My voice was a whisper.

"That's not possible," Jamela replied with finality.

"I don't know who I am anymore," I said. "I would not have thought I was capable of sleeping with one man then covering it up by sleeping with another. Who knows what else I've done?"

"I know. Listen, I know you think I'm a prude when it comes to relationships, but trust me, I have heard it all. Women do what they need to do to survive. But there's a huge leap from sleeping with a guy you clearly cared for, to murder, Maya. I am quite sure you've killed no one. But I agree that you have to get to the bottom of all this. I've always sensed that there was more to you than what the world sees. From the day we first met. Deep waters flowing beneath the still surface. It's time to figure out what lies there. But don't be afraid." She paused, and then her face brightened. "Perhaps you should go to Jamaica and find out firsthand."

"Go to Jamaica? Hell no." I shivered.

"Why not? If you're ready for answers, you need to go to the source."

Jamela was right. Going to Jamaica made sense, but the thought terrified me. Imagining getting on a plane and setting foot on Jamaican soil made me feel like the oxygen was being sucked out of the room. But with Brian away,

I had legitimate reasons not to go. "I can't leave now. Who would take care of Aunt Marjorie and Tai and Angela? I would have to take them with me."

Jamela smiled. "Maya. My dear friend. I promise you, the world will continue to spin if you put it down for a minute and take care of yourself. You came to me for help with Angela. Angela is taking care of Aunt Marjorie. And as for Tai?" Her voice softened, and I felt calmed by the obvious love she felt for my son. "You spent your life supporting his development into an adult capable of functioning in this world, and guess what? You succeeded. He is a wonderful young man, responsible, holding down a job, confident in who he is. He'll be fine."

"I don't know . . ."

"Just a few days. A few days for Amaya to spend with Amaya. I'll keep an eye on things here. You can be back in a flash if anything goes wrong."

"I'll think about it. Thank you, Jamela. You are a great friend."

"And don't forget that, now that you are discovering all these new sisters."

As I waited for Jamela to finish up at her desk so we could go to see Angela, I mulled over the idea of going to Jamaica. I tried to picture the country as I had last seen it, disappearing into the ground as the plane took off for Trinidad. I had not looked back for long, determined to leave behind everything that had occurred in my life. Was I ready to revisit that? Would I be able to climb over the wall I had built between my present and my past? I recalled how last night the house had breathed quietly as I prepared for sleep. Angela had cooked then put Aunt Marjorie to bed, and Tai had been in his room. Their worlds had settled with very little interference from me. Perhaps Jamela was right. They could manage without me. It was time.

IT WAS THE middle of the morning when I drove down into my neighborhood, Jamela at my side, and so the streets were empty. When we were two blocks from my house, I spotted a vehicle about halfway down our block, and from its position, I was quite sure it was outside of my house. A motorcycle, similar in size to the one I had seen Nate on one week before. Without realizing it, I eased my foot off the accelerator.

How could Angela let him in? I thought. I had explicitly forbidden it.

The motorcycle's keys dangled in the ignition and a helmet hung from the handlebar, both suggesting that Nate did not plan to visit for long.

"Why are you slowing down?"

I started. I had forgotten that Jamela sat next to me. I jerked my head in the direction of the motorcycle.

"Whose?" she asked.

"I have a guess, but I really hope it's wrong."

"The dude with the gun?"

"Yeah."

"Oh." Jamela's mouth held the O shape long after the sound had escaped and dissipated.

"Maybe we should call the police?" I said.

"And let them figure out you're harboring an undocumented immigrant? Let's check things out first."

"I thought only white people in movies walked into situations when they knew for sure there was trouble ahead."

"Funny. Listen. We don't confront him. We don't make any sudden moves. If she wants to leave with him, she goes. Your problems are solved."

"We could have that same outcome just sitting here," I replied, but I had already pulled over, opened the car door, and set one foot on the road.

"Now I know you really care," Jamela said so softly I wondered if she was speaking to herself. I did not respond.

As we approached the house, raised voices cut through the silence of the afternoon.

"The backyard," I said, and broke into a run, sprinting through the gate and around to the back of the house.

I rounded the corner to see a man holding Angela by the shoulders. She twisted vigorously under his grasp.

"Let her go!" My voice rang out with the sharp retort of a bullet released. Angela looked up, her eyes wide with surprise. Nate swung around, at the same time reaching under his leather jacket. By the time he was facing me, his gun was facing me too.

The sound of water filled my ears, and the world blurred before my eyes. I staggered and widened my stance to steady myself.

I struggled to refocus on the present. My vision cleared. Jamela stood next to me. Her hands were raised, palms forward in surrender.

"Listen, man," she said. "We don't want any trouble. Just get on your motorcycle and leave. Nobody has to get hurt. We'll forget we ever met you."

"This bitch owes me money. I'm not leaving without it or her." He repositioned himself, training the gun on Angela's temple.

"There's no need for that," Jamela said. "How about you leave with her and nobody gets hurt today."

"No!" Angela and I shouted in unison.

A grin spread across Nate's face. "Seems we have a standoff."

"How much money we talking about?" I asked.

"Well, it was two grand, but seeing how I had to spend the whole week tracking her down into this fancy neighborhood of yours, I have to add some tax. So now it's ten."

"Ten thousand!" Angela exclaimed.

"What's it for?" Jamela asked. "Why does she owe you all this money?"

"She hasn't told you?" Nate sneered. "How she overstayed her visa then came begging to me to fix it?"

"I'll pay it," I added. Even as the words left my mouth, I wanted to pull them back. Brian would think I had lost my mind when he found out.

Nate's eyes widened and he turned towards me with renewed interest. His expression mirrored the one I had seen in our first meeting at the Shepherd Center. His eyes showed bemusement but behind them it was clear that he was in deep thought.

"You all are related?" He squinted at me. "Don't let her fool you with her sob stories. She's an illegal alien, you know. A criminal."

"Is lie him ah tell," Angela cried. "You is de criminal. Me work off de money me owe you and me still don't have the green card you say you could get for me."

"This man can't get you a green card," Jamela said.

"None of this matters," I interjected.

Nate swung around and pointed the gun in my direction again.

"I'll pay," I continued.

Jamela shook her head slowly. "Amaya, don't. How do we know he won't come looking for more?"

I ignored Jamela's protests. "I'm guessing you won't take a check?" I gave a dry laugh. "You'll have to let me go to the bank for the cash." I took a step back.

"Do I look stupid?" Nate said. "No one leaves without me."

I heard the loud clink of metal contacting a hard surface. Nate sank to his knees before me. He looked up, his expression displaying the "what the hell just happened" that couldn't come out of his mouth. He raised one knee, trying to get to his feet. Angela hovered. She held my garden spade above her head ready to strike again, but it was not necessary. His torso swooned, reminding me of a fairy-tale maiden swaying at some awful news, only without the maiden and without the innocence, and the only bad news was ours. *What do we do with him now?*

"He alive?" Angela seemed horrified by the effectiveness of her assault.

I took a step forward and peered at the fallen body. His carotid artery pulsed as blood moved through the veins in his neck. "Yes," I replied. "I'm pretty sure."

"We have to call the police," said Jamela.

"No." Angela looked terrified.

"If we don't, he's going to come after us. And he's sure not to be happy with ten K this time." Jamela shot a look at me. "Which, by the way, was a bad idea. You never pay the ransom."

"That's what you want to argue over now? Not the unconscious crook in my backyard? We have to call the police."

"No!"

"Angela, we'll find a way to protect you. Maybe they won't even discover you don't have papers. And if they do, we'll find a way. But you have to cooperate."

"Don't make false promises, Amaya," Jamela said. "Even I may not be able to get her out of this one. She's broken the law and assaulted a man."

"We need to deal with this before he comes to. Angela, you go inside. Jamela and I will call the police and tell them I hit him. That he broke in. He has a criminal history, and he's on parole." I thought about Detective Bryant and the fact that he knew I had been asking about Nate. If he got involved, the police would never believe this was a random event. I bit my lip.

Jamela nodded. "A B&E charge with a deadly weapon is a class 2 felony. That's twenty years. It should keep him busy for a while."

"What if he tells them about me?" Angela said.

"Tells them what? That you paid him to forge a green card and he's extorting you?" Jamela gave Angela the stare she reserved for courtroom cross-examinations.

Angela did not respond.

"Listen. We can't help you unless you trust us," I said.

Angela and I locked eyes. A second or two passed, then her shoulders fell. I released a breath, long and slow.

"Aright," she said. "Call de police but don't make them take me away."

"You go inside," I said. "Jamela, stay with her. I'll call the police. I'll take the blame."

Jamela and Angela began walking away, but Angela stopped and turned towards me. "Nah do dat. Tell them sey me is yuh sister. Ah true. That's why me a come to Virginia and find you in the parking lot. Tell them me ah your sister and they go let me stay."

THERE WAS NO time to process Angela's words. After shooting me a look that said "We are going to have a talk about this," Jamela led the sobbing Angela back to the cottage she had called home for the last two weeks. While I wiped the handle of the spade with a cloth, then positioned my hands on it as if I were going to strike someone, I once again contemplated Angela's ridiculous assertion that she was my sister. Then I dialed 911. The police responded quickly, and after taking statements from Jamela and me, they piled a barely conscious Nate onto a stretcher and took him away. We did not mention that a third woman had been on the scene.

When the police and ambulance finally left, I looked around the yard. Although the police had been careful to stay out of my garden beds, it felt like there were footprints everywhere. My garden had been violated, and I wondered if I would ever set foot in here again without remembering Nate's menace, my fear, and the gun, that gun. It had never been discharged, but it might as well have. I sank down to the ground, picked up a handful of soil, and held it, deep brown and soft, in my hands.

Jamela sat beside me. I leaned against her shoulder. "Why does Angela keep saying she's your sister? I tried to ask her, but she clammed up tighter than Fort Knox. I suspect she'll only talk to you."

I shrugged. "It's the second time she's said it, but it makes no sense. My parents died when I was very young. Look at her. She can't be more than twenty-four. Not much older than Tai. She couldn't be my sister?"

"She seems quite convinced."

"And she must be lying . . . or mistaken."

"Based on what you are saying, yes, it can't be true. You two have a strong resemblance, though. And didn't you say Aunt Marjorie thought she was your actual sister, Amaryllis? Maybe she's related. A cousin or something? Maybe you should ask her."

"No!" I shouted, surprising myself with the vehemence in my voice. "It's not possible, and I don't want to hear her lies. I really can't process all this right now." I dropped my head into my hands. "It's just too much."

"I know what just happened was traumatic. But we can handle things here. I still think you should go to Jamaica."

I jerked my head upwards to look at Jamela. Was she serious? How could I leave when a gunman was just assaulted in my backyard?

"Hear me out," she continued. "The police have your statement. Nate is in jail. Brian will be home soon. Going to Jamaica will give you some time away to process things and to find answers. Go."

CHAPTER TWENTY-NINE

I did not put up much of a fight. Two days later, I was on a flight to Jamaica. Jamela thought I was going to uncover difficult truths and that was correct, but it was as much about escape from the truths that seemed to be unfolding in my house in Virginia.

Although I had accompanied Brian on a few business trips when Taiwo was young and easy to travel with, my last flight had been five years before, when Brian and Jamela conspired and surprised me with a vacation to Hawaii on our fifteenth wedding anniversary. I had not flown on a plane since 9-11, and the security process—removing shoes, separating liquids—was all new to me. As I moved through the checkpoints, I felt uncomfortably guilty even though I had nothing to hide, at least not from airport security.

After we boarded, the plane was delayed on the tarmac about twenty minutes past our departure time. As I sat enduring the strange mix of scents: jet fuel and air-conditioning refrigerant, I tried not to interpret the delay as a bad omen. The woman next to me was just as nervous. She tapped her leg so vehemently that my seat shook, and I barely resisted the urge to place a comforting hand on her arm. *She is not your concern*, I reminded myself. *This trip is about you and only you.*

Finally we took off and for the first time, I thought about each of the two hundred thousand pounds that were defying gravity by lifting off the ground and powering thirty thousand feet into the air. The luggage in the overhead compartments shifted noisily. And then we were gliding, free, leaving behind everything, letting go. Tears pricked the back of my eyes.

Hours later, I awoke to the sound of the captain announcing our descent.

My head had fallen onto the window, and my neck was stiff. I looked out and a mass of land lay behind me. Jamaica. I inhaled. Passengers clapped when the plane bumped to the ground, and then many stood to retrieve their overhead luggage despite the air hostess's cautioning that we had not yet come to a complete stop at the gate. I looked out the window and absorbed the surroundings. The colors of the landscape seemed muted. Mountains were impressive, dipping towards a sea that dashed itself at their feet in a white-capped rush, but the green, verdant in the memories that lapped at my brain, was dull like an overused carpet, and the ocean was brown.

I stepped off the plane and paused at the top of the steps. I inhaled a deep breath of warm air. If salty had a smell, this would be it. I waited to feel something, a pull, a memory from when I left, but nothing happened. The woman who had sat next to me nudged me forward with the large crocus bag that had scratched against my leg for the entire flight. I stepped forward. My first steps into Jamaica.

The immigration hall was air-conditioned, yet it still felt too hot. I slipped out of the jacket I had worn on the plane and folded it over my arm as I joined the line for Residents and Returning Nationals. The sounds of talking and rolling luggage wheels filled the high-ceilinged room. I tried to re-attune my ears to the Jamaican patois I had abandoned so long ago. At first, the words sped past me in a jumble, but eventually I was able to decipher and separate them, and by the time it was my turn to go to the counter, I was ready.

The immigration officer looked up cursorily, then he pulled back and took a second look at my face. Although I had nothing to hide, a bead of sweat formed between my breasts and slid down towards my belly. I twisted the beaded bracelet I had slipped onto my wrist that morning.

He looked down at my passport and turned to the detail page. "Amaya Lin," he read. "You don't look like the Lin dem. Who is you family?"

I hesitated. It was hard to tell if he was asking in his capacity as an immigration officer or just out of curiosity. I decided to answer. "My maiden name is Gordon."

A smile lit his face.

"Ah. Gordon. I know you remind me of somebody. You come to see your auntie." It was a statement, not a question.

I stared at him for a beat.

"My aunt? No," I replied. "I don't have any aunt here."

"Kathryn Gordon and you not family? Must be." He looked at me more closely. "You favor she too bad, like she spit you out. I recognize you from the time you step up here, I just couldn't place you."

I shook my head and kept a straight face, but my mind was in turmoil. *Could I really have my first clue handed to me that easily?*

The man continued, glancing back and forth between my passport and my face. "You caan be she daughter. She na'ave no pickney, only that girl she raise."

I smiled politely, and my disinterest seemed to remind him that he was supposed to ask specific questions. He began with a barrage, barely waiting for me to answer one before he shot another at me. "Why are you here? When are you leaving? Vacationing by yourself?" I wondered if it was a test; everything he asked was on the form I had completed while on the plane, a form that was now in his possession.

He flipped through the empty pages of my passport. "When last you been back?"

I hesitated again. I was a Jamaican by birth, so his question had no bearing on whether I should enter the country or not, but he had authority. If I pissed him off, he could probably delay my entrance and I did not have time for any trouble. "Long time," I replied. "1980."

He whistled softly. "That's a long time. Your aunt goan be glad to see you."

"I honestly don't know this woman," I said, trying to keep the irritation out of my voice. I glanced at the people waiting behind me, hoping to remind him that he should not hold up the line.

"Well, you should go see her. I sure you and she is family," he said finally. "Gambit Boutique. Kathryn Gordon."

He stamped my passport with a flourish.

"Welcome home," he said. He shook his head and as I walked off, I heard him comment, "What a way she favor Miss Gordon."

Past that hurdle, I cleared customs with ease and walked out into an open hallway. I stopped, two opaque glass doors separating me from my future. I felt suspended in circumstance. I could not go back. The airline held no further responsibility for me, having expelled me from its bowels. I could only move forward into the next chapter of my life, a chapter in which I would uncover events that were hidden to me now. For over twenty years I had dreaded the idea of returning home. I had been sure my fear would flow from my pores, marking me as prey. Instead I was ignored as if I were just another creature joining the struggle.

I pushed open the doors and the heat seared my skin. I squinted in the sunlight, having forgotten how much closer the sun seemed in the Caribbean.

"Taxi, daughta?" A man in a light-colored shirt and long pants wiped his forehead then donned a yellow, green, and black baseball cap emblazoned with the words "Jamaica Nice."

"Yes," I replied.

"Where you a go?" he asked, holding the car door open for me with one hand and taking my carry-on with the other.

"I'm staying at . . . I'm going to . . ." I paused. I had planned to go straight to my hotel, check in, then figure out my first move. My hotel was in Kingston, not far from the airport, but a three-hour drive from Black River, purposely selected so I would have a refuge if I was overwhelmed by whatever awaited me in my old hometown. But the immigration officer's words played in my head. Gambit Boutique. Could the owner be my aunt? An aunt implied a parent with siblings and who knows how many other family tree limbs. And if I went, what would I say to her? "Hi, I think you might be my aunt?" No, it was not yet time.

"Miss?" The taxi driver shuffled from one foot to another. "Where you going?"

"I'm staying at the Wyndham," I said. I wanted to be on firmer footing before I started shaking on the family tree.

He frowned as I got into the car. When he pulled off from the curb, he looked in the rearview mirror. "You from foreign?" he said. "You look just like one of we."

"I was born here," I said. "But I haven't been here . . . home for a while."

I closed my eyes, hoping to stem any further interrogation, and he took the hint. He raised the volume of the radio. The afternoon news played. I soaked in the sound of the announcer's voice, the rising and falling rhythms and the colloquialisms that snuck into the script even though it was delivered primarily in Standard English. Those phrases sunk into my consciousness, fingers probing into my memory, the tone of the voices changing, morphing into familiar yet unrecognizable sounds.

I reopened my eyes just as we sped past the bauxite factory, the red soil bright, industrial. We drove deeper into the city through narrow streets flanked by colorful houses with blue, yellow, and pink walls. Whenever the traffic paused, young boys walked between the cars, knocking on the windows, selling, begging, skinny hands extended. The driver—his name was Donovan—pointed out some sights: an area called Beverly Hills, the National Stadium, the Crown House, the Wall of Honour. I tried to recall how many of these landmarks had been here the last time I made the trip to the airport.

Once I settled into the hotel, I put the SIM card Donovan had helped me to buy into my mobile phone. I had to call Brian. I had left without telling him my plans, and I dreaded the conversation.

His voice was sleepy on the phone, and I imagined him in a small European hotel room under the white sheets of a narrow bed, his hair tousled and his eyes red from sleep.

"Hey, Brian," I said. "Sorry to wake you. I forgot about the time difference."

"What time is it by you?" he responded. I heard shifting and rustling of the sheets. "It's midnight here, so seven?"

"Actually it's six. I'm in Jamaica. It's an hour earlier."

Brian did not speak, but I felt as if the radio waves that carried the sound between us had moved into a frenzied overdrive. I waited.

"You're in Jamaica?" he said eventually.

"Yes," I replied. "With everything going on in my head, it seemed like the best thing . . . the only thing to do."

"What about Tai? And Aunt Marjorie?"

"I left them in good hands. You yourself said we needed someone to care for Aunt Marjorie, so I found someone." In for a penny, in for a pound. "The woman from the shelter. And Tai's a grown man. He can survive a few days without me."

"You left a strange woman in the house?"

"You have to trust me, Brian." Even as the words left my mouth, I regretted them.

"How can I trust you?" His voice rose, and I waited as he took a deep breath to calm himself before he continued. "I wish you'd told me first. I feel like I don't know you, Amaya."

"I needed to do this, Brian. For me. Just for once, just for me."

I covered the mouthpiece of the phone so that he would not hear me cry. The truth was, I did not know what I was doing. For years I had dreaded even thinking about Jamaica, and now I was here and I felt nothing.

Brian sighed, and I pictured his shoulders sagging and his eyes kind and dark with concern. "Don't cry, Maya."

"How you know I'm crying?" I was sobbing now.

"Maya, darling. I know you. I have known and loved you since you were that scared little girl at UWI with those bottomless eyes that hid so many secrets." He sighed again. "The truth is, I'm glad you went to Jamaica. It's about damn time you stopped running from whatever you left behind. Do I wish you'd done it differently? Yeah, but I have to trust that it had to be this way."

"Oh, Brian."

"And I know things are crazy between us now, but we will get through it. You, me, and Tai. Okay?"

"Okay," I whispered. I hung up the phone. Relief filled my body. Brian and I were going to be okay.

I woke the next morning after a dreamless sleep with Brian's assurances on my mind. *We can get through this.*

I had decided that I would travel to Black River that day and had already made arrangements for Donovan to take me. I liked that he did not engage in much conversation, and his face had lit up when I asked. He was happy to have a guaranteed fare for the entire day.

"You going on de Black River tour?" he asked from the driver's seat.

"No," I said.

We fell into silence. I started reading a historical romance I had bought for the flight but I found it impossible to keep track of the simple plot. I gave up and stared out the window at the constantly changing scenery, from lush landscapes to villages and towns in various states of development.

It was impossible not to know that we had arrived in Black River. The roadsides were littered with signs promoting tours on the swamp.

"You sure you don't want to do the river safari? De tourist dem love it."

"No, just take me to Orchid Drive. I think I can give you directions once we get in the area. I hope."

Black River streaked past. Donovan drove just as aggressively in the quiet, narrow streets as he did in the midst of Kingston, forging a path through the other cars, the pedestrians, and bicyclists. The streets were lined with colorful houses and buildings with wooden facades, peaked roofs, and lattice-trimmed windows. I dug my fingernails into my palms as I forced myself to process the scenery. It felt familiar, but the connection I expected to feel lighting up a circuit that would illuminate the truth of my past did not materialize. Then I saw the sign for Orchid Drive.

"Turn here." As soon as we turned onto the street, my heart caught, and an image of me walking in my school uniform, book bag over my shoulder, pushed its way forward in my consciousness. A wave of loneliness flowed over me, distracting me so much that I almost missed it when we approached the walls of Aunt Marjorie's home.

"Stop here," I called out, leaning forward to rest a hand on Donovan's shoulder.

I got out of the car, my eyes fixed on the house. It looked just as I remembered it, which was a surprise since I expected it would still be in the disarray Christine had described, an overgrown tangle of weeds climbing the walls and forcing themselves into and widening the cracks in the concrete. Instead, the surrounding walls were freshly painted, and through the gate, I could see that the front garden, at least, was carefully manicured. The house looked like love, and it was all I could do not to sink to the ground and succumb to the overwhelming feeling of helplessness that engulfed me.

"I won't be long," I said to Donovan without turning around.

"Seen. Me a go round de corner down dere so. When you ready text me," he said, already revving his engine.

As he drove off, it dawned on me how isolated I was. Donovan had not been much company. He had hardly said a word since he picked me up from the hotel for the three-hour drive, but he was all I had. I had not been so alone since I met Brian. He and Taiwo, Lisa, Jamela, and Geoffrey had filled my life in ways that had allowed me to ignore all else, but now, I needed more. I had ripped the bandage off, and I was going to look at the wound no matter how bloody and ugly it was.

I opened the gate, then waited for the sound of a dog. Ten seconds. Twenty seconds. I took a few steps into the yard and hurried up the short path to the door. The current residents had a doorbell, although the knocker I remembered still hung from the door. I hesitated then pressed the button. A chime sounded inside. I wiped my palms on my jeans, consumed with anxiety about what I would find on the other side.

"Coming," I heard.

I did not recognize the woman at the door, but she recognized me. I began my practiced spiel: "My name is Amaya Lin, and I lived in this house twenty-five years ago. It would be very important to me if you would let me visit for a while." I had considered then discarded the idea of saying I had amnesia to explain my not remembering details I should. But I did not get further than my name before the woman engulfed me in a hug. She held me away, looked into my face, then pulled me close once more.

"Oh my God, Maya." Her voice was tinged with pity. I pulled away.

"It's Raquel. I lived cross the road from you when you used to live up on Zinnia with your . . ." She faltered for a minute, and her round cheeks looked like they would be hot to touch. "Your parents."

I was confused. This woman could not be older than I was. She was dark, smooth-complected, and plump, a combination that might have softened her features, making her look younger than she was, but it was hard to believe she would have been old enough to remember my parents before they died forty years ago.

She must have seen the confusion on my face. "Come in. You wouldn't remember me, I was a likkle girl in junior high when you left."

I stepped into the house and felt like I had entered a time capsule. The furniture was different; the couch in the living room was cream, whereas I remembered that Aunt Marjorie had a brown-and-beige mottled pattern on hers. But the room was arranged the same way it was in the memories that were slowly surfacing. I stopped and spun slowly. Raquel watched me take it all in.

"I have something pon de stove," she said. "You're lucky you catch me home. I work the two-to-ten shift tonight." She paused and pleasure darkened her cheeks. "I'm a nurse now, you know. Is Miss James who tell my mother to make sure I stay in school." Her features clouded. "How Miss James though? She was in a bad state when she left here."

I followed her into the kitchen but said nothing. She was carrying the entire conversation on her own, posing then answering her questions. I ran a finger along the curve of the kitchen table. Images bombarded my brain, images of Aunt Marjorie and me at the table, our hands always busy with steaming cups of tea, schoolbooks, newspapers, herbs curing. My mind filled the table until I was sure it would crumble under the weight of my thoughts. I looked up, and noticed that the back door was ajar. Raquel gasped as I rushed forward and through the doorway into the back garden. I gasped as well, as much from the burst of hot fresh air that hit me as from the new memory that filled my brain.

CHAPTER THIRTY

Black River, Jamaica - June 1980

T here was a time when the gunshots that exploded nightly like clap-pas set off on Old Years' reduced me to tears. There was an unprec-edented level of lawlessness in Jamaica. High unemployment drove people to desperate measures, or at least that was the claim for the increase in holdups and shootings, and the ease with which the fires raging outside could leap a threshold and turn everything to ash filled me with a paralyzing fear. I was crushed by a sadness that encircled me with a presence that was almost physi-cal. And alone. I remembered feeling so alone.

Just months before, I had been looking forward to year two, my last year of high school, when I would belong to the group of students who traversed the school premises with an air that combined accomplishment, seriousness, and an adult weight of the world. But by the beginning of that crucial year, with my circumstances changed, I shrank into myself, only nosing out of my shell when it was necessary to move through life. People avoided me. Even Christine, whose ever-mischievous gaze had always been eager to meet mine with a silent invitation into her latest misdemeanor, shifted her eyes when our paths threatened to collide along the long, unsheltered corridors that connect-ed the classrooms of our school. Her eyes did not display hatred or disdain; instead, I sensed my presence caused her pain too heavy to carry.

I could not face the tragedy that divided us. Whenever the facts wormed their way near the surface, a rage filled me then steamed up and outward, pressing against my ears and mouth in its anxiety to escape my body. Trapped inside, the rage and the truth combined to form terrible nightmares. I would wake, drenched with sweat after bloody night terrors, to find Aunt Marjorie, a shadow at my bedside, barely illuminated by the moonlight that pressed through the sheer bedroom curtains, rubbing my back or holding my hand.

"Hush, sweetheart, hush," she cooed.

The first morning I woke, the shadows of my dream still haunting my head and the imprint of her fingers still on my hand, I noticed that the circles of sleeplessness around her eyes mirrored mine, and I tried to thank her for her sacrifice. She brushed off my words, swatting the air as if chasing away a fly. "You musta drink your cocoa too late. Sits on your stomach churning. Give you nightmares." Her words echoed, retelling my past.

That morning, she let me stay home from school. She took me into her garden, a small plot no more than fifteen feet by ten, but so densely planted that not an inch of soil was visible.

"Each of these 'erbs have a purpose," she said. She gathered the ends of her flowered housedress between her knees and crouched near the ground. She ran her fingers over the green, purple, and blue leaves of the plants as if running her hands over a piece of silk, assessing its fitness to be turned into a garment. Then she settled on a leaf. It shrank from her touch, closing in to protect its soft middle. "Touch-me-not." The phrase erupted in my mind, a melody of a memory, a happy one I suspected, but I never gave it a chance to grow. Instead, I focused on Aunt Marjorie's hands as she picked the reluctant leaves, crushed them between her fingers, and pressed the fragments to my nose. The scent entered my nostrils in a rush, unpleasant with a sulphuric tinge, yet it filled my head like the calming notes of a lullaby. I stepped back.

"This one will make you sleep." She picked another leaf, its thin lamina speared by a thick vein. "This one will calm your nerves. Make you forget the dreams."

I boiled and drank them all. They helped. They helped me to keep quiet and hold in both the rage and the truth, hiding truth even from myself until all signs of the horrible event that had happened, denied oxygen, spit and sizzled and dissipated into a whisper of smoke. I returned to school, walking to classes every day and sitting in the back where I could slip in and out while attracting the least attention possible. Each day after school, I headed straight home, spending the remaining daylight in the garden and the evenings focused on my books.

In the first few weeks of the term, my classmates reacted to me in equal measures of uncertainty and pity. I silenced their stammered apologies and condolences with a shake of my head as I walked away, and eventually they lost interest. The Reggae Boys' attempts at success on the international football scene and the gunshots that dominated the airwaves overshadowed my story. My teachers attempted to draw me out, calling on me, vacillating between good humor and berating as they reminded me of how I used to participate in class, the books I loved, the history I devoured. Their desire to help became increasingly tinged with frustration that grew into anger then disinterest as they reverted to treating me like everyone else, urging us towards our A-level examinations.

Despite my refusal to participate in any school activities, I paid attention and I excelled. I studied like a fiend, controlling my body, using herbs from Aunt Marjorie's garden to stay awake for days and then to sleep dreamlessly when I decided to succumb to exhaustion. Somehow, Dave had graduated the year before, received the island scholarship, and had chosen to study in Barbados. He had found a way to escape and given me hope that if I strained hard enough against the ropes that held me back, I could break them as he had.

When Aunt Marjorie commended me on my performance in school, I mentioned my aim, my plan to get the island scholarship and leave Jamaica for good.

"Maya. Sweetie." Her voice dropped, soothing. "Your daddy." She paused, watching my face for a reaction. I held my facial muscles in check and she continued. "You know how it is ere. Only one person have to suck a sour fruit and for generations, every pickney mouth come out twist up." She paused again, always testing to see if she had pushed too far. "Even if nothing had happened, your daddy was a big JLP supporter. They not going give it to a pickney from Black River two year in a row, and they definitely not going give it to you. Maybe if JLP win election . . . maybe . . ." Her voice trailed off. "But that going be too late for you."

I didn't listen. I still believed that if I got the grades, they could not deny me the prize. Life owed me.

AFTER OUR EXAMS, the sixth form A-level candidates surged into the world. Some of my classmates with worse grades but better connections were hired conditionally—as bank tellers, store clerks, or teachers in Black River or in Kingston—while we waited for the August release of our examination results. I searched unsuccessfully for work. The high unemployment that had plagued Jamaica in the last year under the People's National Party government in 1980 worked against my entire graduating class, but I had the additional problem of my last name being attached to a hearse no one wanted linked to their place of business. I considered leaving Black River, but I could not afford a place of my own anywhere else on the island.

When the first breadfruit began to ripen in the middle of July, when despair of ever getting a job and contributing to the mounting expenses of living in Aunt Marjorie's home threatened to drown me, I was hired as a cashier in a grocery store, and my life's path changed once more. It was a small shop, ten aisles of essentials, but one of many small stores scattered through Black River under the name of Joseph and Sons.

Somehow, despite the shortage of foreign exchange that made it impossible for stores to purchase and thus sell the imported brands their customers had become accustomed to, the shelves of Joseph and Sons remained stocked. There were points during the day in which we were extremely busy, when Franklyn, my boss, would emerge from the storeroom, wiping the sweat from his forehead and closing the buttons of his shirt around his stomach, to sit at the third counter to relieve the line of customers complaining about the wait. In those moments, I was in constant motion, adding, weighing, counting money, giving change, answering questions. Often people wanted to chat, to explain their purchases, complain about shortages, and seek advice. I complied when I could.

In the downtime I was bored, a state of mind I hated because my mind filled the empty spaces of time with unwelcome thoughts, pushing them forward like gag gifts I knew would be awful surprises if I accepted them.

The other cashier who worked alongside me was Brenda, a young woman about twenty-five with such an air of absolute resignation that I feared my extended interaction with her would suck me into a place from which I could never escape our town, much less Jamaica. She pulled up a stool to her counter and sat on it for our entire seven a.m. to six p.m. workday, except for one break for the bathroom after the midday rush. She did not speak to the customers except to answer questions about the location of an item, which she gave with non verbal cues, only giving in to actually speaking if those failed.

I hated the job but I had to stay. I needed the money, and they were the only place that would hire me. I did not plan to be there long; I had applied to the University of the West Indies in Trinidad and had been accepted contingent upon my A-level results. I just had to find the money to go. Restlessness pushed at me, underlining my inertia, but I worked, I smiled, I counted, I read, I stayed, determined to earn the money that would get me out of Jamaica. By the time I had been working in the store for three weeks, Franklyn trusted me. He often sent Brenda home early, leaving me to work the slower shifts alone.

As a result, I was on my own one afternoon when the front door was pushed open and a customer entered the store. He walked past the cashier lanes then stopped and swiveled towards me slowly, rearing upwards on heeled shoes as if he was relishing keeping me waiting as he revealed himself. When he finally faced me, I saw that he was of Lebanese descent, his craggy face browned from time spent in the Jamaican sun rather than from his genes. He was short in stature but carried himself—head raised, chest inflated—like a much taller man. His clothes were well-tailored, designed to flatter his over-weight body in a way that suggested an aging man clinging to a youth in which he had been considered handsome.

"You're new," he said.

"Me start a few weeks ago."

"And Franklyn left you in here alone?"

I nodded. I recognized him now from the photo of him and his wife hanging at a tilt on a wall near the cash registers, as if monitoring the happenings in the store. The photo had clearly been taken years before, when his straight hair was still black and covered his scalp completely, and his stomach fit neatly into his pants. He was the owner of the store, Mr. Joseph of Joseph and Sons. Franklyn had shared that none of their sons had stuck around.

"You must have something special," he said. "What's your name?"

"Amaya."

He took a step closer and assessed me as if looking through my eyes to something on my brain. I was aware of what I was wearing, how I had combed my hair, the scent of my breath. I realized I had slumped my shoulders, and I straightened up.

His investigation of my person complete, he frowned. "You could do office work?"

I hesitated.

"You did A-levels?"

"Matts and accounting. Waiting for results." I longed to look away from his eyes, so much like those of the fish in the ice cabinet, staring up cold and dead, but I held his stare. He dropped his head slightly as if angling to get a better look. A shiver, unbidden, threatened to wrack my body, but I forced myself to remain still.

"Tell Franklyn to send you upstairs. Tomorrow. The old girl left."

He stalked to the back of the store and ascended the stairs leading to the offices.

The next day, I climbed the stairs to the upstairs office. I looked back and met Brenda's eyes, then felt her gaze on my back as I ascended.

The room was small. Three desks sat grouped together, two on one side, one on the other, their fronts touching, the only way they could fit and still leave space for moving around. The room seemed dimly lit despite the twin fluorescent bulbs that hung unshielded from the ceiling. Bookshelves stacked with paper-filled boxes lined the walls that faced the door and the wall to my right. The wall on my left overlooked the store and was filled not with brick but with a large, darkened pane of glass, which I guessed must be a one-way glass because I had never noticed it from down below. From there, the Josephs oversaw everything that happened in the store, and it occurred to me that it was unlikely Mr. Joseph had been seeing me for the first time the previous day as he had intimated.

My first day upstairs, I tiptoed around Mr. Joseph's wife, trying to look useful. I had studied accounting at A-levels but never actually practiced it, and I had no idea what to do with a balance sheet even if I managed to prepare one. I did not need to worry, though; I was assigned basic tasks, the main one, matching the intake from all of the stores to the sales lists and making sure they corresponded.

By the first Friday, I began to regret the move. The pay was better than what I made as a cashier, and better than I would make pretty much anywhere else in Black River, but I was bored, and Mrs. Joseph's constant scrutiny was stifling. She was always around. I didn't think I had ever even seen her eat lunch. And she spoke infrequently. Franklyn had told me that Mr. Joseph had married her on the recommendation of his family in Lebanon, having only met her once when they were children.

"She nice enough," he said. "Yuh just haffe do exactly what she tell you. She never tried to fit in here, though. She never learn no English neither. Only a likkle patois to tell we what to do. She just a focus on she son dem. Now they gone away . . ." His voice trailed off and he shrugged.

I recalled my attempts to learn French in fourth form, the way I hated how the words pulsed on my tongue, refusing to merge, to sound as if they belonged, and at first I empathized with Mrs. Joseph. But my sympathy turned to anger because when she had to speak, it was in a dismissive tone that suggested it was beneath her to interact with me. She did not speak this way to Mr. Joseph, and some days I sensed she was, perhaps, a little afraid of him, and felt just as trapped in the store, trapped in Jamaica as I did.

Mrs. Joseph introduced me to the office tasks quickly. The volume of responsibility she gave me grew steadily, and I began staying at work later and later, preferring being busy in the uncomfortable silence of the office to the prolonged quiet alone in my bedroom at Aunt Marjorie's house. By the end of my third week, Mrs. Joseph delegated to me the responsibility of counting the cash and checks collected from their other stores in Black River.

"Dey must really trust you," Franklyn said the first time he came up to deliver cash after the midday rush and Mrs. Joseph directed him, with a dismissive wave, to hand the money to me.

In our new routine, Mrs. Joseph would count the float every morning and place it in bags of thickly woven olive-green fabric, one bag for each store, to be collected by the manager or delivered by Mr. Joseph, depending on his schedule for the day. Twice a day, the money and long reams of cash register receipts came in from the High Street store and others, midday receipts in innocuous-looking brown paper bags, and I would be tasked with verifying the contents, categorizing the sales, and recording all the information in the ledger.

One Friday night, mid-July, in my fifth week on the job, my second week handling any cash, I couldn't get the books to balance. I was off by twenty dollars and three cents. The money made many stops before it got to me, at many places where twenty dollars and three cents could inadvertently or purposefully go missing, but that evening, I got the blame. Mr. Joseph was unperturbed, but Mrs. Joseph was incensed. At first Mrs. Joseph spoke in Arabic but when Mr. Joseph insisted on responding in English, she began to speak in English as well.

"She haffe pay."

"Is not her fault," Mr. Joseph replied.

"Maybe she hide it in she bag. Maybe she lose it. She careless."

"She here three weeks and she don't make no mistake. And is only twenty dollar."

"She have to pay."

"Why would she steal twenty dollars?"

"And three cents," Mrs. Joseph corrected him. "She don't have no money. Everybody is tief here."

At this point there was a part of me ready to just give them the money, but my pride would not let me do it. Paying up would be admitting to something I did not do, fueling the version of the truth in Mrs. Joseph's head. Plus, I couldn't spare the money. After I helped with groceries, every extra penny I made was hoarded away in my "escape to college" fund.

"It's okay," Mr. Joseph said, finally acknowledging my presence.

"Go home." He directed this at Mrs. Joseph.

"She haffe pay."

"Me say go home. I go finish up here."

"I'll pay." I capitulated, faced with the prospect of being left alone in the small office with Mr. Joseph's piercing eyes.

They both ignored me. "You go home," Mr. Joseph repeated. "I'll help her look likkle longer."

She began to protest but he silenced her with a look. She left the room, her presence leaving a space in the air like a depression lingering on a bed after the occupant rose.

I began to count the cash even though I knew nothing would change. All this fuss over twenty dollars that meant so little to them.

Mr. Joseph walked around the desks and sat next to me, in Mrs. Joseph's chair.

"Sorry about my wife," he said. "She don't trust no one here."

"It's okay. I don't know why the money short." I wished I were on a rolling chair. He was too close. The scent of the coconut oil slicking back his slightly graying hair was nauseating. I slid to the very edge of my chair, knowing if I moved any further I would fall off. My skirt inched up my legs, revealing a bit of my thigh. I contemplated whether to focus on escaping as soon as possible, or to call attention to my discomfort by tugging the skirt down. I fiddled at one of the rubber bands I kept around my wrist to separate bundles of cash when I counted them.

"Don't feel no way. I don't believe you a tief from me." He put a hand, cold and clammy, on my exposed thigh.

A shiver slid down my spine, not unlike the sensation I felt when I danced with boys at parties, their clumsy groping sparking electric waves in my belly. But this was unpleasant, like a coiling low in my stomach just before I vomited.

"Everything cool," he droned, patting my flesh in a rhythmic pattern.

My body tensed, ready to flee, but I did not move. I looked down at my lap. *This is not a big deal*, I told myself. I needed the job. If he went any further, I would run.

"Thank you," I said.

"Gwan home." His hand snaked down towards my knee. I was thankful for the change in direction. I rose, gathering my worn handbag and the paper bag containing remnants of my lunch into a clumsy bundle. I rushed towards the door and ran down the stairs.

The memory of Mr. Joseph's hand on my thigh consumed my thoughts. I went to bed that evening without eating, and lay awake listening as heavy rainstorms lashed at my windows. When the morning light slid between the crack in my bedroom curtains, I did not open my eyes. Eventually, Aunt Marjorie came in.

"You not going to work today?"

I did not respond. The edge of the bed next to me sank under her weight when she sat. I opened my eyes.

"What's wrong? Something happen?" Her eyes were alert, her shoulders thrown back: indomitable.

I wanted to tell her what Mr. Joseph had done. The words formed in my mouth but I tugged them back, unwilling to expose the truth to the light. Aunt Marjorie would be very upset. She had strict rules about the way ladies were to interact with men, and me sitting alone with my boss at night, my skirt hiked up on my thigh—even accidentally—would not fit her view of decorum. In the morning light, the event seemed so petty; I had exposed myself, and he had not really done anything more than place a hand on a proffered leg. Perhaps it had been a mistake, an unplanned connection of flesh with flesh.

"Some money went missing, and Mrs. Joseph think is me tief it."

Aunt Marjorie steupsed. "They don't know a good thing when they have it. You need the job, though. How much money it is?"

"Twenty dollars . . . and three cents," I remembered to add. "But Mr. Joseph say is okay. He not making no fuss."

Aunt Marjorie's eyes met mine and I held her gaze.

"So why you a stop in bed then, girl? Get out and gwan to work before they accuse you of being lazy on top of everything else."

CHAPTER THIRTY-ONE

Mr. Joseph spent the next day dealing with an issue at another location. I was left alone with Mrs. Joseph, who was even more hostile than she had been in the past. Whereas her eyes used to slide past me as if I were a bowl of boiled dasheen amid a table of delicious desserts, she now regarded me with open distaste.

I made it through that day and the next, holding on to threads of the idea that I would be leaving for university, although I did not have a clear plan for how I would pay tuition, room, and board. Mr. Joseph did not touch me again that week, but he devised a constant stream of reasons to be in my presence, checking on my work, leaning over me, his coconut-oil-slicked hair close to mine, the smell filling my nose and throat almost choking me.

"I sending you to the Central Street store to help the girl there take stock," he said the following Monday morning.

I looked up in surprise. I had many questions—*Who is the girl? How exactly am I supposed to help this woman do something I have never done before? Is this a test? A promotion?* But I relished the idea of leaving the office, and I did not want to hesitate and have him reconsider.

"When?" I asked instead.

"Now. She waiting."

I stood to leave. I wondered if I should ask for bus fare, but I was willing to spend my own money if it meant escaping, even for a few hours.

"I go take you," Mr. Joseph said. "I haffe introduce you to the manager."

I hesitated. Scenes from the previous Friday night leapt to mind. I was eager to avoid entering a small space alone with him again.

"Let's go," he said. He turned and walked out the door. I grabbed my handbag and followed him down the stairs.

"YOU DON'T LOOK like the kind of girl who should be counting penny the rest of her life," he began once we were settled in his car and pulling away from the sidewalk. "You have some ambition, at least more than de gyal dem working for me now."

I was already near gagging from the heat that had not fully escaped through the open windows, so it was easy to mask my repulsion. Mr. Joseph was Jamaican, born on the island and raised here. He spoke like a local, yet in the presence of his fair skin and wavy hair, it was hard to imagine that his disdain for the women he hired was not racially motivated. I said nothing.

"What you going to do with your life?"

"I'm going university in Trinidad," I said. He looked at me as if I had claimed I owned a million dollars. I continued defensively, "Yes. I applied and they accept me. I'm just waiting for my A-level result dem."

He laughed, a short sound halfway between a clearing of his throat and a chuckle. "Where a girl like you going get money for university?"

I shrugged. "Work until I have the money." I tried to look like I had it under control. I did not say that all of my hopes hung on being awarded the island scholarship. I tried to hide the fact that I would probably die if I was not able to accept the position at UWI, but my desperation must have been obvious in my voice.

"I could help, you know," he said. With one hand on the steering wheel and without taking his eyes off of the road, he put a hand on my knee. "We could help each other."

"I don't think so." I moved his hand from my leg. I saw my job and my escape slipping away in his withering look.

He pulled up to the sidewalk in front of the store. "Think about it," he said as we entered the grocery together.

MR. JOSEPH DID not approach me again and as that week passed, I convinced myself that he had lost interest. He sent me to the Central Street store every day that week, but after the first day, I traveled alone by bus, the exact fare folded into a tiny wad and pushed across the desk by Mrs. Joseph, her eyes never meeting mine.

The store on Central Street was a duplicate of the one on High Street in layout and scent. The trainee was Candy, a high school graduate like me, but two years older. She had moved from Brown's Town to Black River one year before. The first time we met, I braced myself for the glimmer of recognition and pity I had come to expect when I met new people, but she did not flinch when I told her my full name. She knew nothing of my past and showed no curiosity about who I was or where I came from beyond what I shared willingly. She seemed quite happy to accept me as I was that day in the office with her. I returned the courtesy.

That Friday afternoon, she invited me out.

"Wha you a do after work?"

I shrugged. "Ah going home."

"Gyal, you should come out with me this weekend. J's Cool Spot having a pre-Independence fete. All de good-looking man dem going to be there." She winked. Her enthusiasm was palpable, like a host of colorful streamers undulating in the air between us, reaching out to touch me, to transfer her passion to me if I just stepped forward to receive it.

I thought for a moment. Seriously considered it. I enjoyed working with Candy and was regretting my return to the tomb-like atmosphere of the High Street office. Going out with her would extend our burgeoning friendship beyond the office and sow the seeds for us to continue meeting after I was no longer required at Central Street. On the other hand, I would have to sneak out of Aunt Marjorie's house, speak to strangers, invite someone into my immediate space, engage in the intimate movements we called dancing, and be stuck in a place without an escape if being there became untenable. These possibilities sent my mind into a whirlwind, and I had to hold on to the back of a chair to steady myself.

Then a single thought sounded in my head. At first I did not recognize the voice, low-pitched and youthful. I scrolled through my memory's Rolodex of vocal timbres to find a match until I realized the voice was mine, a quiet whisper repeating until I would listen. *Amaryllis would go.*

Candy stared at me, the skin on her forehead wrinkled into small rolls. Her eyes, normally sparkling like Sirius and Canopus in a clear dark night, were dimmed with concern. "You okay?" she asked.

"Yeah. I'll come. What time?"

ALTHOUGH I HAD often passed the blood-red and white walls of J's Cool Spot on my way to and from school, I had never been inside a bar at night. It did not look a lot different after dark, an open space with a long bar, high stools, and tables. I had never seen so many people there, though. They filled the inside, sat on the ledges of the window openings—large gaps in the color-fully painted exterior walls—and they flowed out onto the sidewalk in front of the building, a sea of green-and-yellow Independence T-shirts. Music filled every gap, pounding their backs and pushing and pulling their bodies to con-form to the rhythm. It seemed like every adult in Black River was there, old, young, Black, Chinese, Lebanese, and a handful of white tourists. For a while I worried I might run into Mr. Joseph, but after Candy shoved my first drink into my hand, a bottle of beer with ice running down the sides, thoughts of Mr. Joseph evaporated and all I felt was the beat of the music.

Candy introduced me to her friends, mainly men, who looked me up and down with appraising eyes. I felt dowdy. I had not updated my wardrobe since leaving high school. There had been no money for anything but the basics, so I had chosen a pair of plaid pedal-pushers, which sat loosely on my hips because I had lost weight in the last year. I matched them with a green shirt that covered the parts of me the pants refused to hide. I contemplated adding eyeshadow and lip gloss, but when I looked at myself in the long mirror in my bedroom at Aunt Marjorie's house and saw the plainness of my outfit, my hair, my face, I realized adding anything would only highlight how ordinary I was. On the bus to the bar, I had worried that Aunt Marjorie might wake and notice I was missing, but under the buzz of the beer, the thumping of the music, and the interest of the men jostling to grind against my hips, I filed all my cares in the back of my mind to be dealt with in the next morning's light.

"You look real criss, gyal." Hot breath blew past my right ear and I looked back to find one of Candy's friends behind me, his eyes half-closed. Candy had told me his name but I could not recall it. He pushed his body against my back and moved in time to the slow Barrington Levy tune that was blasting from the speakers. He was short—an inch or two shorter than me, and older than I was. The slight bulge of his belly fit soft and comfortable like a puzzle piece into the curve of my back. I turned forward and caught Candy's eye. She was a few feet away, dancing with a tall young man. She winked.

I closed my eyes and sank into the music, boldly matching his movements. He slowed his gyration to a seductive half beat and I followed, pushing my hips into his groin.

Barrington Levy's "Like How You Kiss and Caress Me" blasted from the speakers and my dance partner crooned the lyrics about discovered love, his mouth still close to my ear, startling my eyes open. I focused on the crowd around me for a minute and my eyes lit on a familiar body at the bar, a young man leaning over to get close to the bartender's ear, a crooked smile on his lips as he relayed his order. The long line of his body stretched over the bar, the fingers of his outstretched gesticulating hand, the long narrow face and square jaw, each one of those features was duplicated in the room plentifully, but together they could only belong to one person, Dave. I stopped moving. My partner, entranced by the music, did not notice. I blinked slowly. School was on vacation, so it was not unlikely he would be in Jamaica and in his hometown. When I opened my eyes, the bartender was dealing with another customer. The space Dave's body had filled at the bar lingered in my vision, a chalk outline. My heart rate quickened.

"I have to go," I said to the guy dancing behind me.

He gestured towards his waist and gyrated in an exaggerated circle. "You leaving this?" He smiled. He was not a bad-looking guy and might actually be nice away from the seductive influence of the music and alcohol, but all I wanted was escape.

I mustered a nod and walked away. Dave, if it was Dave, had just ordered his drinks. He would still be near the bar waiting for his order. I could walk over to the counter and look for him, find out for sure. Instead I moved in the opposite direction towards the back of the building. I entered the bathrooms and stood inside a stall. I placed my forearm against the wooden wall and let the images engulf me: Dave laughing with Amaryllis; Dave holding her hand, splashing her with water at the beach. Dave dancing close to Amaryllis, her head buried in his shoulder, his eyes piercing mine. I couldn't see her face, only his. Only Dave's. The beginning and the end of life.

I didn't fight it, didn't wrestle the memories into the ground. By now I knew the memories could find their way into oblivion if I ignored them, pretended they weren't mine to remember at all. Maybe I never had a sister, or a mother, or father. Maybe it had just been Aunt Marjorie and me all along. I lay my head on my wrist, and the pounding in my head and the pulsing of my radial artery gradually melded and slowed to match the rhythm of the bass.

"Maya?" Candy's voice echoed in the bathroom. "You there?"

I considered not answering, but the doors of the stall began about one foot off of the ground and Candy could easily bend and see my feet. In addition, I felt guilty that she had left the dancing to check on me.

"I'm in here. I'm okay." I flushed the toilet unnecessarily and exited the stall. She stood next to me as I washed my hands at a tiny sink. Her gaze rested on my face, studious as if she were reading a book. *Are my feelings really that transparent?*

"You ready fi go? I am." Candy smiled as she spoke, trying to appear flippant, as if it was no big deal that I was melting down in the bathroom, but I could see pity in her eyes. She faced me but her right foot pointed towards the door as if the music was pulling her back into the dance.

"I'm fine. Me goan be okay. Mek you stay."

"Nah. The music nah sweet tonight. Let's go."

CANDY AND I had taken separate buses to the bar, but we walked back home that night. Moonlight flooded the streets, finding corners, uncovering shadows, and I was happy to be outside, to feel the night air only slightly cooler than the daytime temperatures but cooler nonetheless. Out in the open, away from any confinement, the possibility that I had seen Dave seemed increasingly unlikely.

Our decision to walk was objectively reckless. Political turmoil was worsening as Jamaica neared the 1980 elections, and the violence that had kept me indoors at night since my last year of high school was at its peak. Gunshots added a syncopated beat to the music blasting from the bars we passed along our route, punching at least five stuttered bursts into the air during our fifteen-minute walk. The third cluster of shots rang out just as we passed a person moaning in the drains that flanked the empty roads. We hastened our steps, not stopping to investigate if the shots and the moaning were connected.

We walked along the road, sticking close to the sides in single file where there was no sidewalk, and where there was, we walked side by side. The air was heavy with the smell of salt. On a long stretch where a concrete sidewalk separated the street from the houses that crowded its edge, Candy grabbed my hand. At first I thought she was afraid, that she shared my apprehension walking the streets alone just before midnight, but her eyes were bright with emotion and her face was full of a childlike wonder. The sea hummed, a quiet roar just one street south of us, and when she swung my hand I felt renewed, as if I had discarded one skin and found that the new one was lighter in weight. My behavior tonight, drinking, flirting, dancing, was uncharacteristic of the old me in the old skin, but this me was not a complete foreigner either. She was my mirror image, a bold me, somehow brought out by the thrill of the night air. She was unafraid of shadows and ghosts. She could have faced Dave. I hoped she would stay.

Then Candy began to sing and I was transported to a memory of walking hand in hand with Amaryllis, our hands swinging while we sang a nursery rhyme. I tried to dig the image up completely, to hear Amaryllis's voice strong and clear as I was sure it must have been, but I could not. I only recalled my own voice echoing the refrain: *Tra-la-la-la-la*.

"You always so serious." Candy's voice broke into my meanderings. I reluctantly released the moment and felt the memory slipping away like pan grease descending into a kitchen sink, thickening over the water, gurgling and protesting on its way down.

"And you always so happy. How come?"

"I been sad a lot," she said. Then she shrugged. "Got tired of it." She paused, stopped, and dropped my hand. Her face was the one that grew serious. "How Mr. Joseph a treat yuh?"

I looked at Candy, trying to gauge the reason for her question.

"Don't watch me so. He's a man. I figure he's a letch. Me a hear de cashier them talking bout him. Im try anything with you?"

"No. Not really," I mumbled.

"Watch your back. Im is de type who start slow, sweet-talk you and make you feel like is you who foolish to think anything wrong with what he doing. Then im ease in when you nah watch." She laughed, the sound hard like Busta, the dark candy she told me she had been named for. "Thank God he hardly come in de Central Street store. Him nuh come near me. Maybe I'm not im type." She rubbed the back of one hand against the other, the paleness of her palm bright against her ebony skin. She laughed again. "Lucky me," she said. Then, the laugh gone, she repeated, "Lucky me."

Candy and I parted ways where Lovers Lane bifurcated into the roads that led to our respective homes. There were no streetlights along the road Candy took, but she insisted she would be fine, that everyone knew her and she would never be harmed. I believed her, believed that her upbeat disposition would keep her safe from all but the most irrational criminals. As I watched her walk away, I imagined a glow around her dark skin, blurring the edges of her body, and when I blinked to clear my vision she had disappeared into the night.

I FLOATED ON the high of the weekend for days. My new armor kept my back straight and when I looked in the mirror, the young woman who looked back had a slight smile on her face that suggested there was more to her than what was visible on the surface. Mrs. Joseph gave me a strange look when I walked in on Monday and during that day her attitude towards me shifted, her instructions requests rather than orders.

Mr. Joseph did not send me to the Central Street store the next week. I had completed my task there and the Independence celebrations, like a clot in the middle of the week, kept us busy. The stores were flooded on the Monday and Tuesday with customers, and when I finally found a moment to slip downstairs to the main floor of our store and use the phone there, I realized I did not know Candy's real name. I called, asking tentatively to speak to Candy, a question in my voice, and the woman on the other end replied, "She? She don't work here no more." I felt deflated. If the woman hadn't acknowledged Candy's existence in her response, I might have wondered if I imagined her entirely. But she had been there, a supernova, an intense presence in my life then gone, collapsing into a hole, though the residual brilliance she left behind persisted all week.

THAT SUNDAY, I entered the kitchen to find Aunt Marjorie sitting at the table. A cup of tea, so newly poured that steam wisped in lusty gusts into the air, sat unattended, drips of liquid leaking down the gray enamel sides as if the cup had been dropped onto its saucer. She held the Sunday newspaper in her hand. She looked up when I entered the room.

"Sorry, sweetie," she said. She shoved the newspaper across the Formica-covered surface with enough force that it almost tore against the table's metal frame.

I read it standing. My finger traced the list of names, the top fifty performers in A-levels in the country, my heart falling as I scanned the list then surging when I saw my name at the very top. There were three people with the same results, but my name was first. I had outscored them all; my three As in Math, Accounting, and English topped the list as if the accomplishment belonged to the whole country.

I looked up at Aunt Marjorie, wondering why she did not share the joy that made me want to rush out of the room and leap into the sky, into the freedom I knew would come with the island scholarship.

I looked at the paper again. The article to the right of the exam results was titled "1980 Island Scholar" and showed the photo of a stranger, a glasses-wearing boy, shiny and well-groomed except for some visible hand-me-down wear in the tips of his shirt collar. I placed a hand on the table to stay myself from tumbling forward. The Formica felt red-hot under my fingertips.

"It's okay," I said. "Ain't is what you said would happen? It's what I expected."

Auntie nodded. I waited for her usual words of wisdom, the intermittent drippings that had fallen from her lips serendipitously and sustained me over the last year, an assurance that this was God's will and there was another blessing, a bigger blessing, waiting for me to grasp just around the corner, but she was silent. She blew into her tea, holding the cup with two hands as if to keep them steady—the cup and her nerves. She held it so tightly I thought she might crush it.

I walked past her, pushed open the back door, and exited into the back garden. It had rained the night before, one of those drenching downpours that sounded like the end of the world. The smell of salt was thick in the air, cloying like hands clinging to me, holding me to this land I so wanted to leave. I pulled at a leaf, and the entire plant emerged from the waterlogged soil, the roots moving with the desperate swing of someone hanging on to life by a slippery edge. I grabbed at another plant then another, holding them in my fists, crushing the leaves to release their failed magic. A pair of arms enveloped me from behind, as much to stem my destruction of the garden as to embrace me. Aunt Marjorie stood, pulling me to my feet with her. It was the first time she had held me since dispensing the herbs that had subdued my nightmares. I let myself tilt backwards into her arms. I let a few tears fall.

THAT TUESDAY, THE third time Mr. Joseph approached me, I had figured out his strategy: to keep me off-balance, make me wonder why he was not pursuing me, make me doubt my self-worth so that I was relieved to receive his attention. Candy's words, her description of the way he waylaid women, stayed in my mind. I recalled his words, "We could help each other," and weighed that against the impossibility of remaining forever in Black River. I was ready for him. Taking advantage of an after-Independence sale, I had put my savings into a tape recorder, promising myself that the investment would pay for itself. The red Record button was smaller than the others, so it was easy to identify it, to isolate it through the thin vinyl of my handbag and depress it when he made his pass. I let him kiss me. I protested at first then moaned in response. I made him speak the things he wanted to do to me, his longing to feel my brown body against his. I giggled a sound like water falling pure and transparent onto rusted galvanize then running off tainted, brown, and unsavory.

"MR. AND MRS. Joseph paying me way to St. Augustine in September."

Aunt Marjorie's eyes widened. I could almost see the thoughts going through her head, evaluating the reasons the Josephs might decide to make such a generous contribution to an employee. "Really?" she said when she finally spoke.

"Yes." I twisted the rubber band, now a permanent fixture around my wrist.

"I see," Aunt Marjorie responded. We stood in the kitchen, the table at which we had shared many meals and discussions now a chasm between us. She had rescued me, supported me, comforted me, taught me, but in that moment, looking at her rigid stance and calculating expression, I felt like I was looking across the room at someone I had just met.

"You have more to say?" I asked.

"I'm happy for you. This is what you wanted. This is what I been praying for."

THE RUSH TO get ready to leave for Trinidad allowed me to suppress judgment on what I had done to get to this point. Aunt Marjorie must have known the Josephs would not send me to school without some sort of return on their investment. But she said nothing, she who was the overseer of right from wrong, of dignity and purity. I convinced myself that her silence meant that what I had done, leading Mr. Joseph on, touching his sinuous skin, then twisting it all back to attack him, was not so bad. Or that she understood that I did what I had to do to escape, and she was willing to turn a blind eye, to let the value of the ends outweigh whatever path led to them.

For months, until I was able to push the episode with Mr. Joseph out of my mind's reach, I remembered his reaction when I played him the tape I had made of us together.

"Me nah go end up like your father, in a mug shot in the papers in my underwear."

That sentence had almost derailed my plan to execute my takedown calmly. I could still see my father's photo in the newspapers, looking defeated the way I had seen in many mug shots before. Before my father's fall, I had studied grainy newspaper photos of criminals and wondered how anyone could ever have trusted these faces. How could they not have seen their evil nature lurking so obviously in their expressions? When I saw my father in their place, in his undershirt, uncombed, I realized it may have been fear and shock rather than guilt that I had seen in all their eyes. When Mr. Joseph let my father's name fall from his lips, I wanted to scratch his face and scar him, make him hideous, make him suffer as I had. I believed he deserved to be in that mug shot more than my father did, but my rage was reserved near-equally for them both.

CHAPTER THIRTY-TWO

Black River, Jamaica - September 2003

I don't recall how I made it out of Raquel's house and texted Donovan to take me back to the hotel. On the drive back, I sat with my eyes tightly shut, imagining Candy that night, her brilliant eyes shining, caring. *What became of her?* I wondered. I thought of Candy so I did not have to think about my blackmail and subterfuge. I did not know how to process my actions so they fit in with the person I was now. Had I been pushed into blackmailing Mr. Joseph, or was I a pure opportunist? No wonder I never finished university. As Aunt Marjorie would have said, "What start bad a mornin' cyan end good a evenin'." But my story had been going well . . . until now.

Back in bed in the hotel, I tossed and turned. Despite all I had remembered, I really was not much closer to finding out about Amaryllis or my parents, or why I was alive and they were not. My father was some sort of a criminal, it seemed. He had backed the wrong political party and ended up in prison. My belief that my parents had died when I was an infant was inaccurate, a fable I had concocted to survive whatever the truth was. *What's left when everything you believe about your genesis is taken away?* I needed more answers and made up my mind to follow my next lead, the aunt I supposedly had at Gambit Boutique.

I had paid Donovan so handsomely for our day together that he actually smiled when we parted ways and asked, "Yuh need a ride tomorrow, Miss Lin?"

Then, unsure of my plans, I had said no, but once I made up my mind to check out Ms. Kathryn Gordon, I texted him and asked him to pick me up at ten.

I PUSHED ON the buzzer and smiled up at the security camera on the door-jamb. The echo buzzer sounded, and I pushed the door open. Cool air rushed past me, beating a hasty retreat from the gloomy atmosphere into which I stepped. I supposed the dim lighting with spotlights on the clothes was meant to suggest exclusivity, like some of the trendier stores in the United States, but somehow it did not quite hit the mark. I walked past several displays and racks of dresses, blouses, skirts in an array of colors and styles, all made from flowing silky materials. I was the only customer and the young woman who was tending the store must have sized me up as an unlikely prospect, because she did not once look up or offer me help.

"Is Mrs. . . . Ms. Gordon here?" I asked.

The young woman sighed heavily before she lifted her head to look at me. Her eyes widened slightly in surprise. "Miss Gordon not here, but she go come back soon."

My disappointment or maybe it was desperation must have been obvious because she reached under the counter and held out a small rectangular piece of paper.

"Here's her card. You could call her."

I stepped forward to take the card, getting close enough to the young woman that the smell of her perfume immersed me. The scent was so famil-iar. I sensed a memory awakening, moving towards me like a fast-approaching thunderstorm, dark, full, and unavoidable.

Black River, Jamaica - June 1979

I was curled in the middle of a queen-sized bed. The house was empty. There were sounds, things moving, creaking, rattling, whistling, echoing sporadically through the walls, but the only human sound was my breathing. I wanted it to stop—not my breathing, not then, but the other noises. I wanted rhythm, structure, normalcy. A second bed was in the room, a twin bed, the source of spaces in my world, shadows in the room. I curled into a tighter ball. I moved closer to the wall.

I was alone in the world.

Just days before, the house had been filled with voices, people crying, laughing, eating, stomping in and out of the living room, resting plates of food and un-coastered drinks on the furniture. Chaos. I said nothing. I did not chastise them for their carelessness. I had not wanted them to stay but I had not wanted them to go, to leave me in the quiet, alone with the house.

A door opened downstairs and a strong scent of lavender found me all the way up in my bedroom. I felt nausea, loathing. I ran out of the bedroom and to the bathroom. I emptied the contents of my stomach into the sink.

"Amaya? Oh, sweetheart." My aunt entered the bathroom and placed a hand on my back. I wriggled away from her touch and turned so that my next hurl landed in the toilet but not without some soiling the seat.

"The sink was already dirty. You had to mess up the toilet too?"

That reaction was more in character with my Aunt Kathryn—never Auntie and never Kathy.

She bent and opened the cupboard beneath the sink to retrieve cleaning supplies. She turned on the tap full force and began to clean my vomit from the sink, all the while holding her body, clothed in a light-colored linen dress, as far away from the mess as possible. I closed the toilet seat and sat on it. Worn.

"Jesus, Amaya," Aunt Kathryn said. "I know you had a terrible shock, but if you think I going and clean up behind you indefinitely . . ." Her voice trailed off.

A number of retorts came to mind, but I had no fight in me. All I wanted was to return to bed, but her perfume, so strong, so familiar, filled me with so much longing, and I was not sure I would not throw up again. I tried to remember if lavender had always been her scent and I just had not noticed because whenever I spent time with her my mother was always there, or if she had raided my mother's belongings and bathed herself in the scent, seeking her own form of comfort.

"When you come to town, you'll have to fend for yourself. I never had to mind a child before, and I have a business to run."

I nodded then slid off the seat to my knees in front of the toilet. This time I aimed better.

"Oh, Amaya. It's going to be all right." She patted me on the back again as I heaved. My stomach was now empty, and it seemed to be trying to expel my organs.

When I was able to speak, I said, "I can't leave."

I did not want to live with my aunt. I had unpleasant memories of our visits to her house in Kingston. My dad refused to drive the three-hour trip and would hire a taxi to take us. He sat in the front, engaging the driver in conversation, usually about politics, while my sister, my mother, and I sat in the back. The last time was in 1973. I was eleven. The back of the car was hot even with the windows turned down and I sat in the middle, fidgety and itchy in the dress my mother had insisted I wear. The back of my legs sweated where they rested against the vinyl seat. My mother was visibly pregnant and uncomfortable. By the time we arrived in Kingston, she had to be rushed to the hospital. We spent three days at my aunt's house, tiptoeing around its museum-like interior filled with things children were not allowed to touch. I played a game in my head that each time I entered a room and did not disturb or break anything, I was buying my mother some grace from God and hastening her return from the hospital. When she finally came home, no longer pregnant, her eyes withdrawn as if searching, hoping to rekindle the life that had been growing inside of her, I had pleaded with God never to make me have to stay in that house again.

"You can't stay here, Amaya," Aunt Kathryn said, interrupting my reverie. "You're only seventeen and everyone . . ." She paused, and I knew she was searching her mind for the right euphemism. That's what everyone had been doing for days, whispering words and phrases like "lost," "gone," "passed," but more often "resting now," "at peace." If death was such a comfortable place then why should I stay here? I considered banging my head against the toilet seat until my forehead bled, my skull cracked, and my brains seeped out for Aunt Kathryn to clean up. But I was not strong enough.

"Everyone is gone," Aunt Kathryn completed her sentence.

I emptied some more of my insides into the toilet.

"It's been three weeks. We have to go," she pleaded. "This hard for me too, you know."

This isn't hard, I wanted to say. Hard was failing a test, breaking a bone. I'd lost everyone I cared about. We needed another word for that. But I just looked at her and maybe she understood, because her voice softened.

"It's hard, but we have to go. It's temporary. Patsy—" She stopped as if the word had tripped on something on its way out of her mouth. "They going to look after your mother. Besides, I'm sure she'll get better after she has the baby. We'll visit every week until she's well enough for you to come back."

I looked up from where I sat on the floor and wondered if she was serious. Had she not seen what I had seen on our last visit to my mother in the asylum? She had been sitting in a colorful armchair in the corner of her room in the Eventide Home, staring out the window into the garden. From the door, I could see a rock dove on her windowsill. Most of its body was a pale color, closer to a dirty white than gray, but its neck, which it held upright in a proud display, was covered in iridescent green and pink feathers. It cocked its head, turning one orange eye towards my mother as if trying to decide what to make of the woman inside, how to interpret her motionlessness in the face of his obvious beauty. It hopped closer along the sill, then raised its wings and lofted itself out of sight. My mother never moved.

I had crossed the distance from the door to her side and sank to my knees in front of her chair.

"Mom?" I said, unable to reconcile this aged woman with the person who had managed a household and a business just a few weeks before. This woman looked like someone who had been pushed down a steep slide into a bottomless pool and had chosen not to even flounder or try to pull herself up to the top. Her cheeks sunk in, forming deep creases on either side of her lips like permanent dimples but without any trace of a smile. Above her cheeks, dark smudges shadowed the skin, making her eyes look as if they had sunk deep into their sockets in their attempt to unsee the horrible scene that had sent her into this dark place. Her hair seemed thinner, individual strands visible, easily counted. Had it always been so gray? I placed my head in her lap, barely finding space between the edge of her pregnant belly and the end of her knees.

"Mom," I said again. Tears flowed from my eyes, and I lifted my head so that I would not soak the cotton nightgown she wore.

Her eyes were watery and unfocused. She looked in my direction, but she was not really seeing me. I thought of the times I had dived deep into the ocean and for a moment, just before rising and gasping for air, looking up to see the sun and the clouds wavering and realizing I could make them look like whatever I wanted. I wondered if that was what she was doing, forming a kind, beautiful world in her mind, a world where she had not lost so much. Despite her dramatic deterioration, I envied my mother. I wished I could descend into my head and produce my own version of my life, in which my family still existed as a unit surrounding me. Then anger replaced envy. She was protecting herself, protecting the baby still in her womb. How could she leave me behind?

"Mom?" I was more insistent now. I wanted her to see me. If I had to be on this side of reality, I needed her with me. I grasped her by her upper arms; they were thinner than I recalled, already having lost some of the fleshiness that had engulfed me in hugs not long ago. I was afraid to hurt her, so fragile she seemed, yet I shook her, gently at first then more violently.

"Mom!"

Her eyes widened and she looked at me. She saw me, I could tell. She opened her mouth and ran her tongue over her dry, cracked lips, but it provided little moisture. She cleared her throat and reached a hand towards my face.

"Amaryllis," she said. "My sweet Mari."

I fled from the room. I pushed past Aunt Kathryn and did not stop running until I was outside, leaning against her car. I heaved and heaved, trying to slow my breathing. My mother had always been the one on my side. From the day we were born, Amaryllis had demanded all the attention in the room, and my mother had been the one to ensure that there was space for me, space for my accomplishments to shine, space for me to be loved. She had been my gift, mine. I was the one left behind, but I was not who she wanted. The scent of my skin searing on the sun-scorched bonnet of the car smelled like betrayal.

IN THE BATHROOM that afternoon, I wanted to tell Aunt Kathryn that her sister-in-law was gone, trapped where she had fallen, and returning would be an impossible climb. I did not expect my mother to return to me, and neither would I return to visit her. Right then, I decided that I would never visit her in my memory either. From that moment, I decided, I had no mother.

A knock at the front door, sharp and businesslike, prevented me from having to find the words to explain my decision to Aunt Kathryn. I thought it was the police, come to set right the impossible wrong that had stopped my life as I knew it, but then again, police in Jamaica were not reliable that way.

Aunt Kathryn said, "I coming back. Rinse your mouth, I beg you, and start putting your things in a bag. Please. I really can't take being here another minute."

Left in the bathroom alone, I cleaned myself up then made my way to the top of the stairs and looked over the banister to see who was at the door.

I heard a familiar voice: Marjorie James, a woman who lived in our neighborhood. Auntie Marj, as all the children on the street called her to her face. She was a tall woman, large and stately, an early widow. Parents trusted her; she knew what was happening in every household and ruled the few streets of our neighborhood, one hand an iron fist and the other hand open with generosity. We called her "Strictly Decent" behind her back, but there was only affection in the term. Many of the girls in Black River aspired to her height and her posture. She had taught all of us at one time or another, either in school, or later, after her early retirement, at the kitchen table in her house for extra lessons.

I wondered what she wanted. The stream of visitors had almost dried up by then. There was a time when I would have hoped she was bringing over one of her famous pies, an unusual vegetable combined with minced meat and topped with a mix of bread crumbs and grated cheddar cheese. But that day, the thought of food was untenable.

My knees grew weak as I waited. Aunt Kathryn was talking for a long time, which suggested to me that this was not just a food drop-off. I wanted to know what was going on. I sensed it was about me.

Aunt Kathryn stepped back inside and stopped when she saw me at the top of the stairs. Mrs. James, who had been directly behind her, stopped just in time to prevent a collision between her breasts and Aunt Kathryn's back.

"Come down, Amaya. Miss James wants to say something to you."

Steadying myself with the railings, I descended, trying not to think of a time before when I had walked down these stairs, the only problem in my life my annoyance at having to spend an evening with Amaryllis and Dave entwined in each other's arms. I joined the two women in the small open area between the door and the bottom of the stairs, next to the empty umbrella stand. The space was small, and I fought not to react to Aunt Kathryn's perfume. I focused instead on Mrs. James's breathing, steady, even.

"Good morning, Amaya," Aunt Marjorie said. "Your aunt and I have been discussing the possibility of you living with me."

"What?" I said.

Aunt Kathryn spoke. "Miss James suggested that you live with her instead of moving to town. That way, you can finish sixth form without disruption. You'd be close to your mother as well."

I sank down onto the bottom stair. As much as I did not want to live with my aunt in Kingston, I was not sure I wanted to stay in Black River, where my present would never become my past. I would never escape the pitying stares, the questions posed to my face, and the fingers pointing at me behind my back. Our house had already become local legend. If I stayed, I would be a part of that spectacle.

"You don't have to run way," Mrs. James said. "They won't forget but they'll soon stop talking and you will heal. Better you face it here. I'm living alone. We can keep each other company . . . for as long as you need me."

"I agree." Aunt Kathryn had found an option that involved neither my living with her nor her abandoning me, and she seemed determined not to let it slip away. "That's it, then. You'll move in with Miss James, and she will keep an eye on you. I'll check on you soon."

CHAPTER THIRTY-THREE

Black River, Jamaica - September 2003

The tinkling of the bell of the door to Aunt Kathryn's store pulled me out of my vision, but before I could even begin to process all I had remembered, someone entered the store and announced, "I'm back." The voice was melodic with a tinge of fake syrup, reminding me of a villain from one of Taiwo's favorite Disney movies.

The woman who entered the store was slightly taller than me, statuesque, wearing a flowing black and purple top that draped over her frame, granting her an air of regality. She looked at me and stopped moving. I stared as well. It was not like I was looking in a mirror, but it was obvious that the woman and I shared a common ancestor. One of her hands flew to her neck. Her chest heaved, then she shook herself slightly and lowered her arm.

"So, you finally come to look for your aunt," she said.

When I did not respond, she came forward, her arms open to envelop me in a hug. I did not move. I focused all of my energy on staying present in the moment even as the scent of her lavender perfume pulled me towards the past.

"You can't be vex with me," she said. "You run way to America and never look back."

"You left me with Aunt Marjorie. Did you ever come back?"

"I couldn't come to Black River. After everything . . . I couldn't come back. Then when Mrs. James told me you went to school in Trinidad, I figure is best to leave you be."

"But my mother had the baby. And you came back for her. You came back for Angela. My sister Angela." The words felt unexpectedly normal on my tongue.

"She was a baby."

"I was only seventeen."

"I did what I could, Maya. I raised her. She could have stayed and worked with me to run the shop, but she wanted to go to America so badly I let her go. Then when things fell apart in New York, I told her about you."

"She didn't know about me before?"

"What would I tell her? From the time she turn a teenager, I couldn't control her. She was running round with some real vagabond, talking common, not taking on her schoolwork. If I had told her about you, she would have wanted to leave long time. And I was right. Since I told her about you, she has not called me even once. But I'm glad she found you." Her voice softened. "She was all I had of your parents."

"What happened to my mother?" I asked, brushing past the selfish motivation my aunt was so readily admitting.

"Oh, Maya, that's all in the past. Let it rest." She stepped closer and I stepped back. "You look like you've done well. Let the dead bury the dead."

"What happened to my mother?" I repeated. I pressed my nails into my palms to keep me from sinking to my knees with the exhaustion I felt.

"She is dead. Talking about it will not bring her back." She inhaled deeply and her carefully penciled-in eyebrows drew close together. She seemed to tower even higher over me but I remained unfazed.

"Did she die in the Eventide fire?"

Aunt Kathryn pressed her palms against the sides of her face. She squeezed her eyes shut for a moment, and when she opened them, she spoke with a slow, quiet intensity. "Are you hard of hearing? I will not talk about this. Get out, Amaya. Get out." She never raised her voice, but I heard the threat behind her words and I obeyed. Donovan's face was filled with concern when I exited Aunt Kathryn's store.

"Yuh look like you a see duppy. Come, drink some water. I have bottle in the car," he said.

"Thanks. I'm okay . . . I know this is a big ask, but can you take me back to Black River?"

"Black River?" he echoed, his brow furrowed as he looked at his watch. "If we leave now, we not goin get dere until two. You a stay long down dere?"

"I don't know for sure."

"We go have to leave by four so night don't catch we pon de road."

"Please, Donovan. I have to do this."

He took off his cap, scratched his head, and put it back on, pulling the visor low on his face.

"All right. Mek we gwan."

I had to see the house I had just envisaged. Raquel had mentioned knowing my home, and from my remembering, assuming it was memory and not a dream, it was clear that while the photo of Aunt Marjorie and I holding hands was real, it was a single photo that I had stretched and pulled like a thick rubber band to encircle the ten years between the time it was taken and the point, when I was seventeen, when Aunt Marjorie had actually taken me in. And my mother. I dropped my head into my hands. I pictured her in the chair, her mind so unhinged by loss it had caused her to abandon her children: me, and the one growing in her belly. I thought of Angela. She really was my sister.

I strained to recall my mother before she'd ended up in the Eventide Home, to imagine her stroking my hair or holding my hand to cross the road, but nothing came. I had to finish this. I had to face it all, and somehow I knew the only way was to go to the place where it all started, my childhood home. I closed my eyes and fell into a dreamless sleep in the back of the taxi.

By the time we arrived at Aunt Marjorie's old house, I felt better, energized by the nap. I ran up the driveway and pounded on the door with the old knocker. I hoped I was in time to catch Raquel before she went to work. She came to the door in a white nurse's uniform, one hand holding the cap she had been in the process of pinning on.

"Wha gwan, Maya?" Her surprise was obvious in her expression. "I was just leaving for work."

"I know this is a strange question, but can you tell me where my parents' house was?"

She tilted her head slightly to the left. Something in my eyes, or maybe the memory of the haunted look that must have been on my face when I left her house the day before, must have stemmed her usual gregariousness.

"On Zinnia. I'm not surprised you never recognize it. They change it so much, paint it pink. And is a business now, car rental. Go down there so, then turn left."

I walked in the direction in which she pointed and up to the house she had described. It was a concrete monstrosity with pink walls that butted right up against the brick enclosure surrounding the property. *This can't be it,* I thought. This building did not trigger even the slightest memory. I walked to the steps painted in white and stood looking up towards the door. I closed my eyes, trying to imagine myself as a child running up these steps, sitting on them, playing a game. The sound of the door opening startled me. I looked up. A man stood in the doorway, a silhouette as he had not yet stepped all the way outside. He reached down and pulled something out of a tall vase. The item he removed was long and slim, and the memory it evoked sliced into me like a sword . . . I was in the right place.

Black River, Jamaica - May 1979

I was seventeen when my father bought the gun.

I was afraid of the violence that plagued Jamaica. People were being shot in the streets, and our parents, who had been models of bravery all our lives, hunkered down. They drove us to and from school, no longer allowing us to stroll home with friends to stretch and unwind after a long day of sitting in classes while trying to understand the relationships between our schoolwork and the world we were experiencing. When we complained about our movements being restricted, my dad would say, "A bullet don't need your name on it to find your head."

This sort of talk about guns and death had become quite normal around our house. While my father found fault with both of the warring political parties, he supported Edward Seaga's Jamaica Labor Party and abhorred what he saw as the socialist policies of our Prime Minister, Michael Manley.

On evenings when we gathered after dinner to watch the news, Daddy punctuated the newscasts with his own commentary.

"Dem two politicians. They supposed to be leaders, setting example, but they start dis fight in the streets and nobody want to stand down even though all of we tired of it."

"They love watching people fight over them," my mother added. "Remember how they had look pon the stage with Bob Marley?"

I remembered watching the Freedom Concert on TV, Bob Marley's last concert in Jamaica. He called our two political leaders onto the stage, practically shamed them into coming forward. I understood their reluctance to climb the stairs and expose themselves to the crowds. Someone had made an attempt on Marley's life just a year before, so being on a stage with him in front of thousands of people must have felt as dangerous as walking through downtown Kingston naked. As I watched, my heart caught in my throat, even though I was not watching it live and I knew that it ended without incident. Manley stood on Marley's left, and Seaga on his right. The musician raised their hands in the air as if he were declaring them victorious in a race. The gesture was meant to be unifying, but the handshake between the two leaders was tentative and their smiles cold enough to freeze a block of ice in the Jamaican heat. Their reluctance to interact, to show camaraderie in a moment when Jamaica's consummate hero requested it, spoke volumes, and the strife continued.

"They could stop this," my father said. "Jail all of them who a threaten us. They know who they are. But they won't do nothing."

My mother picked up the story. "And meantime, people can't get no groceries. You shoulda see de shelf dem today. Empty!" She nodded at me for confirmation, and I nodded back.

That scared me most: the scarcity of groceries. Every time we passed a store, the lines of people seemed to outnumber the quantity of items on the nearly bare shelves. We could hide, maybe dodge bullets, but what if food ran out? What if my mother's ability to avoid the long lines by paying extra for flour and potatoes no longer kept our shelves stocked and we ended up starving like the children I had seen in Save the Children ads on TV, with ribs so close to the surface of the skin that it seemed only moments before they pierced through?

"You have people starving here, too," Amaryllis said when I confided my fears later that evening. She was frustrated with my parents' adherence to what she saw as their bourgeois status, and tired of being forced by association to participate in their response to the political turmoil. She wanted to rebel, to don army boots and stand with the masses who were demanding a more equal distribution of wealth. "Don't bother listen to Mommy and Daddy. They grow up dirt poor. Some days Mommy never know what she was going to eat. Is like she forget is the same socialist policies she afraid to support now that give she an education and put her where she is today, able to look down her nose at poor people."

"They don't hate poor people," I said, but I said it quietly. I knew there was no arguing with Amaryllis, especially since she had started dating Dave, whose family supported Manley's PNP. I recognized there were flaws in my parents' views but that made them conflicted, not bad people.

"You think just because they support Garvey and make we wear our hair natural for a likkle bit, that they side wit everyone here a yard? They could talk, until is time to give up any of their precious money."

"They pay Anne-Marie son school fee," I countered. Anne-Marie had been our helper for as long as I could remember and a part of the family, as far as I was concerned. "They just don't like nobody to tell them what to do with their money."

"So the poor man must suffer while they living in luxury?"

"Those people should work. Pull themself up instead of looking for hand-outs. You know Mommy and Daddy worked hard. Whatever we have—what they have—it wasn't no handout."

"Listen to you, eh?'Those people.'" She mocked my intonation. "Dave was right. You're so naive, Maya."

My face grew hot at the thought that she and Dave had been discussing me.

"Dave, Dave, Dave. I tired hearing bout Dave. Is like you don't have a single thought of your own anymore," I shouted.

"At least I have a man."

I wondered if she had any idea how deep a wound her words cut.

THEN ONE NIGHT, the lawlessness came too close to home for any of us to deny.

"Why you come home so late tonight, Daddy?" Amaryllis asked.

There was a beat, a quick one, just long enough to fit in the pulse of a heart. There was a challenge in Amaryllis's voice; there frequently was when she spoke to my father. The relationship between her and our dad, which had always been indulgent on both sides, had grown increasingly combative as the political situation worsened. They challenged each other on every issue, and somehow I had been promoted to the role of favorite child.

That night, however, the tension was all external. We sat in the living room, the TV uncharacteristically silent, my father in his armchair, and Amaryllis and I on the green-and-yellow floral-patterned couch, curled into our mother as a pair of cubs might snuggle with a lioness when night fell. On another night, the scene would resemble a standoff, my mother's body a shield between us and our father's verbal tirades. That night, Daddy was in a cheerful mood, equally loquacious and magnanimous, and I felt safe, protected, in part because my father was happy and in part because of the presence of the gun. It stood at his side, balanced on the handle, his finger on the top of the barrel as if daring it to fire. The pose was a sign of my father's boldness in the face of danger. He would not be intimidated. He would protect his pride.

He told us how three men came into his office that day. They burst in the door, brandishing guns and demanding money.

"I don't know what they expected," he continued. "Since this madness start, nobody in they right mind keep cash in they office, except a little vex money to appease the tief dem."

"You was scared, Daddy?" Amaryllis asked.

"I was worried bout Janice. She had been in the outer office, working. I never hear nothing before the tief dem bust in. I was worried they had hurt her. And they nah wear no mask, so I know they didn't plan to leave no witness. I look bout the office for a weapon."

I searched his office in my memory as he told the story. I hunted the cherrywood desk, which would be covered in neat piles of papers, some held down with picture frames filled with images of us at various vacation spots in Jamaica and in Philadelphia, where his sister lived. The boxy monitor on his desk could act as both a shield and an object to shove into an approaching attacker. A "Small Businessman of the Year" trophy from the Chamber of Commerce, tall, wooden, was a potential stake. My father had survived the encounter. He was sitting uninjured just feet away from me. I could reach out and touch him, verify his aliveness, yet I felt a deepening of the fear that had been building in my gut since the first gunshots rang out in our neighborhood.

"They look round my office," my father continued. "Put their filthy hand dem over me desk, open de drawer dem, de cupboard, pull down de painting dem looking for safe. 'You thought I was rich?' me ask them. I laughed at them. 'Nobody rich no more.' I spoke to them so they could understand. 'Oonu done tek way everything, destroy everything. Everybody leaving, nobody building. I in construction, so what dat leave fi me? Nutting.'" His voice had a sharp edge that cut into the fabric of my being.

Do we really have nothing? I wondered. I had never before contemplated the implications of the stories I had heard of people fleeing and selling their houses for cents on the dollar, or simply abandoning beautifully opulent houses. My stomach churned with fear. I swallowed hard and fought to keep the rising bile down. My mother would force me to take a teaspoon of castor oil if I complained of a stomachache or nausea, no matter how I explained that the smell made my symptoms even worse.

"Don't worry, sweethearts," my father said with a laugh in response to the concern that must have shown on my face. "Election coming next year. Jamaicans will come round. We can't fight up with ourselves forever. Something haffe give, and somebody haffe be here to sweep when the dust sekkle. That going to be me. Meantime we just a wait."

I realized now the real reason we had not gone on vacation to the US that year and the reason our parents said "no" much more readily than they had in the past. It had been easy to ignore the changes as the external trimmings stayed in place. Amaryllis and I continued to attend extracurricular activities, we kept our household helper, and my mom dressed like the wife of a successful businessman. Looking back, I saw the stress this had placed on our household, stress that had been increased by the fact that our mother was pregnant again at forty-two.

"They had guns?" Amaryllis's face was filled with awe rather than fear.

"Yes," my father replied, then he recounted how one of the men had held a gun to his face and demanded that he hand over all of the cash in the office.

"I asked them if me look stupid. 'With oonu tief around,' I said, 'me keep me money in the bank.' They didn't believe me. They search again, throwing everything on me desk, inna me desk, on de walls, they throw everything pon de floor. One youth, not more dan twenty, he eye dem red with ganja and rage, lean inna me face. 'Ah lie dat. You a Jamaican,' im say. 'You don't trust no bank.

Yuh must ave likkle something hide away here so. You think is joke I making? Save yuh life. Show we where de money be.'"

My father insisted that he had nothing, and they said they would give him a chance but return the following week for cash. My father told them that no matter when they came and how often they came, he wasn't giving them anything.

"Then they threaten you girls." His eyes darkened now, and for the first time in his recounting, I saw real anger in his eyes. "They know where oonu go a school; a what time you left; a who pick you up; a what time you have piano, Maya; the teacher name; and when oonu go dance class. Dat's why they nah bother wear no mask dem. They nah fraid me." He looked at my mother. "They know you're pregnant." His voice faltered.

No one dared speak in the silence that settled in the room. This was my mother's fourth pregnancy since Amaryllis and I had been born, at least the fourth that had survived long enough for us to know about it.

So my father caved and told them to come back the following week and he would have the money. He told us how he was calm on the inside, but roaring like a lion inside at the audacity of these men to even carry the names of his girls in their mouths.

My mother spoke, a tremble in her voice I had never heard before. "We have to leave, Horace. I been telling you this for months. We can't ignore it no more. This is madness. You don't hear sey how last week somebody tell on Ted and Joan? They tell the police how they been hollowing out their Bible and stuffing it with money to send to America. Now Ted lock way in jail and Joan don't know what to do. And now they threatening we children? We children, Horace?" She rested her hands on the slight bulge in her belly. When she spoke again, her voice was softer, calmer, the voice she used when she had made up her mind and would not be swayed. "We have likkle bit of money stash way up there. We could stay with your sister in Philly. Until we sekkle. She already said so. She begging us to come."

I tried to picture myself in the United States, sitting in the dimly lit living room in my cousin's house, struggling to get enough air in their house with its windows that seemed to be permanently shut. Sleeping on the mattress they laid out on the floor of my cousin's oversized bedroom, going to school with her friends, who always seemed to be laughing at some joke I did not quite understand. I could not decide which fear was more potent, gunmen in Jamaica or a trip to the US without the comforting knowledge of a fixed date for our return.

"You see me doing some menial job up there in America?" my father snapped. "See me doing janitor work? Bus driver? Man with university degree digging in the hot sun in somebody else yard? No sah. You gwan. Run. I not going nowhere. These people, these lazy, money-grabbing anarchists. These socialist." He said the word as if it was the worst of a long line of horrible curses. "They not getting nothing I work hard to earn. Not one cent." My dad's voice rang out, bouncing off the china cabinet filled with the china and crystal my mother had accumulated over the years.

"That's not fair, Daddy. You here living in big house, owning all the businesses, sucking poor people, poor Black people, dry, and not giving them no chance to prosper. No wonder we taking up arms to take back what's ours."

"Oh? You one of them now? You planning to go tief and kill and smoke ganja?"

"Not every poor person doing drugs."

"And I not Black too? I don't know what it is to be poor? I been poor. I know how to work hard though." He let out a sharp breath. "All this coming from that boy you friending. That Dave. How he feel bout you driving bout inna me car and eating me food when your poor people suffering so, eh?"

I felt movement next to me and when I looked to my left, I saw that my mother had placed a hand on Amaryllis's leg, calming and restraining in one gesture. Amaryllis's body was rigid, but she did not speak.

My dad's hand shook as he placed it on the upturned barrel of the gun.

He turned it over and I noticed it was old, caked with dirt. The gun had a history, and I wondered where my father had acquired it. He slammed the barrel onto the ground.

"This is how I dealing with them robbers. They think me a puppy? A scared mongrel? This will show them—every dog have teeth and could bite."

"I don't want no gun in this house," my mother said. "Suppose somebody break in and shoot one of we with it? Is better we leave. Come back when things calm down."

"Me nah keep it inna the house. It'll stay in my office. For when they come back."

"And what you going do then, eh? You going kill somebody child? Is better we leave, me a say." She stood, her body between my father and us girls.

Amaryllis and I huddled together in the indentation left in the spot on the couch my mother had abandoned. We put our arms around each other. I held her as the shaking brought on by her anger at my father's words subsided. Then she stroked my hair for the first time in years, and for a moment I was transported back to simpler times when we were young and I understood our relative positions in the world. She was my protector, and I was still afraid that one day she would tire of the job, that she would expect me to grow up and defend myself.

The men never returned to my father's office to follow up on their threat. They were bound to have heard that he had armed himself, and perhaps they found easier marks. Perhaps they had been among the fatalities we read about in the newspapers every day. As the event receded into our rear view, my mother stopped agitating about leaving Jamaica. A few weeks later, without any discussion, my father brought the gun home and stood it in the umbrella basket just inside our front door. It blended right in and I soon forgot it was there, except on the days when he had a new audience and pulled out the tale of the holdup to showcase how he had triumphed over evil in the troubling times in which we lived.

CHAPTER THIRTY-FOUR

I looked at Amaryllis's reflection in our bedroom mirror. Her makeup was perfect. Her face powder smoothed the edges of her skin into an even surface. On my face, the powder sought out every ridge, sliding into it and caking in, emphasizing the unevenness of my skin. But I still put it on.

School was on vacation, and we were relegated to spending our days entertaining ourselves in the house. Although two months had passed since the attempted robbery of my father's office, the political and economic situation remained tense, and our parents maintained tight control of our movements. My father questioned every request, especially if there was money involved, weighing its benefit against his dwindling business prospects. But their main concern remained our safety.

The intensity of their protectiveness was higher that night. Our mother had tried to renege on her agreement to let us go out and had only acquiesced to Amaryllis because Christine's father was picking us up, driving us the mile to their house, and bringing us back before ten.

I did not want to go.

Although Amaryllis had not mentioned his name, I knew from the care with which she chose her dress, made up her face, and spritzed on her birthday perfume that Dave would be there, and I would spend the evening talking with Christine or fending off her brother's advances. He was fascinated by the idea that he and his best friend would be "doing" twins. The idea of doing anything with him disgusted me, but my mother insisted Amaryllis and I go out together. She could not leave the house at night without me, and so I acquiesced.

Amaryllis stood in front of the mirror, shifting her body this way and that, avoiding the crack that split the bottom half of the glass. One Sunday morning, when we were six, she had protested having to wear a frilly church dress—matching mine in style though not in color—and black leather Mary Janes by throwing one of the offending shoes at the mirror. The shoe heel had hit the mirror in the center, causing it to splinter downward, sending spidery cracks outwards on either side. Her punishment had been that the mirror had never been replaced, and we had had to live with that reminder of the differences between us for the last eleven years. The crack seemed to foretell a bifurcating of our lives' paths, Amaryllis on the left: confident, defiant, and me on the right: mousy, demure.

Finally, Amaryllis was satisfied with how she looked and she said, "You ready?"

"Is early still. Why you don't make him wait likkle bit?"

Amaryllis gave me a withering look. "Like you know something bout keeping man. Dave not going wait around for a woman."

I had noticed this change in her speech, the way she spoke of herself as a woman and moved with a womanish sashay in her body. Her attitude towards me had also changed. She'd always reminded me that I was five minutes her junior, but since she met Dave and subscribed to his political views, where she used to treat me with playful tolerance, she now treated me with true disdain.

I glanced in the mirror again and smoothed my hair, which had been plaited into two cornrows. I looked like what I was, a schoolgirl trying to look grown. With a sigh, I followed her out of our bedroom, down the stairs, and through the living room, where Daddy sat listening to the radio. All of the lights were off except for a table lamp whose heavy shade rendered it ineffective.

I held my breath as we made our way towards the door, heels high off the floor, careful not to call attention to our passage through the dark room. I turned my head in my father's direction only once, sweeping a glance past the ornate, heavy wooden furniture that dominated the living room and toward the cushioned rocking chair that was my father's sole domain.

We weren't sneaking out, not exactly. My mother had given us permission to go, and it was a tame excursion on the surface, just a change of scenery, a relief from our prisonlike existence. My father generally followed my mother's lead when it came to handling us girls, but he was as mercurial as the light bulb that flickered in the dark hallway, producing huge shadows that grew whenever the light dampened. That night, he had been unusually silent at dinner, and I sensed some deep distress lurking under his quiet demeanor.

We were almost at the door when his voice boomed across the room. "Where you two off to?"

Amaryllis swore softly, "Damn," but not softly enough.

My father was standing when he replied, "A what you a say?"

"She said we going by Christine," I replied, shooting a glance at Amaryllis, begging her to hold her tongue. "Mommy said we could go."

My father stood in front of us now, his face glowering in the hall light. "Oonu a spend too much time a Christine yard. I struggling to put roof over oonu head. Tonight you staying right here so. It's too dangerous out there."

He turned towards his chair, signaling the end of the discussion.

I saw words forming behind Amaryllis's eyes and racing towards her lips.

"That's why we going together," I preempted. "And Christine's father coming for us, Daddy." I formed my lips into my sweetest smile. I was unpracticed in persuading my father. Sweet-talking him used to be Amaryllis's role.

He spun on his heel, looked at me, and laughed. The sound was short yet indulgent, and I was hopeful.

"My dear Maya, how you going protect Mari from a gun? Just last night Mr. McClure daughter dem was . . ." He shook his head and released a heavy sigh. "Just know is dangerous out there. And I hear your sister still keeping friend with that PNP fella, Dave. Who knows what kind of trouble he mix up in."

That time I could not preempt Amaryllis's response.

"Dave not like that," she blurted.

"So is true. You a see him." The red glow from the lamplight behind my father seemed to grow with his anger.

"We're friends, Daddy. All of we. Just friends," I said.

But it was too late.

"You not friending any guy mix up with those thugs. Robbing and shooting people in the street." Daddy paused and lowered his voice. "Raping young girls."

Amaryllis should have backed down then, but she persisted. "You don't even know Dave, Daddy. He's real smart. He's probably going to get the island scholarship."

"I don't care if he is the King of England, oonu not going nowhere tonight," he growled. He was close to us now, towering over us. His voice was low. His anger reddened his brown complexion and set his face in determination. I saw a mirror of that resolve settle onto Amaryllis's face like something hardening inside her. I knew the look well, and I feared the hardness would become permanent one day.

Her hand was still on the door handle and every moment seemed staccatoed, playing frame by frame like one of the black-and-white movies Daddy loved. Amaryllis's hand twitched on the handle then opened it. In a fluid motion, she stepped outside.

"Where the hell you think you going?" my father yelled.

The next minutes were a blur. I remembered my father's shouting but few of his words. I remembered sensing someone on the stairs behind us, probably our mother, but she would not intervene then. I remembered standing frozen, in awe of my sister's defiance. In that one moment, she embodied everything I thought freedom meant. Her yellow dress flashed brightly in the streetlights as she ran down the front steps. I was mesmerized by the movement of her skirt, the speed of her feet in her saucy red high-heeled shoes. I was caught between being the obedient child and grasping at that bit of freedom, defying my father this one time. Distracted by indecision, I didn't see the gun in my father's hand until the flash of yellow in Amaryllis's dress was challenged by the brighter flash near her head, and then covered in a long red tear that flowed down her back as she fell.

"Oh my God, oh my God, my Mari, oh my God." The words repeated in a cycle, first quietly, then louder and louder until I covered my ears so that I could hear only the screaming inside my own head. My mother rushed past me and out into the garden. She dropped to her knees and held Amaryllis's head in her lap. Her round robin of pleas to Heaven turned into a loud wail.

My father dropped the gun then fell to his knees. His mouth opened but no sound emerged.

My mother rose from Amaryllis's side. The front of her nightgown was soaked with blood, so much blood. She cradled her pregnant belly as she ran to my father and picked up the gun. She hit him on the shoulder with the butt of the gun as if she were knighting him, but with such force that he fell to the ground and curled into a ball.

"What did you do?" she screamed and hit him again. "What did you do to my child?"

"Nothing," he said, finding his voice.

"Nothing?" She hit him again. "Nothing? She dead. She over there dead."

"Is only stop a mean to stop her. Shoot inna the air. I aim to miss her."

The night descended into a blur of red: red blood; red flashing lights; red, tear-filled eyes.

My father was taken away to jail in handcuffs, fingerprinted, and photographed. Two nights later he was found dead in his cell, having strangled himself.

SO THIS WAS me. This was the family I had had then lost, each one of us a little culpable, my father, my mother, Amaryllis, and me . . .

CHAPTER THIRTY-FIVE

Kingston, Jamaica - September 2003

For three hours I held back the tears, twisting my bracelet again and again until the beads pressed tiny circles into my wrist and the wire began to cut into my skin. I had seen a softer side of Donovan after each of my trips into my ever-darkening past, and did not want to experience his response if I dissolved into a sniveling mess in his back seat. Few people knew the right words to say or gestures to make to someone in crisis, and I doubted Donovan was one of them.

Finally alone in my hotel room, I sat cross-legged on my bed and let the full reality of my discovery wash over me. A gun had gone off and my family had disintegrated. My sister dead, my father incarcerated, my mother institutionalized, and her baby shuttled off to a disinterested aunt. The fiction I had created about my parents dying in a fire, about being raised by Aunt Marjorie, had been just that: a backstory to hide the truth, which I had then absorbed into my being until I believed it myself. I no longer felt the urge to cry. The tears that corresponded to what I had discovered would have to be hurricane-force and flood-inducing. I had nothing inside to give.

When I lost my family, I had buried the truth in the most inaccessible regions of my mind. Was I any different now, twenty-four years later? Did I have any new tools to manage? A stronger support system? I had Brian, but then again, did I? How would he respond to this news of my murderous family history on top of everything else? Would he understand that I had not been keeping secrets from him? That this was as much a revelation to me as it was for him?

Jamela's words came back to me: "The world will continue to spin if you put it down for a minute and take care of yourself." I had done as she said, and the world had spun ahead to a place I no longer recognized. When I left Virginia, I knew nothing about my parents or my sister. Now I had clear images of them, our lives together in Jamaica, and the abrupt way in which that had ended. When I left Virginia I had one photograph of Aunt Marjorie and me. Now I remembered photographs chronicling our lives as a family, hung around the house and in my father's office. My family's faces cycled through my mind as if I were in a broken time machine. I saw them in vivid detail, expressions of joy, love, happiness, then ultimately concern and horror. The images that had haunted me all of my life now had names and backstories. I had been digging holes in the garden, manifesting the missing parts inside me. Now that I knew the whole truth, a part of me wished to bury it once more.

I picked up my phone; there were three missed calls from Lisa and Jamela each and a text from Taiwo. One word: "Mom?"

The question mark stopped my heart. I had been gone for three days and had not been in touch with him except to say I had arrived safely. There were so many ways to interpret that question mark: *Do you still exist? Are you okay? Are you still my mother?* I thought of my last words to my own mother, pleading with her to respond.

The text grounded me. My present rushed in, temporarily assuaging the impact of my discoveries about my past. I pressed the buttons on my phone. Taiwo picked up on the second ring.

"Hi, Mom." His voice was subdued. If it had been possible to transport myself through the phone line, I would have.

"Hey, sweetheart," I replied. "What's going on?"

"Aunt Lisa told me the first thing I am to tell you is that I have everything under control."

"And do you?"

"I do . . . now."

"What's going on?"

"I've been doing some research online. Reading about illegal immigration, the penalties, how people hide, that sort of thing. And I looked for information about you. I found out why you did not want to go back to Jamaica. There was a newspaper article online, a picture of one, and it said that your father ..."

"It's okay, Tai." I was not ready to hear those words spoken out loud.

"I guess the FBI didn't like the words I was searching, because they came to work today and questioned me about it."

"They did what?" It was difficult to breathe despite the air conditioner that circulated cool air through the room. I sat up straight in the bed, my blood bristling close under the surface of my skin.

"Oh my God, Tai. Are you okay?"

"I'm okay. It was scary. They were dressed in black with lots of weapons like they expected me to have a ... I don't even know if I can say the word B-O-M-B," he spelled, "on the phone. They may be listening. But I'm okay, Mom. I told them the truth. They checked the computer, and they left."

"Did they say why they picked you? How did they find you?"

"They said they got a tip."

"A tip? From who?"

"They didn't say, but José thinks it must be Ralph. And I think so too. He isn't a very nice person, Mom."

"No. It doesn't seem so," I replied.

"But it's all over now," Taiwo added, his voice lighter. "It's under control."

"Have you spoken to Daddy?" I imagined Brian's anger that I had not been around to help Taiwo through this crisis.

"Yes. He'll be here in the morning. He said he's going to sue somebody."

I ached to be with Taiwo. He had faced a huge hurdle and overcome it. Facing off the FBI would be daunting for anyone, but for Taiwo, it would be much more difficult to process. But he had done it. A tear slipped down my cheek. I had been feeling so much anger towards my parents for abandoning me, but everything they did up to that point had helped me to survive, one way or another, when I found myself on my own.

"I'll be home in a few days, Tai. And we'll talk about what you want to do next."

"Okay, Mom. I love you."

"I love you too."

I slept that night, soundly for the first time since that day three weeks before when I'd seen Angela in the parking lot. The next day, I braved the drive to Black River one more time and had Donovan drop me at the cemetery. It took me almost an hour, walking through hundreds of graves, reading the names and epitaphs until I encountered three concrete slabs side by side. They were unadorned, no loving words, only the names and the years. I sank to the ground with my legs crisscrossed and read each name out loud:

Horace Gordon 1936–1979

Patricia Gordon 1938–1980

Amaryllis Gordon 1963–1979

The grass was low around the tombs, except for a few plants that had evaded the grounds crew. I read the names again, pausing after each to yank up the wayward weeds. The earth was damp after a night of showers, and it yielded up the plants with a sound like a sharp intake of breath. Tears streamed down my cheeks as the weeds emerged, roots intact, and when I had removed them all, I found myself scraping at the damp earth until a trench formed in front of the graves. My tears fell, further softening the soil. I dug until the trough was inches deep. A light sheen formed over the tears that layered the bottom of my hole, and sunlight fractured the surface into reds, greens, and golds. I stretched my arms from side to side to encompass the tombs.

This had been my family. Once upon a time, these three people had been my world.

BOOK CLUB DISCUSSION QUESTIONS

1. How long did it take for you to figure out the truth of the tragedy that befell Amaya? How much did you guess beforehand and were you surprised when you learned the truth? What did you think of the way the events led one to the next until the tragedy occurred?

2. How would you describe Amaya's relationship with Taiwo? How did Taiwo's character impact how you felt about Amaya?

3. The story touches briefly on some of the challenges of being neurodiverse in the Caribbean and in the United States. What did you think of Taiwo's role in the story?

4. How would you describe Amaya's relationship with Brian? How did Brian seem to view her role as wife, mother, and employee? Did she seem fulfilled in the marriage? How might this change beyond the end of the story?

5. Angela is tight-lipped about her connection to Amaya and Nate. What do you think are some of the fears that stop her from confiding in Amaya until the showdown with Nate forces her hand?

6. Amaya convinces herself that planting false memories in Aunt Marjorie's head is harmless and even helpful. What do you think of the way that Amaya handles Aunt Marjorie's dementia even as she is struggling to recover her own memories?

7. In each place that Amaya lives, she builds a garden. In fact, the original title of this book was *Amaya's Gardens*. What do you think is the significance of these gardens to Amaya? How do they impact her life and development?

8. The book observes a variety of migrant experiences through the eyes of Amaya, Mrs. Lin, José, Angela, and Aunt Marjorie. How do the factors that push them from their home country or the ones that pull them to the United States impact the way that they respond to their new lives?

9. What do you think about Amaya's involvement with Dave and the confusion it causes? Did she do the right thing in telling Brian about Dave? What do you think is the truth of the outcome of her encounter with Dave and does it matter?

10. What do you learn about the relationship between Amaya and Amaryllis? What is the impact of Amaryllis's personality on Amaya's development as a person? How does Amaya change once Amaryllis is no longer a part of her life?

11. What did you think about Aunt Kathryn's response to the tragic events? Was her response understandable? Justifiable? What other actions might she have taken?

12. Do you think counseling or some other intervention would have changed Amaya's trajectory? What does it say about Caribbean culture that no one offered Amaya counseling after the event?

13. The start of Amaya's story is set in a turbulent time in Jamaica's history. How did Jamaica at that time, with the political unrest and violent events, factor into the plot?

14. The story jumps in time between the present and the late 1970s into the 1980s, with the earliest events being revealed in reverse chronological order. How did this storytelling approach impact your reading of the story?

15. What did you think of the way the story ends? How do you envisage Amaya's future?

ACKNOWLEDGMENTS

This book's journey from start to publication reminds me of a Makonde Ujamaa Tree of Life sculpture. These sculptures embody the idea that each person should be supported by their community and in turn, lift others up. Unselfish support and generosity has been essential to bringing *What Start a Mornin'* to fruition.

Amaya's story was born in a George Mason University MFA class taught by Helon Habila, who later became my thesis advisor. This book had its genesis when I wrote about Taiwo in response to a writing prompt Helon assigned. I am indebted to him and the rest of the George Mason University MFA Faculty, including Bill Miller, Susan Shreve, Tania James, and especially Courtney Brkic, whose thoughtful guidance and belief in this story kept me moving forward for the five years from conception to delivery.

Courtney's advice led me to the Virginia Center for Creative Arts (VCCA), where I finally finished the book and found an incredible network of support. My VCCA peeps, you know who you are and what you should be doing.

From this group, I must single out Caitlin Myer for championing Amaya's story and connecting me to Murray Weiss after knowing me for just a short time. You did this!

And thank you, Murray, for truly believing in Amaya and for working on my behalf to get the story published. You were so confident about selling the book, I had no choice but to believe it as well.

Murray led me to Michelle Halket and Central Avenue Publishing where Amaya's story found its home. My appreciation to you, Michelle, for your enthusiasm, your vision, and your boundless and gracious patience. My indecisiveness over the title and the cover art must have been torture, but I'm so happy with the outcome.

And to my editor, Jessica Peirce, I am grateful for your careful attention to and respect for my work and also for gently leading me away from the abyss of overthinking on multiple occasions. Further gratitude goes to Molly Winter for proofreading with such a careful eye.

A small part of *What Start Bad a Mornin'* takes place in Jamaica in the late 1970s to early 1980s, and to write it, I did a lot of research: reading, watching videos, and interviewing people. I'm grateful to my late uncle and aunt Lindley and Phyllis Germain, Geoffrey Philp, my cousin John Gordon, and Deborah Arabtig for taking the time to talk to me about their experiences in Jamaica during those times. Your stories all influenced the direction of the book.

Another challenge I faced was untangling the language. Several Caribbean languages live in the same place in my brain, which makes it difficult for me to distinguish among them. Thank you to my cousin Judith Lee, publishing guru Tanya Batson-Savage, and Pamela Wells Russell for helping me work through the vernacular and affects so that the dialog is as realistic as possible.

Thank you to friends, readers, supporters, some of whom agreed to read despite not knowing me at all, some of whom I've yet to meet in real life. Elizabeth Nunez, Cleyvis Natera, Katia Ulysse, Opal Palmer Adisa, Joanne C. Hillhouse, Nerissa Golden, Jewel Daniel, Charmaine Rousseau, Caroline de Verteuil, Lauren Francis-Sharma, Eugenia O'Neal, and my first readers (and chosen sisters) Lesley Cassar and Patti Meek.

What Start Bad a Mornin' will be launched at the 2023 Brooklyn Caribbean Literary Festival, again at Sankofa Video and Books in D.C., and one more time at the Shadwell Great House in St. Kitts. Thanks to you all for embracing Amaya's story so willingly when I approached you.

Thanks to Livingston Jackson (Jaxon Photography), a lifelong friend and photographer extraordinaire who is responsible for making me look great in my photos.

Although the seedlings that grew into *What Start Bad a Mornin'* had their start at George Mason University, the roots have been there from the very beginning. My parents, Clive and Carmen Ottley, have always nourished my creativity and never doubted me whichever direction my life has taken. My husband and children have supported me tirelessly in my writing pursuits and endured my physical and mental absences. My extended family of aunts, uncles, cousins, and chosen siblings who are almost as happy about this publication as I am. I'm indebted to you all.

The existence of this book is a testimony to a lesson I relearn every day. Talk about your dreams. Let people know what you need. Help someone else when you can. Together we can reach great heights.

Photo: Livingston Jackson, Jaxon Photography

Carol Mitchell describes herself (in jest) as being in self-imposed exile from the places in the Caribbean that she considers home: St. Kitts & Nevis, Trinidad, and Jamaica. She holds an MFA and teaches writing in Virginia. She is also a fellow of the Virginia Center for Creative Arts. Her short stories have appeared in various Caribbean journals, and four of them have been long-listed for the Commonwealth Short Story Prize. She has written 18 children's books. *What Start Bad a Mornin'* is her debut adult novel.